TEAROOM
Mysteries

Dear Reader,

Christmas is a joyous time of the year. Lights are hung, trees are draped in ornaments, and carols play everywhere you go. It's the time of year when people's hearts turn toward spiritual matters, and we Christians celebrate the fact that Jesus came to earth to save us all. One of my favorite things about the season is seeing people who wouldn't otherwise have anything to do with faith willing to sing songs about Christ incarnate. It's a holy time—a season of anticipation and expectation.

In this Tearoom Mysteries story, strange things start happening around Lancaster. Someone starts robbing businesses in town, dressed as Santa Claus. It's both the perfect disguise and unspeakably creepy. That makes it fun for me as the author to bring it into our quaint small town's holiday season. As part of my research for the story, I discovered that the Santa we know—round belly, red suit, beard—was largely brought into popular imagination by Coca Cola, which used the image in their advertising, and by department stores. But the real Santa—also known as Kris Kringle, Sinterklaas, and Father Christmas—seems to be derived from Saint Nicholas, a fourth-century Greek bishop who was famous for his generous gifts to the poor. This explains why our modern Santa gives away gifts, but it also reminds me that—behind all the trappings of the season—the true spirit of Christmas is found in turning our hearts toward the coming of Christ and passing on His gift of love to others.

May Christmas be always in your heart, all year long.

Best wishes,
Elizabeth Adams

Tearoom Mysteries

Tearoom for Two
Tea Rose
To a Tea
Crosswords and Chamomile
Burning Secrets
O Christmas Tea
On Thin Ice
Tea Is for Treasure
Trouble Brewing
Mystery and Macarons
The Tea Will Tell
Tea and Touchdowns
Steeped in Secrets
Stealing Santa

TEAROOM
mysteries

Stealing Santa

ELIZABETH ADAMS

Guideposts
New York

Tearoom Mysteries is a trademark of Guideposts

Published by Guideposts Books & Inspirational Media
110 William Street
New York, New York 10038
Guideposts.org

Acknowledgments

Every attempt has been made to credit the sources of copyrighted material used
in this book. If any such acknowledgment has been inadvertently omitted or
miscredited, receipt of such information would be appreciated.

Scripture references are from the following sources: *The Holy Bible*, King James
Version (KJV). *The Holy Bible, New International Version.* Copyright ©1973, 1978,
1984, 2011 by Biblica, Inc. Used by permission of Zondervan. All rights reserved
worldwide. www.zondervan.com

Cover and interior design by Müllerhaus
Cover illustration by Ross Jones, represented by Deborah Wolfe, Ltd.
Typeset by Aptara, Inc.

Printed and bound in the United States of America
10 9 8 7 6 5 4 3 2 1

Stealing Santa

CHAPTER ONE

S now fell gently as Jan Blake eased out of the driveway on to Main Street in the little town of Lancaster. She tried to keep her eyes on the road, but the lakefront village, beautiful in all seasons, really cleaned up nicely at Christmastime. Most of the houses had wreaths on the doors and greenery on the porches, and a healthy dusting of snow made the entire town look peaceful and calm. White lights were draped on fences and strung up over the road. There were already two inches of snow on the fence posts, with more predicted to fall this morning.

"*Ooh*, those icicle lights look pretty," Elaine Cook said from the passenger seat, pointing to Gift Me, the shop across the road from their home. It was only two weeks until Christmas, but many of the neighbors were still decorating, and every day the little town looked more festive. "And look, some kids built a snow family in front of the library. Isn't that cute?"

Jan looked and nodded, then focused on the road again. A plow had come through not too long ago, and Main Street was pretty clear, but you still had to pay attention on the icy streets. Christmastime in Maine was beautiful, but it could also be bitterly cold and brutal. Suddenly she spotted some-thing strange up ahead.

"What's that?" Elaine asked, pointing down the road.

Jan had a sinking feeling she knew. The way the blue and red lights bounced and reflected against the snow, they could only come from one source.

"Is there a police car in front of Murphy's?"

Jan was afraid there was. Jan and her cousin Elaine had planned to make a quick run to the little general store to stock up on some necessities, hoping to avoid a trip to the big supermarket in Waterville. Now that she saw the police were here, she hoped everything was all right. She pulled into the small parking lot beside the white clapboard building and parked in an empty spot next to a snowbank. Jan stepped out and followed Elaine, who was already heading across the wet parking lot toward the entrance on the side of the store.

Jo Murphy, who owned the store with her husband, Des, was standing outside, huddled under the eave, bundled up in a dark-purple parka. Her curly brown hair fanned out beneath a fleece hat. She gave a rueful smile as Jan and Elaine approached. "Fun way to start the morning, huh?"

"What happened?" Elaine's own red knit hat had slid down over her forehead, but she hadn't seemed to notice. She was focused on the area at the rear of the store, away from the road, where they could see Trooper Dan Benson looking around in the snow that covered the yard. Elaine saw that Des Murphy was inside the store, talking to another officer.

"When we got here this morning to open up, we found the back door standing wide open," Jo said, shaking her head. Jo had a direct, plainspoken manner, and she chose each word carefully. She was thoughtful, and sometimes seemed overshadowed by her gregarious husband, but her calm demeanor seemed to serve her well today. "At first we thought maybe Nick had just forgotten to lock it when he left last night. That's happened before."

Jan nodded. Nick was one of the Murphys' twin teenaged sons who helped in the store. Jan supposed both of the boys must be at school on this Monday morning.

"But then we found the office door jimmied open," Jo said. "That's when we knew something was wrong. When we got inside, we saw that the safe, where we put the cash after we close the registers, had been opened."

"What do you mean?" Jan asked. "Someone had the combination to the safe?"

"No." The police officer was now taking a picture of something in the snow behind the store. "The safe door had been torn off. They say probably with a crowbar, but they're not positive yet."

"Oh my." Elaine's face had gone pale, and her eyes were wide.

"What...? How...?" Jan stammered. She couldn't believe it. A crowbar? That was so—that meant—how could this—

"How did this happen?" Elaine asked.

"That's what they're trying to figure out." Jo gestured at the officers.

Lancaster was a peaceful town. Sure, there had been a few mysteries that had come up since they'd lived here, just like you'd find anywhere else. But overall, it was pretty much as close to idyllic as you could find. But this—

"A crowbar?" Jan repeated. "I didn't know you could open a safe that way." She couldn't help the shiver that ran through her. The cousins ran a tearoom out of their grand Victorian home, and they also kept their cash in a safe in the office.

"I didn't either," Jo said. "I thought the point of a safe was that you couldn't open it without the combination. But it seems that you can."

"But…" Elaine was sputtering, as Jan still was. "How did whoever it was get into the store?"

"Des found a little piece of metal in the snow before the police arrived," Jo said. "Thank goodness he found it when he did, because it probably would have gotten buried with all this coming down." She gestured at the falling flakes, which just a few moments ago had seemed so peaceful. Now, Jan wondered what other evidence they were helping conceal.

"Metal?" Jan asked.

"We didn't recognize what it was," Jo said. "But Trooper Benson immediately saw it was a lock-picking tool."

"Goodness. Someone knew what they were doing."

Jo nodded, keeping her eyes focused on the officer behind the store. For a moment, they all stood and watched. Jan started to wonder if they should head inside and give Jo space. But then Jo spoke again.

"You know what the weirdest part about all of this is?" She rubbed her gloved hands together, trying to keep warm in the frigid air.

"There's something weirder than someone opening your safe with a crowbar?" Elaine asked. She met Jan's gaze, her eyes wide.

Jo nodded. "Faith Lanier came over when she saw the police car show up this morning. She wanted to see what was going on." Jo pointed to the house next to the market, a beautiful colonial-style wooden home that was one of the oldest in town. Faith Lanier, who owned the gift shop A Little Something farther down on Main Street, had grown up in that house, and she and her husband were good, solid, hardworking people. "And she told me that she'd been woken up in the night by a noise, so she got out of bed to see what was going on. She looked out the window"—Jo pointed to the second-story window that overlooked the store's parking lot—"and she said she saw Santa Claus walking across the parking lot."

Jan didn't know how to respond. Santa Claus? She couldn't have heard that right.

"She saw Santa Claus?" Elaine repeated.

"That's what she said. Red suit, red hat, beard, and all. Walking through the parking lot. Obviously she didn't think he'd just robbed our store, or she would have called the police. But she swears that's what she saw."

"What in the world?" Jan looked toward Elaine, but her cousin seemed to be as confused as she felt. "Did Santa Claus really rob your store?"

Jo let out a soft laugh, but it sounded more like a moan. "I'd guess someone dressed as Santa Claus, not old Saint Nick himself. But yes, it does appear that way."

CHAPTER TWO

Elaine and Jan chatted with Jo for a few more minutes, and then, as Dan Benson headed over to speak to Jo, Jan asked, "I guess you're not open for shopping at the moment?"

Jo smiled. "I don't see why not. It's hard to turn down a sale. As long as customers steer clear of the office it should be all right."

They thanked her and headed inside the store. The wide-plank pumpkin pine floors were scarred and scuffed but polished to a high sheen, and the wooden ceiling arched above the small space gracefully, creating the sense that the store was bigger than it really was. The small market had been a fixture in Lancaster for more than fifty years, and it carried a little bit of everything, from hardware to clothing to toiletries, as well as a small grocery section. Even though the store was small, Elaine was constantly amazed by how they always seemed to have exactly what she needed.

"Shall we divide and conquer?" Elaine suggested, holding out a handbasket for Jan.

"That probably makes the most sense," Jan said, and took the basket. Elaine took one for herself, and while Jan wandered over to the grocery section, Elaine located the small section of Christmas supplies. They already had plenty of decorations for the tearoom, which they'd draped in evergreen boughs and white lights and hung with wreaths. They had put up a large fir tree in the west parlor and a smaller one in the east parlor, and had even set up a small tree in their private sitting room upstairs.

Today, Elaine was looking for wrapping paper. Elaine was already done with her Christmas shopping. She was quite pleased with herself, if she was being honest. She'd been planning all year for this, making purchases for each of her children and grandchildren and friends as she thought of them. Now she could just enjoy the holiday season instead of rushing around trying to get everything done in time.

She stood in front of the rolls of wrapping paper. She reached for a roll of elegant heavy paper printed with silver snowflakes. It caught the light and sparkled a bit. It would look beautiful under the tree.

She placed the roll of snowflake paper in her basket, one end sticking out awkwardly, and saw a cute roll with a fun Santa print that she could use to wrap the presents for her grandchildren. As she reached for it, she remembered what Jo had said about Santa robbing this store last night, and she shivered. She knew it was silly, but she put the Santa roll back and reached for a roll that featured little snowmen in hats and red scarves instead. After she'd picked out matching ribbon, she went over to the section of the store that housed toiletries and selected a new bottle of hand lotion. The air was so dry indoors this time of year.

"Hi there, Elaine. Finding everything you need?" Des Murphy had appeared at her side.

"Of course. As always," Elaine said. "How are you doing?"

Des gave a rueful laugh. "Well, I've had better mornings, if I'm honest."

Des was in his midforties, with brown hair and green eyes and a kind smile. He was outgoing and gregarious and loved to make everyone feel welcome.

"No doubt. Jo told us what happened. I'm so sorry to hear it."

"We're hopeful the police will catch him," Des said.

"Do they have any leads?" Elaine asked. She couldn't help it. Her radar had perked up. She and Jan had solved a few mysteries since they'd moved to Lancaster a year and a half ago, and she couldn't stop herself from trying to find out more about this one.

"Not at this point. Nothing aside from the guy in a Santa costume. But that's pretty hard to use to track down a thief, you know?"

"Certainly." Elaine couldn't imagine how that fact could be used.

"But I have to admit, the image of Santa Claus breaking into my safe with a crowbar is enough to give me nightmares."

"You and me both." Elaine looked up at the ceiling. "You don't have any security cameras?"

Des sighed. "It never occurred to me we'd need them."

Elaine could understand that. They didn't have them at the tearoom either. She hoped that the lock-picking tool Jo had mentioned outside would provide some clue. Maybe they could get fingerprints off it.

"Let's just hope they catch him," Elaine said, and Des agreed, and then said goodbye and wandered off to check on some other customers who had come in. Elaine headed over to the food section and found Jan reading the label on a bottle of salad dressing.

"I think you grabbed the wrong kind," Elaine said. She reached for a similar bottle on the shelf. "That one's fat free." She stuck out her tongue to show her feelings about low-fat dressing, but then she saw Jan's face.

"Actually, I'm trying to eat healthier," Jan said, placing the bottle in her basket.

"Oh." Elaine looked down and saw that Jan's basket was filled with low-fat versions of all her favorite foods: skim milk, packaged egg whites, margarine, and sugar substitute. "Wow. You're serious about this."

"I am." Jan pressed her lips together. She nodded. "I realized I've put on a few pounds the past couple months, and I need to be more careful about what I eat. So I'm going to try to eat better."

Elaine looked at her cousin. Sure, she'd probably put on a few pounds recently, since her boyfriend, Bob Claybrook, had moved to Baltimore for a job. Her cheeks were a bit rounder, her arms a bit fuller. But it wasn't much, and it looked good on her. She looked healthy. Come to think of it, Elaine had no doubt gained a few pounds too. But what did they expect?

Jan spent every morning turning out delicious baked goods to serve in the tearoom. Of course they had to sample every once in a while.

"You can feel free to continue to use the full-fat versions of this stuff," Jan said. "It won't bother me."

Elaine didn't know what to say. She wasn't opposed to eating better. It would be good for her to lose those few extra pounds. Her doctor would no doubt approve. But was this—

Elaine tried to phrase this carefully.

"I'm glad for you," she said. "It's wonderful that you're taking charge of your health. But do you think..."

She paused, and listened to the holiday music playing over the store's loudspeakers. She looked at the wreaths on the walls, the lights strung up around the trees. The plates of premade cookies and Yule logs and containers of eggnog.

"Maybe it would be best to wait until after Christmas to start the diet."

"I'm not dieting," Jan said, her chin held high. "It's a healthier lifestyle." She kept her eyes down as she rearranged the items in her basket. "And as much as I would love to put it off, I don't think there's any reason to wait. You start getting the benefits of eating better right away."

Elaine nodded, but inside, her mind was spinning. It sounded like Jan had swallowed a bunch of platitudes from women's magazines. Of course, what she was saying was absolutely true, and it would be good for both of them to take better care of their bodies, but Elaine still didn't see why she was insistent on starting this diet—fine, "healthier lifestyle"—now, at the absolute worst time of year for such things. And what about the tearoom? Was Jan's new health kick going to mean all the pastries they served would taste like cardboard?

"Will your health choices extend to the baking for the tearoom?" Elaine asked this as kindly as she could.

"For the tearoom, I'm still going to use real butter from Richardson's dairy, and real sugar," Jan said. "Our customers want to eat something delicious, and I'll oblige. I just won't be sampling quite as much as I normally do."

Elaine was relieved to hear that. "Well, good for you," she finally managed to say. And she was glad for Jan. Good for her for taking charge of her health. Maybe she'd join her in this new healthier lifestyle in the new year. Truthfully, though, Elaine thought it was a tiny bit futile to start a new diet before Christmas.

Jan gave her a resigned smile. "We'll see how it goes."

Elaine watched as her cousin started toward the checkout counters. She had a smile on her face, but there was something defeated in her eyes, and the slump of her shoulders as she walked past a display of hot cocoa and mini marshmallows gave Elaine pause. Elaine watched her for a moment. Jan didn't seem to be any more pleased about the idea of this diet than Elaine was.

Still, just to be safe, Elaine grabbed a package of butter and added it to her basket before following Jan to the front of the store. Maybe she would worry about her weight in January. For now, it was Christmastime. Elaine was going to enjoy the season.

CHAPTER THREE

Jan was just putting whole-wheat bread in the toaster for her breakfast when the doorbell rang. She brushed the crumbs off her hands and walked down the hallway toward the door.

Jan opened the door and found Max Arrington, their regular delivery guy, on the doorstep. He wore a heavy coat dusted with snowflakes over his brown uniform, and the ends of his dark hair were just visible under his wool hat. He was a jovial guy in his midthirties, and Jan was always glad to see him— and not just because it meant whatever goodies they'd ordered had arrived.

"What do you have for me today?" Jan asked, ushering him inside the door.

"Just this." Max held out a package. Jan looked down and saw that it was the new batch of candles she'd ordered to line up in hurricane lamps on the mantel. There was something so striking about lighting a room with the warmth of candlelight, especially in these cold, dark days of winter.

Jan took the package and set it down on the counter. He held out the little handheld scanner for her to sign, and she used the stylus to scribble her name on the pad.

"Thank you so much," Jan said. "This must be a busy time of year for you."

"Oh yeah." He laughed. "But I'm grateful. It keeps me out of trouble." He took the scanner from her hands, gave a little salute, and turned to go. Jan closed the door and started to carry the package toward the kitchen, but she'd only gotten halfway there when the doorbell rang. She turned back and opened the door again, and this time it was Bristol Payson on the doorstep. Max was just climbing into his truck, which was parked at the curb. Bristol was bundled up in a puffy down parka and had a scarf pulled up over her nose. Winter in Maine meant learning to recognize your friends from their eyes and outerwear.

"You guys are popular today," Bristol said, pulling down her scarf.

"Please come in," Jan said, ushering her inside. Bristol owned the Bookworm, the charming bookstore next door to Tea for Two, and she had become a good friend as well as a neighbor.

"Thank you." Bristol stomped the snow off her boots and then stepped inside and unwound her scarf. "Oh, it's so beautiful in here." Bristol pulled off her knit hat and gazed into the east parlor, where the tree in front of the window was hung with silver and blue ornaments and ribbons. "I love that tree topper. Where did you get that?"

Bristol was pointing at the antique hand-blown mercury glass star that topped the tree.

"Isn't it gorgeous? Elaine found it at this little stall at Mainely Bargains," Jan explained. They'd found so many treasures there, including the painting of a woman drinking tea that usually hung in the west parlor. The painting was with an art authenticator at the moment, but they'd made an eleven-by-fourteen print of the painting to keep while it was away. She took Bristol's coat and hung it on the hooks by the door.

"Come in. Would you like some tea to warm you up?" Jan led Bristol down the hall toward the kitchen. "We're just about to eat a late breakfast. I could make you something if you'd like".

"No, thank you." Bristol opened a bag that she had slung over her shoulder as she entered the kitchen. "Hi, Elaine."

"Hello, Bristol." Elaine was just stepping in from the covered porch, where she'd gone to set out fresh food for Earl Grey, the stray cat who called their porch home. During the cold winter months they set out a little cat house they had made for him out of a styrofoam container with straw in it, and he seemed content. Through the glass door, Jan could see Earl Grey happily parked in front of his bowl. "How's everything at the Bookworm?"

"Things are going well. The holidays are always a good time for book sales." Bristol saw the plates sitting on the counter. "Please don't let me stop you from enjoying your meal," she said.

Jan looked down at the plates and up at Bristol. Rose Young and Archie Bentham, their two employees, would arrive shortly to open the tearoom, so they should eat pretty quickly.

"Are you sure you don't mind?" she asked.

"Not at all. I don't mean to interrupt. Should I come back another time?"

"Don't be silly," Elaine said. She was washing her hands at the sink. "We're glad to have you. But I insist that you have something too." She moved away from the sink and reached into the cabinet to pull down a plate, then set one of Jan's freshly baked cranberry scones on it.

"*Ooh.* Well, if you insist." Bristol laughed. "I certainly won't turn down one of those." She followed the cousins to the dining table, where Jan set down her plate of dry toast next to Elaine's breakfast.

"That looks delicious." Bristol was looking at Elaine's plate—which was loaded with fried eggs and sausage links and a scone on the side. Then she looked over at Jan's toast, and her smile faltered for a minute, but she recovered quickly.

"I'd be happy to make you some," Elaine said.

"Oh no, thank you. Really." Bristol picked up her scone. "I already had breakfast. I don't know how you guys do it. If I worked here I'd be a thousand pounds," she said, smiling. Jan didn't meet her eye. "Did you hear about the fund-raiser I'm organizing?" Bristol continued.

"Sure. The one where you're collecting money to buy gifts for children who have parents in prison?" Elaine asked. She took a big bite of her sausage and used her napkin to wipe a little dribble of juice from her chin. "We've seen the articles about it in the paper."

"That's right. They do such good work, and this charity really helps these children know that someone cares about them. A bunch of businesses in town are setting up boxes to collect donations."

"We'd be happy to set one up," Elaine said.

"Thank you," Bristol said. "I sure do appreciate that. But I was actually going to ask if you would be willing to do something else."

Jan took a bite of her toast. The bread was a bit dry, but it did taste pretty good. It wasn't a bad breakfast.

"What's that?" Elaine took another bite. Jan could smell the sausage from here.

"The collection boxes will be out for the next week and a half, and there's supposed to be a big fund-raiser event to get one last big push at the end, next Tuesday night." She looked from Jan to Elaine and back again.

Jan nodded. That was just over a week from today.

"I saw that. The newspaper said it was going to be pretty fancy."

"People have been very generous. A local caterer heard about it from Mark, and she's donated her services for the event. Food, serving ware, servers, everything."

"Wow." Jan did enough cooking and serving to realize how generous this donation was.

"And an anonymous donor has agreed to match whatever funds we raise at the party itself."

"That's quite generous." Jan suspected Will Trexler to be the donor. He often was for this sort of thing. He had more money than he knew what to do with and was always looking for ways to help.

"It truly is. So naturally I'm very anxious to make sure the event goes off smoothly."

Jan nodded and waited for Bristol to go on.

"I had rented out the Old Grange Hall for the event, but they apparently had a lot of water damage when a pipe froze and burst a few days ago. They called me today to say they can't host the event after all."

"Oh no." Jan hadn't heard about that. A lot of community events were hosted at the facility, and it was a shame they'd had damage. "I'm sorry to hear that."

"They said insurance was going to cover the damages, thankfully. But in the meantime, that leaves me without a space."

"Oh." Jan saw where this was going now.

"I was wondering if you'd be willing to host the party here," Bristol said.

"Host the party?" Jan asked. "You mean here at the tearoom?"

"That's what I was hoping for. Maybe push the tables to the side, or move them out altogether, or something. Everything would be handled—setup, cleanup, food, everything. I would just need to use the space for the actual party itself."

"How many people were you thinking?" Jan's mind was racing. A week was not a lot of time to plan an event like the one Bristol was proposing. Even if Bristol really did handle all the details, it would still impact their business and their personal lives at this busy time of year.

"I'm not really sure, but probably somewhere around fifty?"

Jan looked through the open doorway and into the east parlor. Both of the parlors were good-sized, and with the furniture pushed back or removed, it wasn't too much of a stretch to imagine a large crowd in here. And with the Christmas trees draped in ornaments and fairy lights and evergreen boughs wrapped around the mantel, it did look like the perfect setting for a holiday party. She was pretty sure they didn't have anything on the calendar that night.

"Of course, you should take some time to discuss it between yourselves," Bristol said. "And I would totally understand if you need to say no. I'm sure that like most women, you both already have enough to do at this time of year. But I just thought—well, it really is a perfect space, and you have it decorated so beautifully, and it's for such a good cause, so I wanted to ask."

"Of course," Elaine said.

Did they have time to take on a project like this? Jan wasn't sure. But then again, it *was* for a good cause. And it would take her mind off missing Bob. After all, before he'd taken the new job so far away representing people who'd been wrongly imprisoned, she had thought he would become her husband at some point. So yes, she missed him even more than she'd imagined she would. She was counting down the days—seven—until he came home for Christmas. At least if she had a big project like this to focus on, it would serve as a distraction.

"I think we should go for it," Jan said. Elaine's eyes widened, and a smile spread over her face. True, Elaine was usually the one more prone to making impulsive decisions, but Jan felt good about this one.

"Really?" Elaine asked. Jan nodded. "Good. I do too."

Bristol clapped her hands. "Oh, thank you so much. This is really wonderful. I so appreciate it."

"We're glad to help," Jan said.

They chatted for a few more minutes, and then when Rose came in, Bristol excused herself so they could get things ready to open the tearoom for the day. Jan headed to the kitchen to start making finger sandwiches, but her mind was thinking about the party. She knew the caterer would have the food under control, but Jan had a recipe for these wonderful little mini grilled cheese sandwiches that would be just perfect. Maybe she should suggest that—

Now she was hungry again. Jan looked around. She knew she was supposed to grab a healthy snack in moments like this—a handful of almonds, or a few carrot sticks. But who could seriously go for carrot sticks when there was a whole tray of freshly baked gingersnaps sitting on the counter? One wouldn't hurt.

Yes, Jan thought. This party was going to be fun.

CHAPTER FOUR

Later that evening, after dinner, Elaine settled down on the couch in the sitting room on the second floor of the house. Jan was in her bedroom, Skyping with Bob. Elaine had called her own boyfriend, Nathan Culver, who owned an auction house specializing in antiques, but he'd had a long day and wanted to get to bed early. Elaine was curled up watching snow fall gently out the window. The white lights on the Christmas tree in the corner bathed the room in a soft glow, and the air was perfumed with the fresh scent of evergreen. She had a mug of chamomile tea in one hand and a mystery novel next to her on the couch, but she found herself staring out at the falling snow.

Elaine had grown up in Maine, and though she'd traveled the world with her late husband, Ben, she'd never found anyplace more beautiful than Maine in the winter. The way the snow fell in giant gentle flakes, catching in the white pine and balsam fir branches, blanketing the world in a layer of white, was evidence that God loved beauty.

Finally, her eyes were getting heavy, and she placed her bookmark inside her book and closed the cover. Jan's bedroom light was off; she must have gone to bed as well. Elaine took her mug downstairs and rinsed it out, and then she checked to make sure the doors were locked and turned off the lights. The fairy lights on the trees in the parlors went dark, but the electric candle in each of the front windows continued to burn. Traditionally, a candle left burning in the window of a New England home was a sign that inside, weary travelers would find rest. Elaine loved the symbolism of that, and she loved the way the lights cast golden light over the snowy yard. She took one last look at the yard, and then she turned and headed up the stairs. A few minutes later, she was curled up under her down comforter and drifting off to sleep.

WHAT WAS THAT? Elaine sat upright in bed. She'd heard a noise. A scraping sound. She knew that sound. That was the sound of the back door opening. She listened carefully, and heard something else. It sounded like the noise the door made when it swept open across the kitchen floor.

Elaine hopped out of bed and pulled her flannel robe around her as she ran down the stairs. To the right, the front half of the first floor was bathed in the low light from the electric candles, but the back half of the house was dark. Elaine hurried into the kitchen and flipped on the light.

It was—

No, it couldn't be—

But before Elaine knew what was happening, she let out a terrible scream.

CHAPTER FIVE

Elaine was still breathing hard when Jan made it down the stairs and found her in the kitchen.

"What is it?" Jan looked around. Her heart was pounding. "What happened?"

Elaine didn't answer at first, just looked toward the back door. That was when Jan realized it was standing open.

"Was someone here?" Jan stepped toward it. She'd been in a dead sleep less than a minute ago, but now she was wide awake.

"Santa," Elaine stammered. "I just saw Santa Claus."

"What?" Jan stopped and looked at Elaine, who seemed to be frozen to the spot.

"Santa Claus was in our kitchen."

A cold wave of fear washed over Jan as she registered what Elaine was saying. "You mean someone dressed like Santa broke into our house? Like at Murphy's?"

Elaine nodded.

"And you caught him?"

"I scared him away. I flipped on the lights, and he ran for the door."

Jan stepped toward the door. She used the sleeve of her nightgown to touch the doorknob—if there were any fingerprints on it, she didn't want to mar them—and peered out. The door to the screened-in porch was also open, the screen sliced open. Jan turned on the light and stood on the porch and peered out over the snow-covered yard. It had stopped snowing sometime in the night. She didn't see any movement—but then, she couldn't see much, as most of the land that sloped down toward the frozen lake was pitch black. Only a small section by the porch where the kitchen light threw off a small glow was visible. Jan had no clue which way he'd gone.

"Do you see anything?" Elaine asked, coming up beside her.

Jan scanned the small patch of ground around the porch. "No." Usually she was grateful for the serene setting—no ambient light to block out the view of the stars. But tonight, she wished for a little bit of light pollution. She flipped the switch that turned on the light on the back of the house, but the light didn't spread very far in the inky-black night.

Earl Grey cautiously poked his head out from his nest. His fur stood on end and his tail was twice its normal size.

"Hey there, buddy." Elaine reached down and stroked his head. "That must have been scary for you, huh?"

The cat started to purr.

"Too bad he can't talk. It would be great if he could tell us what he saw," Jan said.

"He's useless," Elaine said as she picked him up and cuddled him to her chest. His purring got louder. "I'm sorry. I should have gone after him."

"You certainly should *not* have," Jan said, indicating Elaine's bare feet and robe. "You would have frozen to death. Besides, he's probably armed and dangerous. I'm just grateful he ran away. There could have been another outcome here, and I'm glad you're safe."

"Thank you." Elaine stared out at the dark night. "Speaking of freezing to death, we should go back into the house. We need to call the police."

Jan realized she was right. She was barefoot, wearing only a knee-length flannel nightgown. Goose bumps had raised all along her legs and arms.

"How about you go in and call them? I want to check something out."

"Jan, please come inside where it's safer."

"I will." Jan stepped toward the screen door and pushed it open gently.

There, just like she suspected. "Do you have your phone handy?"

"It's charging in an outlet in the kitchen. But we can just use the wall phone..."

"Could I borrow it for a moment? Mine is upstairs."

Elaine gave her cousin a strange look, but then shrugged, set the cat down gently, and headed back into the kitchen. She came back out a moment later with her phone.

"You go call the police. I'll be right in."

"You're not going after him, are you? It's not safe. He could still be out there somewhere."

"No." Jan shook her head and pointed the phone at the ground. "Unfortunately for our thief, he came to rob us in the dead of winter. Which means he had to track through snow to get to our door." Jan tapped the camera app and moved the camera so a footprint was framed on the screen.

"Ah. Brilliant."

"I'll get some photos, and you get a state trooper here ASAP."

"Sounds like a plan."

As Elaine headed inside, Jan moved into the open doorway. She knew there had to be a footprint if he'd gone out this way, and there it was. A whole series of them, some coming toward the house, close together, as if he'd approached cautiously. And then spaced farther apart as he ran away. Jan wasn't sure if they would be able to use the photos of the footprints to help track him down somehow, but she suspected that once the police showed up they'd traipse all over the backyard and mess up the prints that were there.

Jan took several pictures of the footprints in the snow, and then she handed the phone back to Elaine. She hurried back into the kitchen and closed the door. Even the cool air inside felt warm after the unheated porch.

Elaine had used the wall phone to dial 911, which routed the call to the main state trooper office in Augusta. That was no doubt so they didn't have to disturb Dan Benson at this hour. What time was it anyway? Jan craned her neck and looked at the clock. It was 2:37 a.m.

While Elaine explained the situation to the police, Jan filled a teakettle with water and set it on the stove. By the time Elaine had hung up, Jan was setting two steaming mugs of soothing mint tea onto the table. She had taken a Pendleton blanket off the wingback chair in the corner of the formal dining room and had wrapped it around her shoulders.

"They'll send someone now. They should be here soon." Elaine sat down and wrapped her hands around the mug. "Thank you for this."

"I figured we both need some help calming down," Jan said. She settled into the chair across from Elaine. "So did you get a look at him?"

"Not really." Elaine blew on her tea as small wisps of steam curled up. "I was too stunned to really notice much of anything."

Jan could understand that. She also would have been too terrified to be able to recall much of anything, she was sure.

"He was wearing the full-on Santa suit," Elaine said. "Red suit, hat, boots, gloves, white beard, and wig. A black bag. And unless I saw it wrong, I'm pretty sure he had a crowbar tucked into his belt."

Jan laughed because she didn't know what else to do. "Santa with a crowbar. Now I've heard everything."

"Not exactly a Norman Rockwell image, is it?"

"I'm just glad you're all right. It's a very good thing he ran away instead of coming at you." Jan watched the steam curl up from her tea for a moment. "I would imagine he was going for the safe, right?"

"I assume so. But he was on his way in when I caught him. I think I scared him away before he got there."

Jan pushed herself up and went into the office just to check. Everything looked normal, and the safe behind the desk was intact.

"It looks like he probably intended to open the safe, but he didn't get that far." Jan sat back and felt a shiver go through her. "My goodness. It's one thing for him to rob the general store when no one was there. But to break in to rob us while we're here?" She shook her head. "That's bold."

"I wish I'd gotten a better look at him," Elaine said. She took a sip of her tea and closed her eyes for a moment, no doubt replaying the events in her mind. "I think the beard was false, though I can't be sure."

"Why do you say that?"

"He didn't look old enough to have a white beard, and the coloring was wrong. I would guess he has dark hair under the wig, but I can't say for sure."

"Did he fill out the suit?"

"Do you mean, did his belly shake when he laughed like a bowl full of jelly?" Elaine shook her head. "No, he was thin. Not rail-thin, but average."

"I would imagine you didn't see him doing much laughing." Jan smiled.

"No, mostly I saw him lunging for the door." Elaine took another sip and was quiet for a moment. The night was still, and the only sound was the soft ticking of the clock on the wall.

Just then, the doorbell rang.

"That'll be the police," Jan said and stood up.

"I'm glad they're here," Elaine said. "But . . . " She hesitated. "We're going to try to find this guy, right?"

"Definitely." Jan nodded. "Of course the police will be on the hunt as well, but now this is personal. We're going to find him."

"Good. I'm glad we're on the same page. We'll find this creep."

CHAPTER SIX

They both slept late Tuesday morning, and when Elaine finally made her way downstairs, she found Jan drinking a cup of English breakfast tea and shaping the dough for the day's scones. Judging by the number of used tea bags on a plate on the counter, it wasn't her first of the morning.

"Good morning. Did you finally get back to sleep?" Elaine asked. She walked around Jan and moved toward the espresso maker on the counter. After a night like that, tea wasn't going to cut it. She needed the hard stuff.

"Eventually," Jan said. "It took me quite a while though."

"Me too," Elaine said, as she took down the espresso blend from the cabinet. The low whine of a snowmobile came in from over the lake. They were common enough this time of year, and she'd almost gotten to the point where she didn't really hear them anymore.

"But the upside is, as I lay awake in bed, I came up with a plan."

"Yeah?" Jan used a long knife to slice the dough into triangles. "What is it?"

"First off, we change our locks." Arnie Sheffield, the sheriff's deputy who had responded to their call last night, had told them it wasn't strictly necessary, but Elaine knew it would make her feel better.

Jan nodded. "Absolutely."

"Then, we use what we know. We use the pictures of the footprints to try to track him down. But I don't know how far that will get us, so I say we start with the most obvious clue we have." Elaine measured out the espresso blend and tapped it down into the portafilter.

"Which is?"

"The Santa suit."

"How are we going to use that?"

"Think about it. How many people own a Santa costume?"

"Probably not that many," Jan said. She lifted one of the triangles onto her baking sheet.

"Right. And there can't be too many places to get one either. So my thinking is, we should start by tracking down people who have Santa suits and places where people can buy them, and see if we come up with anything."

The look Jan was giving her made Elaine feel slightly less confident in her plan than she had when she'd conceived of it just before sunrise. But still, it was the best idea she could think of.

"And how do you propose we do that?" Jan asked.

"There's one very obvious place to start," Elaine said.

"By asking the neighbors if they saw anything last night," Jan said, at the same time that Elaine blurted out, "At the mall!"

Jan looked at her like she was nuts.

Oh. Right.

"Okay, probably the first thing we should do is talk to the neighbors and see if anyone saw anything," Elaine admitted. "But then, I think we go right to the source and find out about Santa costumes, straight from the horse's mouth." She didn't even care that she was mixing metaphors.

"You want to talk to the Santa at the mall?"

Elaine could see that Jan wasn't buying this. "Why not?"

"You think the mall Santa broke into our house last night, hoping to open our safe with a crowbar?" Jan finished setting the scones on the baking sheet.

"Not necessarily." Elaine wasn't sure if it was the lack of sleep or what, but this idea had sounded better when she'd run through it in her mind last night. "Come on. No one will have a better sense of where to get Santa costumes than Santa himself."

"Okay…" Jan was still dubious, clearly, but she sighed and wiped her hands on her apron. "All right. I'm not sure how that's going to help us, but I need to do some Christmas shopping anyway." She picked up the tray of scones and slipped them into the oven. "Why don't we clean up and get dressed, and then we can start off by talking to the neighbors. After that we'll head to the mall."

"Sounds like a plan." Elaine sipped her espresso and immediately felt a tiny bit better. They would catch him.

HALF AN HOUR later, after Rose and Archie had arrived to open the tearoom for the day, Elaine followed Jan down the steps of the front porch and across the snowy yard. Jan had called Eldon Carter, a locksmith in town, and he had promised to come by just after lunch. For now, they walked toward Sylvia's Closet, a boutique vintage shop run by Sylvia Flood. The shop was on the first floor of a cute Victorian-style house, while Sylvia lived on the second floor. There was a chance she might have heard something.

They crossed the ground between the buildings carefully, sinking into a few inches of snow with each step, but when they got inside, the small shop was warm and inviting, with racks of dresses, skirts, and blouses in one front room, men's shirts and pants in another, and a small room of accessories and housewares in the back. While Jan was more practical and tended to favor simple, functional pants and turtlenecks and fleeces, Elaine could be tempted by a stylish vintage piece, no matter how impractical. Elaine mostly restrained herself, but she had bought several well-made purses and silk scarves here.

"Hello there!" Sylvia called brightly. She was in the front room, setting up a display of snazzy, sparkly dresses in front of the window. "Elaine. Jan. It's good to see you."

"Hello, Sylvia," Elaine said. Sylvia looked fabulous as always in a chunky knit sweater and form-fitting pants with a pair of patent-leather heels. Her dark hair was pulled back into a low ponytail and she wore dark-rimmed glasses. "That's quite a dress."

"Isn't it?" Sylvia held up a long-sleeved, knee-length, tomato-colored sheath covered in red sequins. "I was thinking it would be perfect for a holiday party or New Year's Eve. I bet you could pull it off."

Elaine laughed out loud at that. "I think my sequined dress days are well behind me."

"It sounds like your New Year's Eve plans must look pretty different from ours," Jan added. Elaine nodded. Last New Year's Eve, she'd worn sweatpants and been in bed by ten o'clock.

"Oh, I don't know." Sylvia gave the dress one last look before she hung it on the display rack next to a champagne-colored silk hourglass dress that looked like it came from the 1940s. "I think you guys underestimate yourselves."

"And I think you are an excellent saleswoman," Elaine said. "Sadly, we didn't come here to shop. We came to ask if you'd heard or seen anything out of the ordinary last night."

"No, not that I remember." Sylvia straightened the dress and picked up a black silky sheath from another rack. It looked like the sort of thing you'd see chic women in Paris wearing out to dinner. "Like what?"

"Well, there was a bit of an incident at our place last night," Jan said, and explained what had happened. Sylvia gasped and her eyes widened as she heard the story.

"Oh, goodness, I'm so sorry. I must have slept right through it," Sylvia said. "I'm fighting a cold and I took a dose of Nyquil before bed, so I was pretty much dead to the world. I didn't hear or see a thing. That must have been so scary."

"It was pretty frightening. And I don't know if you heard about what happened at Murphy's General Store the other night, but this appears to be the second time he's struck."

"Oh, wow." Sylvia shook her head. "I've been worried I'll be next."

They chatted for a few more minutes, and Sylvia promised to keep them posted if she remembered anything more from last night or if she heard of anything that might be a clue.

They crossed the street and chatted with Priscilla Gates, the head librarian at the Lancaster Public Library. They knew from experience that the library had a security camera in the front and you could see the sidewalk in front of their house from it, so they asked Priscilla for footage from last night, and she gladly downloaded the night's video and handed them a thumb drive. She'd already made a copy for Dan Benson, the state trooper who lived and worked in Lancaster, so she had it handy. Elaine and Jan were both glad to hear that he was already investigating. They would look it over when they got home, but for now, they headed back across the street to the Bookworm, which sat on the other side of their house.

As Elaine pushed open the door, she was hit with the familiar scent of paper and glue and ink and coffee. The front table held a beautiful display of holiday books, and greenery and cheery velvet ribbons festooned the ends of the bookcases. Elaine noticed a wooden donation box—basically a small locked box with a slot on top that rested on a waist-high wooden stand—for the charity Bristol was supporting. Next to that, there was a larger cardboard box for collecting toys.

"Well, hello there." Katelyn Conrad, née Grande, was behind the counter and greeted them as they walked inside. They had gotten to know Katelyn when she had received a crossword puzzle from a mysterious suitor, and they had tracked him down and matched her up with Frank Conrad, a music teacher at a local middle school who had long had a crush on her. "How are you guys doing?"

"We're all right. How you are you?" Elaine asked. Instrumental Christmas music was playing over the store's sound system.

"I'm all right. Enjoying the Christmas season," Katelyn said.

"How's Frank?" Jan piped up.

A pink flush crept over Katelyn's cheeks. "He's great. He's really busy with all the school holiday concerts coming up, but he's doing well."

"I'm glad to hear it," Jan said.

"So what can I help you ladies find?" Katelyn asked. "We've got a new one in that English mystery series you like, Jan." She gestured toward a display of books on a small table on the end of one of the rows.

"Oh dear. I'm supposed to be shopping for other people, not myself," Jan said, but she moved toward the table anyway. Jan picked up the book and turned it over to read the back cover. Then, with a sigh, she tucked it under her arm. "I love this series. I can't resist."

"A bookworm's dilemma," Katelyn laughed. "Now, Elaine, is there anything I can help you find?"

"We're actually just here looking for Bristol," Elaine said.

"Ah. She's in the back office. Hang on." Katelyn pushed herself off the stool behind the counter and started toward the back of the store. A moment later, Bristol came out of a room at the back of the shop, adjusting her glasses.

"Hi there!" She smiled when she saw Jan and Elaine. "I was actually just talking to the caterer for the big fund-raiser.

34

I'm hoping to finalize the menu over the next few days. Thank you again for hosting."

"We're glad to do it," Jan said. "If you're talking about the menu, I have an idea. I have a recipe for these great mini grilled cheese sandwiches that would be perfect."

"That sounds wonderful. Want to pass the recipe along?"

"Sure thing," Jan said before turning back toward the front of the store. "I saw the donation box at the front of the store. How's it going so far?"

"Shockingly well, actually. We've gotten a steady stream of small bills, but we also got a really large cash donation in the box at the library. Even if that's all we get for the rest of the fund-raiser, we can consider it a success."

"That's wonderful," Elaine said. It was nice to hear that generosity was alive and well in Lancaster. Then again, this town was full of good people, so she wasn't surprised.

"But you all didn't come here to hear me babble about this. What can I help you with?"

Elaine remembered what they had come to ask Bristol about, and her mood turned a bit. Yes, Lancaster was full of good people, but sometimes bad things happened as well.

"I'm afraid we have some not-so-great news," Elaine said. "Did you hear about how Murphy's was robbed by someone dressed as Santa Claus?"

"Oh yes. It's on the front page of the newspaper this morn- ing," Bristol said, gesturing toward a copy of the *Penzance Courier* folded on the counter. "It's so terrible."

Elaine hadn't seen the paper yet this morning, and she glanced over at it and cringed. *Santa Thief,* the headline read.

"Santa broke into our house last night too," Jan said.

"What?" Bristol's eyes widened, and Katelyn, who had settled back behind the counter, gasped.

Elaine quickly told them the story and reassured them that they were all right, though shaken.

"We're hoping someone heard or saw something," Jan said.

"I'm afraid there was no one here last night," Bristol said. "So I'm no help. But wow. I just hope we're not next."

"I'll keep my eyes open," Katelyn promised, and Bristol said she would do the same.

The cousins also checked in with Anita Picard, whose house across the street had a view of Tea for Two, but she hadn't seen anything, nor had Marie Shenvi, who owned Gift Me.

Then, when they were back at home, they sat down in front of Elaine's laptop in the sitting room and reviewed the footage from the library's security camera. The grainy image was in black and white, and you couldn't make out much because of the falling snow. They started the footage at about midnight and quickly skimmed through the tape.

"Quite the happening town, no?" Elaine said as they watched nothing move for long stretches of time.

"Snowy Monday nights in December aren't the most exciting time around here," Jan agreed.

A few cars drove past. A plow came by just after 1:00 a.m. Finally, just before 2:30 a.m., a pickup truck pulled up in front of their house. Their house was mostly blocked by hedges, but they could see that the second floor was dark except for the single candles in each of the front windows.

"Freeze it," Jan said, and Elaine quickly paused the video. You couldn't tell much from the picture—just that it was a pickup truck of some kind. The blurry black-and-white image didn't give them much more to go on, and the license plate was obscured by snow for the very short window it was on the screen. Elaine started the video again, and they held their breath. Flurries of wind-driven snow obscured the screen for a moment. Was this when the thief was cutting the screen door and picking the locks to get inside the house? The snow stopped. Then, the light in Jan's bedroom flicked on, and just a moment later, the truck zoomed past the house again. Elaine paused the video, but like before, they couldn't make out much.

The thief had arrived and left in a pickup, though the make, model, and color were impossible to make out in the footage they had. The video was so dark you couldn't tell anything at all about the person driving the truck.

"I didn't even hear the engine as he got away," Elaine said, shaking her head.

"You probably couldn't hear anything over the sound of your own screaming," Jan said with a smile.

"Hey now. I would like to see how you would have reacted," Elaine said, feigning indignation.

"I would have been doing pretty much exactly the same thing you did," Jan said. "Only I would have screamed even louder."

They started the video again, but after the truck had left the screen, there was nothing—not even a stray vehicle—for the next hour. Finally, Elaine stopped the video.

"Well, at least we learned something new. We now know that our Santa drives a pickup truck."

Jan laughed. "Just like about fifty percent of the people around here."

Elaine sighed. It was true. Four-wheel drive came in handy in the winter, and SUVs and pickups were very common, as most people ended up hauling around snowmobiles or camping gear or firewood at some point in the year.

"I wonder if we might be able to tell something from the tire marks in the parking area," Jan said.

"It's a good idea, though I'm sure the police would have looked into that last night. But we can check on our way out."

"Out?"

"To the mall." Elaine smiled. "Don't tell me you forgot."

"I hadn't forgotten. Though I hoped you'd changed your mind," Jan admitted.

"Oh, come on. It will be fun," Elaine said.

Jan sighed. "Let me grab my shopping list."

CHAPTER SEVEN

A few minutes later, after they'd touched base with Rose and Archie to let them know they were going to be out again, they were in Elaine's car and heading toward Augusta. Jan had lived in Augusta for most of her life, and her son, Brian, still lived there with his family, so she had spent plenty of time at that mall. She wasn't totally sold on Elaine's idea of trying to solve their mystery by talking to Santa, but she didn't mind going to see him. Jan had tried to downplay the Santa story when her kids were young—she and Peter had been sure to teach them the real meaning of Christmas—but there was still something magical about children looking forward to meeting Santa at Christmastime.

They parked and headed inside. The mall was busy, even on this cold Tuesday morning, and Jan followed Elaine past several big-name stores and toward the open gallery in the middle. The smell of melted butter and cinnamon sugar hit her as soon as they walked in. Oh dear. She'd forgotten how the mall always smelled like Cinnabon. Her stomach groaned.

The whole-wheat toast and low-fat peanut butter she'd had for breakfast weren't cutting it.

They followed the sound of jingle bells and soon found a line of children snaking past oversize presents and enormous candy canes. At the end of the line was a man dressed as Santa Claus sitting on a large chair inside what looked like a hut made of candy canes. Young women dressed as elves helped children up into his lap, took pictures, and guided parents toward the cash registers. To the left of Santa was a small building labeled Santa's Workshop.

"Do you think there's a way we can skip the line?" Jan asked uncertainly. How long would this take?

"I don't know how. Should we just ask an elf whether Santa can take a break from delighting children to tell us whether he's a thief?"

"I guess not." Jan eyed the line. It was almost all mothers with young children. She would feel ridiculous standing here without a child. Why hadn't they at least thought to bring along a child? She was sure her twin grandsons, Max and Riley, would have loved to have joined them for this. But they were in school, and Elaine was already getting in line. Jan hesitated. Were they really going to do this? There was no way *this* Santa was the man who had broken into their house, was there?

But there was Elaine, waving at her to join the line. She was already stepping under the candy cane archway. Oh, goodness. She didn't see how she would get out of doing this now.

"So," Jan said when she stood next to her cousin in line, "what do you intend to say to Santa when we get up there?"

"I'm going to ask for a pony for Christmas," Elaine said with a smile.

"I can still get out of line. I'll gladly meet you by the fountain in an hour. There's a sale on those leather gloves I wanted to get Bob at Macy's."

"I'm going to ask him if he's read the paper, and if he knows where one might get their own Santa hat and beard."

"All right then." Jan relaxed a bit. The line was moving pretty quickly. There were only a few children ahead of them now. Right now a little boy sat on Santa's lap screaming at the top of his lungs. Jan had to laugh. She had a photo of her daughter Tara doing the exact same thing. And now look at Tara. She was all grown up and living on her own and designing jewelry. And she was dating Jack Weston, Lancaster's game warden and most eligible bachelor. It seemed like just yesterday she was little. Time passed quicker every year, it seemed.

"How's Bob?" Elaine asked.

"He's good." Jan wasn't really sure what to say. Bob had asked her to marry him at the same time he told her he was taking a job in Baltimore. He'd wanted her to give up everything here and move with him. And as much as she'd wanted to marry him, she hadn't wanted to leave behind her whole life here, and he hadn't been willing to stay. So the past few months had been rocky, and Jan had even considered dating other people, but her heart hadn't been in it. It was Bob she wanted. The time apart made her realize that.

"He really loves the work he's doing. He's got these really interesting cases, like this boy he's defending right now, who was picked out of a lineup as being the one who broke into a house and robbed a woman at gunpoint. The fact that the poor guy wasn't even in the state at the time doesn't seem to matter—he was convicted of the crime and is serving time for something he didn't do. Bob feels good about helping him, and you can see why."

"Absolutely." Elaine shuffled forward as the line moved up. A little redhead with pigtails and a smocked dress was climbing up into Santa's lap, helped by an elf in a tight green suit. "And he's still planning on continuing with this work indefinitely?"

Jan didn't know how to answer. "Yes." Man, the smell of those cinnamon rolls was delicious. It was so mean to pump that smell all the way over here.

Elaine didn't answer, but she placed her hand gently on Jan's back.

A moment later, the redhead was climbing down and they were next in line. Santa Claus turned to them with a big smile and looked around, no doubt looking for a child.

"It's just us," Elaine announced brightly, stepping forward. The poor green-suited elf, who couldn't have been much out of high school, seemed completely at a loss. Elaine stepped up to the dais where Santa's throne rested and waved. Jan followed a step behind. "I'm Elaine Cook, and this is my cousin Jan Blake. We don't want to sit on your lap, but we were hoping we could talk to you for a minute."

The elf with a camera looked from them to Santa and back again. Jan supposed they probably didn't encounter this situation very often.

"Ho ho ho, that's quite all right," Santa said. "Santa loves to talk to grown-ups too."

"Great," Elaine said. The elves still looked uncertain, but they let Elaine and Jan step closer to the throne. "I don't know if you've read this morning's *Penzance Courier*"—Jan would guess he probably hadn't; most people in Augusta got the *Kennebec Journal*–"but there's a thief going around Lancaster breaking into businesses dressed as Santa Claus."

Santa's smile didn't falter, but his eyes registered confusion and concern.

"We were hoping you could tell us where people go locally to get Santa suits and beards, so we can try to track him down," Jan said.

"Yours is really good," Elaine added. "We figured you know all the best places to get Santa gear."

Again, Santa didn't drop the smile, but the elves had frozen in place. No one said anything for a moment, but then Santa let out another, "Ho ho ho." He slowly pushed himself up from his chair and announced, "Santa needs to take a quick break to check on the reindeer."

He gestured for Elaine and Jan to follow him toward a door in the small house next to the chair. He waved to the crowd of waiting children, announced, "I'll be right back. I have to go give Rudolph a carrot," and started toward the door.

Jan looked at Elaine, who shrugged and started to follow him. Jan heard one of the elves trying to placate a mom with two toddlers who was next in line, but then she followed Elaine and stepped into a small room made out of plywood. The inside of Santa's workshop turned out to contain employee lockers, a desk with chairs, and extra camera equipment. Santa sat down on one of the chairs and gestured for them to sit on the others.

Jan looked around uncertainly, but she sat.

"I'm sorry to be so dramatic," Santa said. "I'm not allowed to break character in front of the children. And of course I couldn't have anyone overhearing me discussing other Santas. We all know there's only one, right?" He gave them a wink, and Jan didn't know what else to do, so she smiled. "Now what's going on?"

Jan was heartened to see that this Santa was soft-spoken and seemed to actually be interested in hearing them out. Maybe this hadn't been a terrible idea after all.

"I know this is somewhat unusual," Elaine said. "But for the past two nights, a man dressed as Santa Claus has broken into businesses in Lancaster, where we live. The first night he broke open a safe at a store, and last night I caught him coming into our house. He had a crowbar hooked on his belt, so I assume his intention was to break open our safe as well."

"Wow." Santa's eyes were wide. "That's terrible."

"It is," Elaine said.

"To besmirch the name of Santa like that..." His voice drifted off. Jan thought he must be joking at first, but she soon realized that he wasn't. He seemed to feel genuinely put out to hear this.

"We're trying to track down the thief," Jan said.

"Aren't the police doing that?" Santa's brow furrowed.

"Of course," Elaine said smoothly. "It's just that we've solved a few mysteries in the past, and since this one affects us personally, we're looking into it as well."

"*Ooh*"—Santa's eyes lit up—"I've heard about you! The cousins who solve mysteries! You own a tearoom, right? And figure out mysteries that sometimes the police don't?"

"Oh, we can't compare to the police," Elaine said, but Jan could see she was pleased that he'd heard about them. "But yes, we do enjoy solving mysteries."

"Well, in that case, I'm very glad to do what I can. But I'm afraid I don't have much help to offer. There are probably many places to get a cheap Santa costume, but this is a professional suit licensed by the International Society of Real-Bearded Santas. You have to be a member of the organization to have access to one like this."

Jan looked at Elaine. She didn't even know where to start with this.

"What is the International Society of Real-Bearded Santas?" Elaine asked. "Is that a trade group?"

"It's much more than a trade group," Santa said. "It's a brotherhood. A group of like-minded individuals who believe in the goodness of children, the spirit of Christmas, and the joy of giving. When we get together for conventions, it's like the spirit of Christmas just settles over the place."

Jan tried to hide a smile. She loved the image of a convention floor being overrun with grown men dressed like Santa Claus.

"So...I guess that means your beard is real?" Elaine said it as a joke, but Santa didn't seem to see it that way.

"Of course! What self-respecting Santa has to wear a fake beard?" He seemed to be offended at the very thought.

He seemed so earnest that Jan tried to navigate this carefully. "And do all mall Santas belong to this group?"

"Many do." He nodded. "Of course, there are other groups as well, but the International Society of Real-Bearded Santas is the most respected."

"What…" Elaine was trying to hold back a chuckle, Jan could tell. "What are the other groups?"

"The biggest ones are the World Federation of Real-Bearded Santas and the International League of Real-Bearded Santas, but there are some smaller ones as well."

"Wow." Jan just didn't know what to say. She'd had no idea there were multiple groups of real-bearded Santas. "And do you all work together?"

"Oh no." Santa shook his head. His real beard swung with his head. "The groups don't exactly get along."

"Oh my." It took everything in her to stifle a laugh. The idea of rival groups of Santas was too much. So much for the spirit of Christmas. She met Elaine's eyes and she could see that Elaine was close to losing it. She had to focus here so they could get what they needed without offending Santa.

"So you're saying that the average person couldn't get a suit like yours? That only professionals have access to one like this?"

"That's right," Santa said, nodding. "I'm sure there are many places where normal people can buy Santa costumes. Probably online would be easiest. But not one like this."

Jan couldn't think of how to respond. She was still fighting back a giggle that threatened to come out. Thankfully, Elaine stood up, held out her hand, and said, "We've kept you from the children long enough. Thank you so much for your help."

Santa nodded and led them to the door. Jan waved to the elves, who still seemed stunned, and hurried after Elaine, who was already making a beeline for the area outside Santa-land. They walked away quickly, and made it past the Gap and the Sharper Image before they both burst into laughter. Jan hunched over, putting her hands on her knees.

"I have to admit, I'm glad you dragged me to that," Jan said. "Rival groups of Santas? Who ever heard of such a thing?"

"It's not funny," Elaine said, laughing so hard she could hardly catch her breath. "I know it's not funny. But it's making me laugh so much."

It took them a few minutes to recover, but finally Jan straightened up and took a deep breath.

"Right," she said, nodding. "So. We know our thief isn't a professional Santa, because if he were, he wouldn't besmirch the name of Santa like that."

This sent Elaine into a fresh fit of giggles, and then finally she took a deep breath, sighed, and said, "Well, that was a total waste of time."

"Not a total waste," Jan clarified. She looked around. "I still have my Christmas shopping to do." Jan had presents for the grandkids all squared away. They were easy and fun to buy gifts for. It was their parents who were hard. "Meet you back here in an hour?"

"That sounds good to me," Elaine said, and after one last glance back at Santa's workshop, sighed and headed off.

CHAPTER EIGHT

When they pulled up at the tearoom later, Eldon Carter's van was parked in the driveway. Elaine was glad to see he was already here, especially after a fairly useless trip to the mall. She hadn't exactly thought meeting Santa would clear everything up, but she'd thought they'd learn something useful. No dice. And since she already had her Christmas shopping done, she had mostly wandered in and out of stores before settling down on a bench to read her book until Jan was done. But Jan had returned to the car loaded down with bags, so at least the trip had been helpful for one of them.

Now, Elaine and Jan made their way to the front porch and found Eldon working on fitting a new lock in the door.

"Hello there," he said brightly. Eldon was in his early forties and had light-brown hair and a cheerful smile. He had the front door propped open as he worked, and Jan and Elaine hurried past him inside. "I hope you don't mind that I got right to work on this one. I wanted to get it done quickly since I know you don't want to freeze your customers."

Elaine glanced toward the fireplace in the east parlor, where a fire was burning briskly, and the two tables closest were occupied with Christmas shoppers and their bags. Archie, who generally took charge of the fireplace this time of year, was currently setting down a fresh pot of tea for one of the customers.

"Thank you so much for coming on such short notice," Elaine said, unwinding her scarf. "We really appreciate it."

"Of course. I hear you all had quite a scare last night. After something like that, I'm glad to be able to help. We want Lancaster to be safe."

"Thank you," Jan said.

In addition to being the town locksmith, Eldon was the chairman of the board of selectmen, and he was always concerned when there was anything wrong in town.

"I'll be done with this one in a jiffy, and then I'll move on to the back door and side door," Eldon said. "And get you a shiny new set of keys."

Jan was already heading toward the kitchen, no doubt checking to make sure everything was in order. Elaine hesitated. She kept her coat on—with the front door open like that, it was chilly in here—but she had started to move toward the kitchen when she paused. She realized she didn't really know how picking a lock worked. Arnie Sheffield had pointed out the scratches on the face of their back door lock as evidence that it had been picked. But was there some way to trace those scratches to find the tool that made them?

"Can I ask you a question about picking locks?" Elaine asked.

"Sure thing. You looking for a side career?" Eldon joked as he screwed the new lock into place. "A life of crime?"

49

"Depends on how much you teach me," Elaine said.

"All righty." He turned the screwdriver one last time, turned the lock to make sure it worked, and nodded. "That's one down." He closed the door and picked up the bag that had been sitting at his feet. "How about if we move toward the back door and I'll show you what I know."

"That would be great. Thanks." Elaine led him down the hall toward the kitchen. Rose was hard at work making croissants, her long blonde braid snaking down her back, and Jan had already set the kettle on to boil and was setting out several of their delicate china teapots.

"Hi there, Rose," Elaine greeted her. Rose was in her midtwenties, and around the time her mother died, she'd decided to make a career change. She'd started working in the kitchen here and was going to culinary school at night. She'd also recently started dating a man she had met in one of her classes, and she was hopeful about their future.

"Hi, Elaine. How was the mall?"

"Jan found some gifts, at least."

Eldon moved toward the back door—the one that the thief had picked the night before. He set down the bag and opened the door so they could see the lock.

"Yep, this has been picked, all right," he said, running his hands over the tiny scratches on the face. "He did a clean job of it too, whoever he is."

"What made the scratches?" Elaine asked. Eldon nodded and bent over to open up his bag. He pulled out a metal box and opened it. Inside was a collection of long, skinny metal tools.

"Think of your lock like a cylinder." He pointed to the circle on the face of the lock. The hole you put your key in was in the middle of the circle. "You slide your key into the cylinder. Inside are tiny little pins on springs, basically. Imagine the pistons in your car, which move up and down. But these pins are moved up and down inside the cylinder by the key."

Elaine tried to picture this in her mind.

"You slide the key inside the lock, and it pushes the pins up based on the shape of the key. Each key is cut differently to line up with pins, or tumblers, inside the lock, and to move them into the correct positions to open the lock."

Rose grabbed a handful of silverware and ducked out of the room. She could always be depended on to see to all the needs in the tearoom.

"So when the right key is inside the lock, the pins are moved to the right position, and the lock turns," Jan said, nodding. Jan always had been better at picturing stuff like this. But Elaine thought she followed.

"Exactly." Eldon smiled at Jan. "So that's when you want to open the lock with a key. But what if you don't have a key?"

"You act like a civilized person and realize you're not meant to go inside," Elaine said.

Eldon laughed. "Well, sure. That's what *you'd* do. Maybe this whole 'thief as a second career' thing isn't for you after all."

Jan gave Elaine a funny look, but Eldon continued.

"Someone who knows what they're doing can manipulate the lock by inserting one of these tools." He pulled an L-shaped metal tool from the kit. "This is a tension wrench. You use it, as well as one of these bad boys." He selected one of the thin metal tools from his kit and pushed it inside the keyhole. He pulled it out and held it up to show them. It was basically a long piece of metal with thin metal barbs on the end. He pointed to the barbs, which seemed to mimic the teeth of a key. "See this bit? You have to find the right one to work for your lock, and sometimes getting the right one in scratches the face of the lock. But you use this to push up the pins inside the lock. With some work, you can get each of the pins inside the lock to release, and then use the tension wrench to turn the cylinder and open the lock."

It seemed like quite a daunting process to Elaine, especially as you couldn't see what you were doing inside the lock. "How long would something like that take?"

"Depends on a number of factors, including the skill of the person doing it. On a cold night, it might have been a bit harder, but a skilled thief could do it in a few minutes, probably."

"Based on what we saw on the security footage, he was only here a few minutes," Jan said.

Elaine nodded. They were dealing with an experienced thief then, for sure. But who? "Is there any way to trace the scratch marks on the door to figure out which tools made them?"

"I'm afraid not," Eldon said. Elaine had known it was a stretch, but she was still disappointed.

"What about the safe? Could he really open the safe with a crowbar?" Jan asked.

"Oh, certainly. Here." Eldon straightened up and pulled his phone out of his pocket. "Safes are generally relatively, well…safe. But sure, it is possible to get one open with a crowbar. Check this out." He held out his phone and she saw there was a video playing on the screen. Elaine took the phone and Jan walked over and watched over Elaine's shoulder. The video showed a man using a crowbar to pry open a home safe in under two minutes.

"Goodness." Elaine had thought a safe meant no one could get what was inside. "So what are we supposed to do to keep valuable things protected?"

"For your most valuable items, a safe deposit box is the way to go. But most of the time, a safe is perfectly fine. There are not too many people who would know how to do what the man in the video just did."

"No." Elaine handed the phone back. "We just happen to have found the one person who does know how to pick locks and open safes."

He gave her a sympathetic smile. "Why don't I get these locks finished up? You'll feel better then."

Elaine wasn't sure she would, but she nodded anyway.

CHAPTER NINE

J an wolfed down her lunch of lean turkey on dry bread. Maybe that was how people survived on diets—by the time they finally got to eat, they were so famished it didn't matter what the food was, it somehow tasted good.

When she'd finished, had some more Earl Grey tea, and tossed some food into the dish for Earl Grey the cat, a fresh surge of customers had started to arrive at the tearoom. Jan tried her best to forget about Santa and lock-picking and safes and focus on greeting each person who walked in that door as if they were family. Soft instrumental Christmas music played, and the gray skies and falling snow outside made the tearoom feel warm and bright.

Among the new arrivals was Sarah Ryder, Pastor Mike's wife, who brought along her niece. Then came Macy Atherton, who ran the Green Glade Cottages, and her friend Rue Maxwell, who owned Northwoods Bed-and-Breakfast with her husband, Ned.

"How about a seat by the fire? It's always so drafty in here, and these old bones can't handle the cold," Macy said by way of greeting. Jan stifled a laugh. Macy was younger than Jan and Elaine. She was one of their most faithful customers, especially in winter when the cottages weren't busy. Though she typically found something to complain about, she kept coming back.

"Right this way." Jan pasted a smile on her face and led them to the table closest to the fire.

"Oh, wow. I love how you've decorated that mantel," Rue said. Rue had perfectly styled blonde hair and was wearing a red sweater that looked so soft it might be cashmere. "It looks fresh and natural and gorgeous."

"Thank you," Jan said. She'd clipped fresh holly branches from the yard, with their glossy green leaves and their bright-red round little berries, and she'd woven them in with pine boughs and pine cones she'd also gathered from the yard. Rustic white pillar candles set here and there between the branches gave the whole thing a soft, glowing look.

"You two always have the most beautiful place," Rue said, settling into her seat.

"Now. Tell us about what happened last night." Macy looked up at Jan expectantly.

Jan held back a sigh. So much for forgetting about it all. She gave them the abridged version of the story, and then went to the kitchen to put in their order for full afternoon tea. More guests arrived, including Andrea McInnis with Sharon Reddick and Maureen Oakley and her daughter. Jan kept busy, greeting guests and fetching tea, but her mind wasn't focused. She couldn't stop thinking about what had happened last night. She couldn't stop trying to figure out who their thief could be. And she couldn't stop thinking about the clue she hadn't looked into yet. She had taken pictures of the boot prints he'd left behind in the snow. Could she use that to track him down?

Jan looked around the tearoom. Archie was chatting with the woman at the table by the front window in the west parlor, and Elaine was just bringing out tea in the east parlor. Rose had things under control in the kitchen. Jan had an idea. She would just run upstairs for a minute to see if she could figure this out.

She settled down on the couch in the sitting room with her laptop. The first thing she did was Google "International Society of Real-Bearded Santas." She read through the site that came up, and she found contact information for the group. She sent off an e-mail, asking if it was possible to get a list of their membership, and quickly did the same for the other groups the Santa at the mall had mentioned. He'd said the thief wasn't a "real" Santa—Jan laughed at the idea—but it was worth checking into anyway.

Then she transferred the pictures she'd taken in the snow from her phone to her laptop and enlarged the photos and brightened them so she could see them a bit better.

She had one good shot where you could really make out the tread the boots had left behind in the snow. Judging by the deep tread, Jan's guess was that these had been left behind by some kind of Pac boot—a boot with a thick rubber sole and a waterproof lower, paired with a leather laced-up upper. For a fraction of a second, she felt triumphant—she'd figured it out. Then, just as quickly, she realized that she'd figured it out because just about everybody in Maine wore some version of a Pac boot in winter. She needed more to go on.

Jan studied the image of the tread a moment longer and turned back to her laptop. She would just have to try to find an image of the treads for all the brands she could think of and see if they matched up. She typed "L.L. Bean Pac boot" into her browser and did a search. It was Maine, after all. L.L. Bean was everywhere. It wasn't hard to find an image of the bottom of the boot, and Jan studied the tread. It didn't match. Her tread was more spiky than wedge-like. What about another brand? She tried Googling "Sorel tread" next. She studied the bottom of the boot that turned up. It was hard to tell, but—she squinted. Didn't look like a match.

She ran through all the brands she was familiar with. Each brand typically made several styles of boot, which made this more challenging than it should have been, but generally each brand had its own distinctive tread pattern. Still, it was hard to compare a picture of a boot online with a picture of a footprint in the snow. She was starting to think she was getting nowhere. She was about to close the laptop and head downstairs when she remembered something. She'd gotten Brian boots for Christmas last year. What were they called? He'd e-mailed her the link to the boots, hadn't he?

Jan searched through her e-mail and found the message from Brian last year. This year, she was chipping in with her other children, Tara and Amy, to buy him a new snowblower, but last year he'd suggested these boots as a gift idea. She clicked on the link. Ah. That was it. Schnee. She'd liked the brand name because it meant "snow" in German. You could probably trust a boot named after snow.

She did a Google image search for the boot, and found one store's website that showed the treads. And, wait—she enlarged the picture. It looked like this could be it. The treads on these boots were like small spikes. They could be the ones in the picture. She looked from one photo to the other and back again. It was possible. But she couldn't tell.

Then she had an idea. She grabbed her cell phone and called Brian.

"Mom?"

"Hi, honey. How's it going?"

"Good." She thought for a moment and decided not to tell him about what had happened here last night. It would only worry him, and Brian was already predisposed to worry about her. "Everything's fine. But I have a strange question. Can you send me a picture of your boots?"

"What?"

"The snow boots you got last year for Christmas. I need a picture of the treads. Or, even better—can you walk on a piece of white paper so I can see what the treads would look like in the snow?"

"It's nice to talk to you too, Mom. How's Bob doing?"

Jan sighed. Fine. Sometimes she got excited and forgot about formalities. "Everything is fine," she repeated. "Business is going great. The house and town are beautiful at this time of year. Bob will be visiting in six days."

"That's great."

"How are you guys? How are my adorable grandchildren?"

"They're awesome. We have Avery's holiday concert at the school tonight. You remember that Kelly has a karate demonstration the first week of January, right? Paula is rushing around trying to make everything perfect for the holiday like always. So overall, pretty normal."

"I'm glad to hear it."

Brian waited a beat, and then said, "Okay."

"Okay?"

"I have no idea why you want me to step on a piece of white paper wearing my snow boots, but I will do it tonight when I get home and send you a picture."

"Thank you!"

Brian laughed. "I'm hoping you'll tell me what this is about at some point?"

He probably thought she had some holiday surprise up her sleeve. Jan felt a teensy bit bad about that. But better than letting him know the real reason she wanted to see it.

"Of course. I'll talk to you later."

"Bye, Mom."

Jan hung up feeling a little better. She didn't know if she was any closer to finding answers, but she felt like she'd made a bit of progress, and that felt good. She stood and stretched before heading back down to the tearoom.

THEY HAD JUST finished cleaning up the tearoom after closing that afternoon when the kitchen phone rang. Elaine grabbed it as Jan set a tray of teacups down on the counter.

"Tea for Two, this is Elaine."

"Hi, Elaine. It's Priscilla Gates, from the library."

Elaine wanted to laugh. How many Priscillas did she think Elaine knew, let alone Priscilla Gateses? Elaine knew she was from the library. But that precision was part of what made Priscilla so good at her job.

"I know you are looking into this Santa thief thing," Priscilla said. She'd given them the library's footage, so naturally she knew. "Well, I overheard something today, and I thought you might be interested."

"Oh?" Elaine didn't usually put much stock in hearsay, but if it came from Priscilla, there was probably a pretty good chance it was solid. Jan gave her a questioning look, and Elaine held up a finger to ask her to wait.

"You know Chris Cosgrove?"

"Of course." The teen volunteered at the library, and was also a star quarterback and a straight-A student.

"He was talking to another teenager who was in here today, someone from the Forrest High football team, I believe. Now that the season is over, I see more of them inside the library."

Sports were a big deal around these parts, and Elaine and Jan had experienced firsthand the excitement of the local team's thrilling win at the homecoming game last fall.

"They were discussing another player who had dressed like Santa Claus for Halloween," Priscilla continued.

"Really?" Didn't teenage boys usually dress like the Grim Reaper or stuff like that? She'd never heard of a kid dressing as Santa. "Did they think he might have been behind the thefts?"

"They were discussing the possibility. Of course, when they saw me coming, they disbanded, so I didn't get anything more out of them. But I thought you might be able to."

"We'd love to talk with Chris," Elaine said.

"I suspected as much. He'll be here tomorrow afternoon if you want to stop by then."

"We'll be there." Elaine thanked Priscilla and hung up, then turned to Jan. "It looks like we may have our first actual suspect."

CHAPTER TEN

Wednesday morning dawned clear and bright. As Elaine tied the belt of her robe around her waist, she pushed aside her curtain and looked out the window. The snow-covered yard sloped down toward the frozen surface of Chickadee Lake, and all of it glittered in the dazzling dawn light. It was stunning. Elaine stood there for a moment, gazing out, thanking God for the beauty He showered them with each day. She felt blessed that He had brought her here and allowed her to enjoy it.

Finally, when the pull of caffeine and the smell of freshly-baked apple spice muffins could not be denied any longer, she padded her way downstairs.

"Oh. Hello." Elaine started when she saw that Faith Lanier was sitting at the table across from Jan. She ran her hand through her hair and tried to smooth it down.

"Hello, Elaine. I'm sorry to startle you. I know you weren't expecting to see me here." Faith was wearing jeans and a sweatshirt, and she looked pale and had dark half-moons under her eyes. She had her hands wrapped around a mug of tea, and she had one of Jan's muffins on a small plate in front of her. Elaine got a bad feeling in her belly.

"That's quite all right." Elaine recovered quickly. She looked terrible, but then it looked like Faith hadn't dolled herself up for a social call either. She looked at Jan for an explanation. She hoped this didn't mean—

"The water in the kettle is hot," Jan said. "And so are the muffins." Jan had just a mug of milky tea in front of her.

"Thank you." Elaine placed a tea bag in her mug, then poured the hot water over it. She set a muffin on a plate, then sat down at the table too. Maybe Faith had come here with news about what she'd seen at Murphy's General Store the other night. But something about the haunted look in Faith's brown eyes made her doubt this.

"There was a break-in at A Little Something last night," Jan said.

There it was. The news Elaine had been dreading. A Little Something was the gift shop Faith owned just a few doors down from Tea for Two. Faith always stocked it with fun things like trendy jewelry, country-themed décor items, and beautifully crafted heirloom-quality stuffed animals. Faith carried the jewelry Jan's daughter Tara made, and it sold well.

"I am so sorry. Was anyone hurt?"

"There was no one there, thank goodness," Faith said. "And none of the inventory was taken or damaged. But he did pick the lock, and he did break into the safe."

"With a crowbar?"

"Definitely with a crowbar." Faith crumbled off a piece of the muffin and put it in her mouth.

"When did you discover this?" Elaine asked.

"When I woke up this morning, I looked across the street at the shop and saw that the door was standing open." Elaine nodded. A Little Something was two doors down from Tea for Two, and directly across the street from the Laniers' house. "I panicked a bit, and I dragged Murphy out of bed and made him come over and check it out with me. When we saw that the safe had been ripped open, we called 911, and Arnie Sheffield showed up and investigated. He promised Trooper Benson would stop by later to follow up." Faith broke off a bit of the muffin, popped it in her mouth, and chewed for a moment. "But I was so keyed up that I knew I couldn't go back to sleep. I saw your lights on here, and I had heard that you guys were investigating what was going on…"

"How'd you hear that?" Elaine asked. They hadn't told too many people, had they?

Faith laughed. "It's a small town. Everyone knows when someone sneezes."

Elaine had to acknowledge that was true.

"But it was Macy Atherton who mentioned it, at our book club meeting last night," Faith continued.

Ah. Well, that explained it.

"Maybe she was speaking out of turn, but we all know you guys investigate most of the things that go on in this town, so I just assumed…"

"She was right," Jan said.

Was Elaine imagining it, or was Jan eyeing the muffin on her plate? "We are investigating. I'm glad you came to talk to us. I'm just always amazed by how the grapevine works in this town."

Faith shrugged. "Welcome to small-town life."

Elaine loved that the people of this town took such an interest in one another's affairs. It meant they cared. But she wanted to get back to the topic at hand. "Did anyone see the thief?" Elaine asked.

"Better than that," Jan said. Elaine looked at Faith.

"The timing is a bit nuts, actually. Remember how I saw that guy dressed like Santa leaving Murphy's Sunday night?"

Elaine nodded. How could she forget something like that?

"I was pretty worried about it," Faith admitted. "And then when I heard what happened here the next night, I decided I had to do something. So yesterday, I went to the big hardware store in Waterville and bought a security camera."

"Wow. You can buy those at the hardware store?" Elaine had assumed you had to get a contract with a security company to set one up.

"You sure can. They're not cheap, but they're not hard to set up, and you can monitor them remotely."

"Really?"

"Sure thing." Faith pulled her phone out of the purse at her feet and touched the screen. "See? Here's the shop right now."

She held out the phone to Elaine. Elaine took it and saw that a camera had been mounted in the corner of the shop and she was seeing a live feed of what was happening inside. Which was nothing. It wasn't even 8:00 a.m. The store was dark and nothing moved, but you could see the whole shop.

"Can you access the video from last night?"

"Absolutely. It stores it in the Cloud." Faith gestured for her phone, and Elaine gave it back.

Elaine wasn't really sure she understood what "the Cloud" was, but had the vague notion that this meant the camera stored the footage on far-off computers somewhere. By tapping the screen a few times, Faith was able to pull up a piece of footage from the previous night.

"Here it is."

Elaine looked at the screen and saw that, sure enough, there was the man dressed as Santa, just like she'd seen the night before. It started with a shadow outside the front door of the shop. He stood there for a few minutes, doing something with the door handle. Elaine knew this must have been when he was picking the lock. And then he came into the shop, looked around a bit, and headed for the small office at the back. He had the same costume that Elaine had seen. It hung a bit on him, and he had a crowbar hanging from the belt. He wore white gloves, and he had a black bag tucked into the belt as well. Just before he got to the back of the shop, he glanced up at the camera.

"Freeze it," Elaine said.

Faith tapped the screen, and the image stopped. Elaine leaned in and studied it. He was looking directly up at the camera, but the full white beard, mustache, and wig obscured so much of his face that it was hard to tell anything about him.

"I think the beard must be fake," Jan said, and Elaine nodded. She was pretty sure of that too. It was hard to tell his age, but something about the way he moved suggested he wasn't old enough to have all-white hair. No real-bearded Santa then. But there really wasn't much else. The full Santa beard and mustache, along with the red-and-white hat, really was an excellent way for him to disguise himself, Elaine had to admit.

"It's the same guy I saw coming out of Murphy's the other night. It has to be," Faith said.

"Yep. It's the same guy I saw," Elaine added.

Faith started the video again and they watched as he disappeared off the screen as he moved into the office.

"The fatal flaw," Faith said. "I should have gotten two cameras, one of the main space, and one for the office."

You could hear a few loud creaks and groans, and then a pop, though nothing registered visually on the screen.

"Maybe it's a mercy," Jan said. Elaine nodded. She didn't need the image of that man breaking open a safe in her mind. She thought about the video Eldon had showed her yesterday that showed someone cracking open a safe with the crowbar. A shudder went through her.

A moment later, the man appeared back on the screen again, and this time the black bag was slung over his shoulder, just like Santa Claus. Only instead of containing gifts for good boys and girls, this bag held the contents of Faith's safe. They watched as he threaded his way back through the shop and toward the front door again. They watched as the man went out of the shop. The whole incident had taken less than five minutes. Then they backed up the footage and watched it all through again.

"Wait. Can you back it up?" Jan asked in the second after the man left the office, the bag of toys—er, cash—hefted over his shoulder.

Faith nodded and backed the footage up, and let it play again from the time he walked out of the office.

"What's that?" Jan pointed at the screen.

Faith froze it again and held out the phone to Jan. Jan pointed to something. Elaine leaned in and saw that now that he was holding the bag over his shoulder, there was a gap between the white glove on his hands and the sleeve of his red suit. And there, in the gap, was a bracelet of some kind.

"How in the world did you see that?" Faith asked.

"Jan notices things the rest of us miss," Elaine said, smiling at her cousin. Elaine was so glad to have Jan on her side. "She always has."

Jan used two fingers to enlarge the image on the screen.

"Can you tell anything about it?" Faith asked. Jan continued to stare at the screen a moment longer, let out a breath, and shook her head. She held out the phone so Faith and Elaine could see it.

It was just a dark band around his wrist. Maybe silver, or maybe something else, she wasn't sure.

"You know…," Elaine said. She squinted at the small dark spot on the screen, willing it to form into some kind of solid clue. "It kind of looks like it could be a military dog tag bracelet."

Jan and Faith looked at her, waiting for her to go on.

"The kind that has your name and rank engraved? Have you seen those? Ben had one like it."

Elaine's husband Ben had been a lieutenant colonel in the army, and together they had lived all over the world before he passed away. "They're kind of like the dog tags you wear around your neck, only way more stylish. Ben was really proud of his military service, and he liked being able to show the world."

"As he should have." Jan sipped her tea. "Our veterans deserve every honor."

Elaine nodded. "And if I'm right about this, that fact may come in very useful. There has to be some way to track down veterans and active-duty servicemen in our area."

"Our thief is a military man," Faith said.

"Looks like it to me," Elaine said. "Or former military man." She wasn't sure how she would be able to use that to find him, but it was still one more clue than they'd had before.

"And check out his boots," Jan said. Elaine squinted down at the screen again. You could see both of his feet in this shot, and Elaine noticed that they weren't your standard black buckled Santa Claus boots. These were black Pac boots. The kind most men in Maine wore.

"I did some investigating on the boot tread of our Santa," Jan said. She walked over to the counter and picked up her own phone and tapped the screen a few times to pull up a photo. "Brian sent me this picture last night."

Elaine and Faith leaned in. It looked like someone had stepped on a piece of white paper and left a footprint behind.

"This is Brian's boot print," Jan said, then toggled the screen so she could see both photos side by side. They matched. The boot print left in the snow was the same as Brian's boot print.

"I don't get it. Your son isn't the thief, I'm sure of it." Faith's eyebrows were scrunched up, and her lips pressed together.

"No, Brian is not the thief." Jan shook her head, and Elaine let out a little laugh. The idea of mild-mannered Brian, father of two girls and manager of an auto parts store, breaking in and opening a safe with a crowbar was so far from reality that it was almost fun to imagine. "But I do know that his boots are made by the company Schnee. This is what they look like." She pulled up a picture of the boots she'd found in an online shop. They were black and laced up the front and had a thick rubber sole that wrapped around the top part of the foot.

"So we need to be looking out for men wearing boots like these," Elaine said.

"Exactly." Jan turned to Faith. "Did you notice any footprints in the snow outside your shop?"

Faith leaned back in her chair. "I didn't even think to look. But I cleared the walkway to the door yesterday after the snow stopped, so if he stayed on the path he wouldn't have left any. And yesterday Murphy was working on chopping up a tree that came down in that big storm a few weeks ago, so he was walking all over the yard from the front to the back of the store and all over the place. So there was a pretty good swath of the yard where the snow was already packed down. Any smart person would have walked on that." She took a sip of her tea and thought for a minute more. "And even if the thief left some, I think they were probably destroyed by me and Murphy traipsing in and out as we tried to figure out what happened. But I can't be sure."

"Did the police look for any?" Elaine asked.

"From what I could see, they didn't seem to pay attention to them," Faith said. "But I don't really know."

Elaine still wanted to take a look outside A Little Something to see if there were traces of the boot prints there. If there were, that would connect the thefts a bit more solidly, even though there was little doubt in her mind that they had been committed by the same man.

"It's a really good thing you had that camera installed," Jan said.

"Well, it would have been better if it had stopped the guy from breaking in altogether, but I suppose it's better to have the footage than not. I'm glad I set it up."

"I am as well." Elaine looked at Jan. For a moment, Elaine thought about installing one here, but quickly dismissed it. This was their home as well as their business. She couldn't imagine many things worse than having every moment of your life recorded. "I assume you've given a copy of this to the police?"

Faith pinched off a bit of the muffin. "Yes, they have it."

Elaine took a long sip of her tea. The video was a huge clue, and she hoped it would lead them to the thief soon. As far as she could see, there was nothing in the video that was a slam dunk, nothing that clearly identified the thief. But they would follow up on every clue that came in. She'd do some research on former and active-duty military in the area later today, and she thought Jan was on the right track with this boot print thing. And if there were any prints left behind by the thief last night, she wanted to try to find them right way.

"Would it be all right if we came over to see if there are any prints that did survive the night?" Elaine asked.

"Sure thing. I need to go back over there now and get ready to open up for the day. And I guess we'll need to get a new safe installed. I'll call Eldon Carter."

"He was here yesterday to change our locks," Jan said. "I'm sure he'll be glad to help."

Eldon might be the only one for whom this rash of thefts was a positive, Elaine thought wryly as she pushed herself up. But then—wait. There was no way…

No. She shook her head. Just because Eldon was getting a lot of sudden new business didn't mean he was behind the thefts.

"I need a few minutes to get dressed," Elaine said, gesturing down at her pajamas and robe. "But then we'll be by shortly."

"That sounds great. Thanks for the listening ear," Faith said as she popped the last of the muffin into her mouth.

"Thank you for coming straight to us," Jan said. "We want to catch this guy as much as you do. We'll see what we can do."

WHEN ELAINE CAME downstairs a little while later, Jan was hunched over the newspaper at the table.

"What is that?" Elaine asked.

"I know. It's terrible." Jan straightened up and closed the newspaper, holding it up for Elaine.

"Huh?" Elaine realized Jan was pointing to the headline on the front page of the *Penzance Courier*. "I was talking about *that*." She pointed to the mug of pale yellowish-green tea in front of Jan.

"Oh. That's green tea."

"I figured. But why?" Elaine didn't mind the tea, which was made from tea leaves that hadn't been oxidized and was said to contain phytonutrients, which were good for fighting cancer. Elaine found green tea bitter and vaguely reminiscent of boiled spinach, but it could be just right in certain situations, like with Chinese food. It was just that Elaine had rarely known Jan to settle in with a cup of green tea in the morning.

"It's supposed to be very good for you." She glanced up. "The water in the kettle should still be hot."

Ah. So this was part of her new health kick then. Elaine tried not to make a face and headed toward the cabinet. She pulled down a tea bag of English breakfast and set it in a to-go mug. "Well, if green tea is your thing, have at it. Now what's so terrible in the paper?" She turned to the headline Jan had pointed out: *How the Grinch Is Stealing Christmas.*

"They've nicknamed this guy the Grinch," Jan said.

"Pretty apt," Elaine said. In the beloved Dr. Seuss story, the Grinch dresses up as Santa Claus and breaks into the homes of the Whos of Whoville to steal their gifts, hoping to stop Christmas from coming. Their own thief wasn't too far off, though he was breaking into safes with a crowbar instead of sneaking down chimneys to steal toys.

"It's awful." Jan shuddered. "Obviously the break-in at A Little Something isn't mentioned since they printed this overnight, but I assume it will be front-page news tomorrow." She looked down at the paper again. "They mention us in the article, saying that you chased him off. When did you talk to River White?"

River was a reporter from the paper they'd worked with in the past.

"He called yesterday afternoon," Elaine said. "I talked to him for a few minutes."

"You're quoted here."

"Do I sound silly?" Elaine poured hot water over her tea bag.

"No, not at all. You say, 'I just reacted when I saw him coming in. The last thing I ever expected to see was Santa Claus breaking into our house.'"

"Borderline." Elaine set the kettle back down. "I'll read the article later." Though she wasn't sure she even wanted to. This whole thing was already casting quite a pall on the holiday season. She would rather not relive those terrible moments when she'd caught him in the act. "Is there anything good in the paper?"

"*Hmm.*" Jan looked down again. "There's another article about the fund-raiser Bristol is heading up. It has a list of all the businesses in town that have a donation box, and she's reminding everyone that donations made at the big event will be matched dollar for dollar and announcing the new location for the fund-raiser."

"We're just all over the news today." Elaine stirred in a little sugar and a splash of milk.

"Apparently." Jan turned the page and skimmed. "Oh, and here's something nice. A disabled veteran was apparently behind in his rent and facing eviction, and someone left his landlord a cashier's check with a note that said it was to pay off the guy's rent."

"A cashier's check?" She took a sip. Ah. Nice and strong, just as she liked it. "Was there anything to say who it was from?"

"Apparently not. The landlord said there was just the unsigned note." Jan held out the newspaper and showed her a photo. The veteran and a woman Elaine assumed was his wife stood on the porch of a small tan house.

"Wow. That's amazing."

"It is amazing." Jan looked down at her green tea for a moment. "Almost too amazing."

"What do you mean?" The caffeine from this tea hadn't kicked in yet, and Elaine couldn't understand how something could be too amazing.

"It's interesting, right? The guy needed a large amount of cash, and suddenly some appeared. The guy's a military veteran, and so's the guy who is robbing places around town."

Elaine saw what she was getting at now. "You think the veteran is the Grinch." It was obvious, once she understood what Jan was getting at.

"I think it's possible." She looked down again. "It says his name is Garrett Ruth."

"We can certainly investigate him," Elaine said. "But first, shall we go see about those boot prints?"

They bundled up and headed down the steps and out to the sidewalk. The morning air was bitingly cold, and Elaine's breath puffed out in front of her as she walked. But the sunlight that filtered through the bare tree limbs was bright and made the snow glisten. Icicles hung from the rooflines of each of the buildings. They passed Sylvia's Closet, still dark at this hour, and reached A Little Something a moment later. The lights were on inside, and as they walked down the short path that led to the front door of the shop, they saw movement inside. Elaine noticed that Faith had been right—the walkway had been cleared, and though there were footprints around the uncleared section off the path by the door, there were so many it was hard to see any one clearly. They probably weren't going to get anything useful from that.

Elaine followed Jan inside and was greeted by the smell of the scented candles Faith had arranged neatly on a cabinet by the door. Along one wall, she displayed locally made scarves, knit hats, and quilted blankets, and the back of the store held display cases of jewelry and trinkets. Along the far wall was an impressive collection of Christmas ornaments, wreaths, and nativity sets. As they made their way to the back of the store, Elaine saw Faith pop her head out of the office at the back.

"Hi, Elaine. Hi, Jan. Trooper Benson is here."

"Hi, Dan." Jan gave a wave as he leaned back into the doorway and nodded.

"I'll be done in here in just a minute, and then you can come in," the state trooper said. Elaine always appreciated that Dan Benson never seemed to be put off when they investigated a mystery alongside him. She knew that not all police would be so amenable to civilians getting involved in their affairs. Of course, it probably didn't hurt that Jan and Elaine had managed to solve a few mysteries themselves; it had helped his record when Jan and Elaine got involved, so what did he have to lose?

While they waited for Trooper Benson to finish up—Elaine craned her neck and saw that he was dusting for fingerprints—she browsed the collection of ornaments. There were some cute ballerinas made out of what looked like doilies. She wondered if her granddaughter Lucy would like them. Elaine had already bought presents for her grandchildren, but she hadn't bought them ornaments. And there were some beautiful ones made out of blown glass. There was one shaped like a drum, and another like a soldier. Would Micah like those? Or would an eight-year-old destroy them?

"I'm done in here." She looked up and saw Dan Benson looking at her. It was just as well. She'd already gotten what she needed for the grandkids. "This thief is really something, isn't he? Dressing up like Santa and then doing that?" He gestured at the safe door, which lay on the floor of the small office.

"It's hard to believe," Elaine said. "Hopefully we can put a stop to this before he strikes again."

"I'll do my best. And good luck to you." He touched his cap and started toward the door. Elaine looked around. Where had Jan gone? "Jan?" She wasn't in the store.

"It looks like she went out back," Faith said, standing in the doorway of the office. She was gazing toward the door that led out to the small yard behind the building. Through the glass panel in the door, she could see Jan.

"What is she doing out there?" Elaine walked toward the door and peered out the glass panel. Jan appeared to be staring down at the ground. Had she found some boot prints after all?

Elaine turned the handle and pushed open the door and followed Jan out into the yard. Faith slipped her coat on and followed as well.

"What is it?" Elaine didn't see any footprints out here aside from Jan's. But Jan had her phone out and was taking a picture of something on the ground with it.

"Look." Jan was a few paces ahead of them, and she pointed at something ahead of her in the snow. Elaine followed the line of her arm. At first she didn't see anything. What had gotten Jan so excited? "They go down to the lake." She moved her hand along in a line toward the lake.

That's when Elaine saw what she was looking at. And that's when she understood why this was such a big deal.

CHAPTER ELEVEN

A re those snowmobile tracks?" Faith asked, coming up behind Elaine.

Jan nodded. The deep gouges in two even lines were unmistakable. There they were, two sets. One running from the ice to the backyard, and then a spot where it had turned around, and another set leading back onto the ice. A set of boot prints that matched the ones at their house led to the places where the snow had already been packed down by Murphy. She saw his firewood in a neatly stacked pile by the side of the yard.

"I'll go stop Trooper Benson," Faith said, and turned and ran back inside.

"He rode in on a snowmobile but no one heard anything?" Elaine's brow furrowed. Jan understood. Snowmobiles weren't exactly silent. Would the thief really have been able to arrive and depart on one without anyone noticing?

Jan shrugged. "We'll have to check with Sylvia." Sylvia's Closet was next door, with Tea for Two just beyond that. "If she took cold medicine again, she might not have heard a thing. And aside from her, we're the closest neighbors. If neither of us heard anything, I don't know who else would have." Jan turned and followed the tracks as far as she could with her eyes. They cut across the lake and veered off toward the left. It was possible the noise could have been heard from the Green Glade Cottages. But the cabins weren't busy at this time of year. "We could check with Macy, I guess," Jan said, but she wasn't sure it would do much good.

"It may not be necessary. We just need to follow the tracks and see where they go," Elaine said.

Jan desperately wanted to. "How? On foot?" She had done some snowmobiling in her younger days, and Peter had always loved it. There was nothing like zipping down a trail covered with freshly fallen snow. It was fast and fun and a fantastic way to see Maine in the winter. But neither she nor Elaine owned a snowmobile.

"Why not?" Elaine asked.

Why not? Jan wondered. Now that she thought about it, she couldn't come up with a good reason. If the ice was thick enough to hold a snowmobile, then they weren't in any danger of falling through. They could cover the ground on foot with no problem, though it would take them a while. Jan wasn't exactly dressed to go traipsing across the ice on a day as cold as this. She hadn't put on her thermal tights, or her Smartwool socks, or brought her good outdoor gloves.

"Now how in the world did we miss this?"

Jan turned to see Trooper Benson following Faith Lanier toward them. He was shaking his head.

"Who would have ever thought to look for snowmobile tracks?" Elaine asked, shrugging. "Besides Jan."

"I wasn't looking for snowmobile tracks," she said. "I was looking for boot prints, and these appeared."

"I'll go get my sled and see where they go," Dan said. "There are a lot of tracks out there on the ice, though, so who knows how long you can follow them. But we'll try."

"We'll see you out there," Elaine said, and started toward the ice.

What was she doing? She was really going to walk it herself?

"Trooper Benson is going to check it out," Jan said. She gestured at the state trooper, who was already turning to go back to the street. He'd be back shortly with his state-issued snowmobile—his "sled," to use the slang term.

Elaine crossed her arms over her chest. "Jan Blake. Are you really going to let a little cold keep you away from solving this mystery?"

Jan sighed. That was exactly what she had intended, actually. But Elaine was right, of course. She needed to see this for herself.

"All right," she said. She turned to Faith. "We're headed out there on a fool's errand. If we don't return, you can have our house."

"*I'm* supposed to be the dramatic one," Elaine called. She was already heading toward the ice. Jan sighed and hurried to catch up to her cousin. A few moments later, they were stepping onto the ice, which was frozen solid and covered with several inches of powdery snow.

Jan had lived in Maine all her life. She knew lakes in winter. She knew this ice was probably at least a foot thick, maybe more. But she had never gotten used to the way the ice creaked and groaned beneath you. She always thought of that scene in *Little Women* where Amy falls through the ice and has to be rescued by Laurie and nearly dies. Then again, Amy got Laurie in the end, so maybe it wasn't all bad for her. But she had heard plenty of stories of people falling through ice, and it didn't usually work out as well for them.

"Isn't it gorgeous?" Elaine asked.

Jan looked up and took in the towering pine and spruce trees topped with snow, the clear cerulean sky, the picturesque houses perched along the shore. She didn't see it from this angle, and she had to admit Elaine was right. From here, it was pretty much perfect.

For a little while, the tracks were easy to follow. They were the only set that led from this spot on the shore toward the middle of the lake. But it wasn't long before they met up with others. There were lots of trails that led to the lake, and the Pine Tree Grill was known as a spot where snowmobilers were welcome, with a special area under the deck for parking the sleds, so a number of treads led off in that direction. The farther they got onto the ice, the more confused things got.

"It looks like this is about as far as we can go," Elaine said a moment later. They had followed the tracks a little ways out onto the ice, but they had met up with tracks left by another snowmobile. The tracks they were following were on top, so they were visible for a while, but there were a lot of tracks out here, and they quickly became obscured. There were several trails that led out to the lake and he could have taken any one of them.

"So there's not really any way to say which direction these tracks end up going," Jan said.

"It doesn't look like it to me." Disappointment was thick in Elaine's voice.

"Maybe Dan will be able to tell something we can't." Jan tried to sound hopeful to boost Elaine's spirits, but even as she said it she doubted it.

They trudged back toward the shore.

"Why would the thief use a snowmobile?" Jan asked.

"Why do half the people in this town use a snowmobile?" Elaine asked. "It's fun."

"Right. But he drove a truck when he came to our house. Why a snowmobile last night? Especially when a snowmobile is louder and more dangerous and way more likely to be noticed."

"Good questions. I don't know the answers, but I wish I did."

When they made it back to the shore, they reported their findings to Faith. After looking around the shop for a few more minutes, and after Jan had taken copious pictures of the snowmobile tracks, they turned and headed back toward the tearoom. Faith promised to report whatever Trooper Benson found on his sled.

BACK INSIDE THE tearoom, Jan got busy in the kitchen getting things set up, and Elaine set the tables, getting the business ready to open another day. Tonight, they were supposed to meet up with Jan's son, Brian, and his family to check out a Christmas light display in Augusta, so they had a busy evening coming up, on top of the crazy start to the morning. Elaine was already ready for a nap.

Guests started arriving shortly after that, and they were busy for the next hour or so. Then there was a lull, and Elaine decided to take advantage of it to work on some invoices she'd been avoiding. She went into the office and sat down behind the computer. She had a whole stack of invoices that needed to be processed and paid. But as she opened her book-keeping software, she kept thinking about the man they'd seen on the camera footage this morning. No surprise there—he was basically all she'd thought about ever since she'd seen him sneaking into their home.

Was he Garrett Ruth? Elaine typed his name into her browser and did some research on him. Facebook told her that Garrett was married, and he had lost part of his leg serving in Afghanistan. He was looking for work but his medical problems were making it difficult because he couldn't stand for long. He was probably in his midtwenties. Her fingers hovered over the keys. How could she find out if he was the Grinch?

She got up and grabbed the newspaper article again. It said he lived on Meadowbrook Lane. That was on the outskirts of town, in a neighborhood of older starter homes. *Hmm.* He rented his place. Maybe his landlord could shed some light on things. But how could she find out who his landlord was? He wasn't named in the paper.

Then Elaine had an idea. It would take some doing, but she could find this out. First she typed "Meadowbrook Lane" into Google Earth. There were only ten houses on the street, so it didn't take her long to click on Street View and look through the photo of each one. The technology that existed these days was creepy if you thought about it too much, but Elaine was grateful for it now. By matching the picture from the newspaper with the Google street view, she'd determined that Garrett lived at 23 Meadowbrook Lane.

From there, it only took a quick search in the county records database to find that the house was owned by a Gabrielle Ayers. Elaine didn't know her, but found her phone number easily enough in the local phone book. She lived in town, and was friendly when Elaine called, but said that she had no idea where Garrett had gotten the money to pay his back rent. She'd found a cashier's check for the full amount she was owed in her mailbox, and the note simply said that the money was a gift and should pay off what Garrett owed.

"In a way, it was a gift to me as well," Gabrielle said. "I felt awful, starting the process to evict a disabled veteran. But I have to pay my mortgage, and I don't have a lot of margin, and I couldn't keep up when he was several months behind. But the last thing I wanted to do was kick him out, so I was grateful when the check showed up."

Elaine asked if she had any clue where the check came from, and Gabrielle said she didn't. The note had been printed on a typical sheet of white printer paper. She gave Elaine the name of the bank the cashier's check had been drawn from, but Elaine knew enough to realize that the bank wasn't going to tell her who had ordered it.

She wasn't sure what else to do on this, so she thought for a moment. "What is Garrett like?"

"Oh, he's the nicest guy. I don't think anyone ever taught him about money, and obviously he's had a hard time the past few months. But he's a good guy. And Tracy is super-sweet. She tried her best keeping them afloat, but her job at the theater doesn't pay all that well. They're good, honest people. They just fell on hard times."

Elaine pondered this for a moment.

"Look, I'm sorry, but I've got to run," Gabrielle said. "I'm sorry I couldn't be more help."

"I appreciate it."

Elaine hung up. She would need to find some other way to learn more about this Garrett fellow. A veteran who needed money. He fit the bill, all right. Could he have robbed Murphy's and gotten enough to pay off his back rent? And then—what? Gotten a cashier's check? And after that gone to the newspaper and made up a story about a mysterious donation to throw suspicion off himself?

On the one hand, it would be a brilliant tactic to stop any speculating about how he'd gotten the money together so quickly. On the other hand, it would be ridiculously dangerous to get his name and face in the newspaper if he was going around robbing people.

She needed more information. And all morning, ever since they'd noticed the military bracelet, something had been bothering her. They knew another veteran, one who'd gotten into trouble before. Elaine turned back to the computer and typed in Reggie's Anderson name. Reggie's mother, Bettina, was a friend of Jan's, but Elaine couldn't see simply calling her up and asking if Reggie was in trouble again. But there was nothing to be learned by Googling him, she found. She would have to find another way to learn more about him. Elaine turned and grabbed the phone book from the shelf behind the desk, found his number, and then picked up her phone and dialed. The line rang and rang before voice mail picked up. Elaine asked him to please give her a call back and left her number. Hopefully he'd call her back soon.

Still, the military connection had led to a useful clue. There had to be some way to track him based on that.

Elaine eyed the stack of invoices, then decided she would just do a tiny bit more research. It wouldn't take all that long. How hard could it be to get a list of all the current and former military men in the area? She pulled up a browser and searched for "Military Lancaster Maine." Huh. Not much came up. She broadened her search and looked for military in Augusta, Maine, and got better results. The first thing that came up was Camp Keyes, a base for the Army National Guard. *Well, there you go*, she thought. *Easy enough.*

She clicked on the website and started poking around. There was a page about the distinguished history of the Maine National Guard, which had been established before the US was even a country, but there didn't seem to be any way to find a list of current or recent members. She clicked back to the main search page and found information for VA hospitals in the area. But surely hospitals wouldn't be allowed to release information about their patients, so she wasn't sure how that would help. There was a VFW hall. Didn't you have to be a member to go into those things? There was a military support group that met in the area. Could she show up at one of the meetings? And then what? Look around and see if anyone was dressed like Santa?

Elaine pushed back from the computer. This was getting her nowhere. Maybe a cookie would help her think more clearly. Besides, it was after school by now. Chris Cosgrove would probably be at the library. She and Jan should go over and try to talk with him.

Elaine walked into the kitchen and saw that Rose was setting out Christmas cookies on one of the tiered silver serving trays.

"*Ooh,* those look good," Elaine said, snatching one that she'd just perched on the edge of the tray.

Rose laughed. "Help yourself. They're *lebkuchen.* My mother used to make them. I made a batch last night with Emma and I didn't want the leftovers sitting around."

Elaine recognized the name of Rose's boyfriend's six-year-old daughter. So she was baking with the girl. That was sweet.

"I am thrilled to take them off your hands," Elaine said, popping it into her mouth. It tasted like ginger and molasses and was delicious. "Wow. Those are good."

"I'm glad." Rose set another one out and laughed. "When I first set them out, Jan told me to hide them."

"Ah. Yeah, she's on a diet kick at the moment," Elaine said, reaching for a second cookie.

"It's a bad time of year to diet," Rose said.

"You're telling me." She popped the cookie into her mouth.

"Have you guys made any progress on the mystery?" Rose asked, setting out a third cookie in the same spot.

"Not enough, I'm afraid. I was just in there trying to figure out how to get a list of all the military men in the area, and it's a bust."

"Huh." Rose adjusted the placement of the cookie on the silver tray and then reached for another. "I would guess the military wouldn't want to give information like that out for privacy reasons. But what if you started with charities that worked with military families?"

"That's not a bad idea." Elaine thought for a moment. Could a group like that have been behind the donation for Garrett Ruth? "I don't have the slightest clue where to find a list of groups like that."

"Neither do I." Rose set the next cookie precisely on the tray. "But when I couldn't find the answer to something, my mom always told me to start at the library. Maybe they would have some resources."

"You know, your mom was a smart woman," Elaine said. She knew Rose's mother had passed away last year, and Rose still missed her. "Maybe I'll try that. I'm headed there anyway, if I can pull Jan away."

"Archie and I have it under control," Rose said. Elaine thanked her, swiped one more cookie, and went out into the west parlor, where Archie was charming a group of women from out of town. That English accent, coupled with that sweater vest and bow tie, could capture just about any audience. Elaine peeked into the east parlor, where Jan was taking an order from a young couple.

Jan straightened up, caught her eye, and walked toward her. "How's it going?" Elaine asked.

"It's just fine. Everything is under control in here," Jan said.

"Would now be a good time to go to the library and talk to Chris?"

"Just let me put this order in and I'll be ready to go."

A few minutes later, they walked inside the Lancaster Public Library. At this hour, the place was hopping, and voices echoed throughout the high-ceilinged space. The children's area to the right of the circulation desk was busy with mothers and children huddled on the big blue carpet reading together. The tables to the left were full of students hunched over books and writing in notebooks. One of the donation boxes for Bristol's fund-raiser was placed by the circulation desk. Elaine's eyes went to the second floor, where the fiction was housed, but had to remind herself that she already had a stack of unread books next to her bedside.

"Hi." Priscilla smiled from behind the front desk. Today she was wearing a cheerful red sweater and had her hair pulled back in a low ponytail. "How's everything going?"

"Oh well, you know." Elaine laughed. "Christmas always seems to be the busiest time of year somehow, doesn't it?"

"Yes it does," Priscilla laughed. "But also the best somehow."

Elaine nodded. "And on top of all that, we're still on the hunt for Santa."

"Ah. So then you must be here to talk to Chris."

"We were hoping to. Is he around?"

"He's reshelving books upstairs. Go on up."

"Thanks so much." Elaine followed Jan up the stairs, which were tucked away next to the video collection, and up to the second floor. The room was lined with shelving, but they found him easily next to a cart in the mystery section.

"Hello, Mrs. Cook, Mrs. Blake." Chris was tall and had sandy hair and an earnest face. "How can I help you?" He held up the book in his hand. "I hear this one is great," he added.

Elaine craned her neck to see what it was. Ah. It was a mystery that took place entirely on a train. She'd heard people talking about this one. It was getting great reviews.

"We were actually hoping to talk to you," Jan said.

Elaine nodded. "But I'll take that book anyway."

Chris laughed and held out the book. "It's yours." Then he turned to Jan. "What did you want to talk to me about?"

Jan froze. Oh dear. Jan was good at noticing details and putting pieces together, but sometimes she got flustered when faced with tricky situations, and this was one for sure. Elaine jumped in.

"I don't know if you've heard about the recent thefts that have happened around town," she started.

He nodded. "Yeah. The Grinch. Totally scary."

"It is very scary. In fact, I met him face to face when he tried breaking into our home the other night. It was one of the most frightening moments of my life." Elaine was pleased to notice that his face was duly shocked by this. "So we'd love to find him and put a stop to this. We're looking into every possibility for who could be dressing up as Santa, and we heard a rumor that at Halloween, one of the guys on one of the local high school football teams dressed up as Santa Claus. Well, we know you're really connected there, so we figured you were the one to ask to find out about that."

One of Elaine's main strategies was to make the source feel important. If people felt like they were under suspicion, they typically closed down, but if they believed you thought their opinion was valued, they were generally happy to help.

"Oh yeah. Cole Holmberg." He picked another book from the cart and checked the spine. Elaine recognized it as part of a series set in a small town in Quebec. She hadn't read that one. But she already had one book...Chris slid it into place on the shelf, and Elaine forced herself to focus. "He showed up at Eli Turner's Halloween party dressed like Santa. Everyone thought it was hilarious."

"Why hilarious?"

"I don't know." He shrugged. "Who does that? No one dresses like Santa."

"Can you tell us anything about Cole?" Elaine asked. "What's he like?"

"He's a nice guy," Chris said. He reached for the next book on the cart. This one looked dark and moody, judging by the cover. Fine for a cold night by the fire as long as it wasn't too scary. "He plays tight end. A junior. He lives about halfway between here and Claremore."

"Do you have any idea why he chose to dress like Santa for Halloween?" Jan asked.

"I think he just thought it would be funny. Most kids dress like zombies or whatever, and the girls mostly wear as few clothes as they can get away with. So he comes into this party dressed as Santa and tossing out candy canes, and people loved it. Everyone likes Santa, right?" He paused. "Well, they did before this anyway."

Elaine smiled, even though she really felt like crying.

"Here. I think I have a picture." Chris reached into his pocket and pulled out his phone. He touched the screen and pulled up a social media app and scrolled around for a minute. "There."

He held out his phone and showed them a picture from the Halloween party. A group of kids was in someone's kitchen—Eli Turner's, apparently—holding red plastic cups. Front and center was a guy dressed in a red Santa suit, with his arm around a girl in a skin-tight black cat suit. Around them, there were teenagers dressed as nurses, celebrities, and the Grim Reaper.

Elaine studied the photo. Could this be the guy she'd seen? It was hard to tell. His hair was light brown, and his coloring could match the man on the video footage. This kid was tall and strong, but he was still a teen, so he hadn't reached that bulk that professional players had. Based on his body size, she couldn't rule him out. It was possible, she decided.

"What did you dress as?" Jan asked.

"Francis Crick," he said. "My best friend was James Watson." Elaine had no idea who Francis Crick or James Watson were, but Jan laughed out loud.

"Have you seen Cole wear the Santa costume since?" Elaine asked.

Chris chuckled. "No, he doesn't typically wear it to school or anything like that."

Right. That had probably been a silly question.

"But if what you're really asking is, do I think Cole could be behind the break-ins, the answer is I don't know."

Jan met Elaine's eye.

"I want to say no way. I mean, he's in high school. He's not a ninja, or a professional thief, or whatever you have to be to pick locks like this guy has been doing. And that's just wrong, right? He's just a kid, like me." He picked up a book and looked down at the spine without really seeming to see it. Elaine nodded, though she knew—as she was sure Chris did too—that high schoolers weren't exactly kids. They were immature, but they were very nearly full-grown adults. "But if I'm honest..." He let his voice trail off.

"Has he gotten in trouble in the past?" Elaine asked gently. Chris didn't want to tattle on a friend, so she would need to draw it out of him.

"Yeah. He's been suspended a couple times for losing his temper in class and for not showing up." Chris was still looking down at the book. "He almost got kicked off the team for taking the petty cash from Coach's desk last year. The captains got together and voted to keep him on as long as he returned it."

Theft, then. He'd stolen money before.

"He must be a good player," Jan said.

"He is. But he's also a good guy." Chris seemed to finally zero in on the name on the book's spine. "I get the sense things aren't great at home. Would that be enough to drive him to rob people?" He shrugged. "I would hope not. I don't think so. But if I'm honest, I can't really say no."

"Do you know how we might get ahold of Cole?" Jan asked.

"He works at the hardware store over in Waterville after school," Chris said. "I don't know his schedule, but I think he's there most days."

"Thank you so much for your help," Elaine said.

"Of course. I want this to stop as much as anyone." Chris reached for the next book. "You won't..." He hesitated. "You won't mention you talked to me, will you? When you talk to Cole, I mean?"

"Certainly not," Elaine said quickly. "We appreciate your help."

"Yes, thank you for your help," Jan said, and then, as she turned to go, she added, "By the way, I love your shirt."

Elaine had noticed that he was wearing some kind of silly T-shirt, but she hadn't understood it. Some joke about something the kids were into these days. How had Jan understood it?

Chris looked down at it and laughed. "Thanks. It's super nerdy but I love it. I got it from this site called Mainely Made. It's like Etsy, but for people in Maine to sell handmade stuff."

Elaine recognized the name Etsy. It was a website where people could sell handmade goods. She'd found a few gifts there through the years. But she'd never heard of the local version. She looked at the T-shirt again. It was a plain black shirt, and the white writing said, *There are two kinds of people in the world: Those who can extrapolate from incomplete data*

That was all. What kind of crazy shirt was that?

"Sometimes I forget how geeky you are," Elaine said. Jan had always been fascinated by science and had loved doing experiments with her kids when she'd homeschooled them. She'd even worked as a chemist at a water-testing lab in Augusta for a while.

"I'll take that as a compliment," Jan said.

"As it was intended." Elaine followed Jan down the stairs and toward the checkout desk. Priscilla smiled and reached for the book Elaine shoved across the desk.

"Find everything you need?" she asked.

"Yep," Jan said, just at the same time that Elaine asked, "Actually, do you know where I'd find information about charities that work with military veterans?"

"*Hmm.*" Priscilla thought for a moment, and then scanned the barcode on the back of the book. Elaine saw that Jan was nodding. She didn't need to explain why she was asking, then. Jan had figured it out. "I'm sure we have some resources here. How about I take a look and call you and let you know what I find?"

"That would be wonderful," Elaine said, and tucked the book under her arm. Together she and Jan walked out the doors of the library.

Elaine pulled her coat closed and buttoned the buttons as they walked. "So. Do we head to the hardware store now?"

The Christmas lights strung up on the trees along Main Street were starting to blink on. It was just after four, but the light was already fading from the sky.

"We'd probably better wait until tomorrow," Jan said. Elaine reluctantly agreed. They needed to help clean up the tearoom and eat something before they had to meet up with Brian's family to see the light display. It wasn't an official display, just a street in Augusta where every house put up over-the-top decorations, and many people made it an annual tradition to see it. Avery and Kelly, Jan's grandchildren, loved it, and Brian and Paula said they had room in their minivan for Jan and Elaine, both of whom loved spending time with the girls.

"We'll go tomorrow," Jan said again, and Elaine could see she was trying to convince herself. She wanted to go hunt down this clue as much as Elaine did.

"You know, we don't have time to go all the way to Waterville," Elaine said. "But it wouldn't take all that long to swing by Meadowbrook Lane, would it?"

Jan turned to her. "Meadowbrook Lane?"

"To see if a certain disabled veteran who suddenly came into a large amount of cash has any answers."

"I like the way you think."

A few minutes later, they pulled up in front of 23 Meadowbrook Lane. It was small, but neat. They made their way up the shoveled walk and rang the doorbell. A few moments later, the door opened to reveal a young woman. She couldn't have been more than twenty, Jan thought. She wore an apron that said "Mrs. Ruth" and had long brown hair that curled in soft waves. Tracy. The landlord had said her name was Tracy.

"Hi," she said. She looked from one to the other.

"Hi. I'm Elaine Cook, and this is my cousin Jan Blake." Elaine stuck out her hand. "We're hoping to talk to Garrett Ruth."

"He's not home." The girl had a Midwestern twang to her speech and big eyes outlined with heavy eye makeup.

"Do you know when we might be able to talk to him?" Jan asked.

"Why?" The girl didn't seem upset or put out, just curious.

"We were hoping to find out whatever we could about the money that was donated for your rent," Elaine said.

The girl nodded. "You from another paper?"

"I..." Elaine coughed. "Not exactly."

The girl opened the door and gestured for them to come inside. They stepped into the small living room, which had beige carpet and an overstuffed sectional and a huge flat-screen television. The small kitchen was off to the right, and Jan saw a pot of something boiling on the stove.

"That was the strangest thing," Tracy said. "We were getting desperate. We knew the landlord had started the eviction process. We just didn't have any way to come up with the money. Garrett hasn't been able to find work, and I work part-time selling tickets over at the theater, but I don't make all that much. We were about ready to have to move back in with his parents, but we did that before, and that's a bad situation."

Jan wanted to ask more about that, but she didn't want to distract her.

"Anyway, then on Sunday Gabrielle called us and said she'd been given a check and the rent was taken care of. Just like that."

"Do you have any idea where it came from?" Elaine asked.

"No." She shook her head and her curls bounced. "No idea. But we were so grateful. Gabrielle seemed nervous about it at first. I guess she thought maybe it was stolen or something, I don't know."

Jan was wondering the same thing herself, but didn't say so.

"But since it was a cashier's check, she knew it was at least legal," Tracy continued.

"How many people knew your situation?" Jan asked.

"Not too many," the girl said. "Obviously we weren't real proud of it."

"Do you have any idea who the money could have come from?" Jan tried again.

"I wish I did." She shrugged. "So I'd know who to thank. But I guess they wanted to remain anonymous. We decided it was just something to be grateful for, and if we ever find out who it is, we'll thank 'em personally."

As Jan listened to the girl speak, she tried to read her. The Midwestern accent made her sound honest and forthright, but that didn't mean she was. It was difficult to believe someone had simply paid off their rent, anonymously, no strings attached. Was that just a cover story? But then, surely they could have come up with a better cover story. Did that mean it was true? And how did the person know how much they owed? They had to have told someone.

"We'd still really love to talk to Garrett," Elaine said, and dug a business card out of her purse. If the girl recognized the name of the tearoom, she didn't show it. "Could you have him call us?"

"Okay," she said. "Nice to meet you."

Jan followed Elaine out the door.

"She's got to be lying," Jan said as they were settling back into the car.

"Really? I kind of got the sense she was telling the truth."

"Seriously?" Jan buckled herself in. "They have no idea where the money came from, but it just happened to be the exact amount they owed in their back rent?"

"Stranger things have happened. This is a town full of nice people."

"That's true," Jan said. "And a town being targeted by a thief."

"I guess we'll just have to wait to see what happens when we talk to Garrett," Elaine said. Jan didn't see what else to do, so she nodded.

CHAPTER TWELVE

A few hours later, Jan and Elaine were in the backseat of Brian and Paula's minivan, taking in the over-the-top lights as Brian drove slowly down the popular street. Jazzy Christmas tunes were playing on the car stereo, and though the world outside was draped in white, it was warm and cozy inside the van. Jan knew the whole thing was an assault on good taste, but she couldn't help loving it anyway.

"Do you think they make you sign something saying you promise to decorate for Christmas before you move to this street?" Avery, Jan's twelve-year-old granddaughter asked. They were driving past a house with a blow-up Santa, snowman, Grinch, and Snoopy in a Santa hat set up in the snow-covered yard. Thousands of colored lights draped along the roofline, wrapped around trees, and hugging the windows blinked on and off at random intervals.

It really was impressive that every single house on the block participated. Jan knew it had started with just one house setting up an elaborate display, and then the neighbors had joined in, and somehow it had become an annual thing.

"I suspect it's more like peer pressure than anything formal," Paula said from the passenger seat. She had offered the seat to both Jan and Elaine, but they both preferred to sit in the back with the girls.

"Check that one out." Kelly was pointing at a yard that had Santa bowling. Lights in various parts of the yard lit up in succession, so it looked as if the parts were actually moving.

"I can't stop wondering how high their electric bills must be this month," Brian said.

"Just enjoy it," Jan teased. Brian had always been practical, sometimes to a fault. Even if it wasn't logical or cost effective, this season was magical, and you had to just take it in.

"Amen," said Paula from the front seat.

"*Ooh*, look at that one!" Kelly pointed to a house on the other side of the street that had a life-size nativity scene set up in the yard. The barn was made of wood, and the figures were made of some sort of molded plastic, and they each lit up from within. Jan looked at Mary and Joseph, staring down at the newborn baby Jesus. Every mother she knew had felt speechless, swallowed up by some deep wellspring of love she had never known existed, when she looked into the face of her new baby for the first time. What must it have been like for Mary, knowing that she was looking into the face of God?

"That's my favorite," Jan said.

"Me too." Paula caught her eye in the rearview mirror and smiled. Jan had been lucky to get Paula for a daughter-in-law. She was a devoted wife and a wonderful mom, and Jan couldn't be happier with Brian's choice.

"I don't know. That one on the end is pretty incredible," Elaine said, pointing at a house that looked like it had been draped in a net of lights. Cardboard cutouts of all kinds of strange characters, from Peanuts characters to Pokémon figures to Smurfs, were lit up with spotlights.

Avery and Kelly laughed, and Jan sat back in her seat as they rounded the corner of the block. Whether or not you liked the stylistic choices they made, you couldn't argue with the devotion the people on that block put into celebrating the holiday.

After stopping at Brian and Paula's house for pie and hot cocoa—Jan reluctantly passed on both—she and Elaine were headed back to Lancaster in Elaine's car.

"That was fun," Elaine was saying as they made their way off the main road and into the outskirts of town. "It was nice of them to let me tag along."

"They were thrilled to have you there," Jan insisted. Elaine and Avery had a special relationship and she knew Avery was especially glad to see her tonight. "And so was I."

Jan knew that Elaine wished her children and grandchildren lived closer. They had all visited at Thanksgiving, and Elaine had loved their time together, but she knew it wasn't the same as having them live close enough to see all the time. Jan really was blessed in that way.

They drove in silence for a while, each lost in their thoughts, while Christmas music played on the radio, until they got back to Lancaster.

"Huh. That's odd," Elaine said as she slowed for a stop sign at the corner of Bayberry Lane.

"What is?"

"There are lights on at the King house."

Jan turned her head and saw that Elaine was right. Abby and Burk King owned the ranch-style house on the corner, as well as the Hearthside restaurant, one of the nicest places to eat in Lancaster. But they shut down in the winter and spent the season in Florida, enjoying short sleeves, outdoor pools, and palm trees. But now, not only were lights on at the back of the house, but the driveway was plowed and there was a pickup truck parked there.

"Maybe they came back early?" Elaine asked.

"Maybe." But Jan didn't think so. She'd never known the Kings to come back midwinter. "Does either of them drive a pickup?"

Elaine shook her head, and Jan knew she was right.

"Maybe they rented the place out." Jan said.

"Or maybe Tag is staying there?" Tag, or Taggert, was Abby and Burk's son, and he ran his own mechanic shop in town, working on both cars and snowmobiles. He loved winter weather and spent the season exploring trails with the Blizzard Riders Club.

"Maybe." Elaine turned right so they would drive past the front of the house. Jan knew what she was looking at. The pickup in the driveway. The thief had driven a pickup when he'd come to their house. Was this the same truck? As Elaine drove past at a slow crawl, they could see that it was a dark color, maybe deep red or gray. But the driveway was unlit, and a pile of snow blocked their view of the license plate.

"Do you think I should stop and check out the license plate?" Elaine asked.

Jan was about to answer—of course she should!—when another light flipped on in the front room. Whoever was inside must have heard their car idling out front. Though they weren't doing anything wrong, it could be quite an awkward situation to have to explain why they were poking around the driveway.

"Maybe another time," Jan said, and Elaine nodded as another light flipped on in the kitchen. She drove away, and Jan tried to remember the details of the truck they'd seen in the security footage of the outside of their place. It could be the same truck, she was pretty sure. Then again, half the state of Maine had trucks, so it was hard to know.

"I'm going to call them and see." Elaine had pulled over and was already scrolling through her phone, looking for a phone number for Abby and Burk.

"Right now?" Jan asked.

"Why not?" Elaine shrugged, and Jan saw that the phone was already ringing. Then she heard it go to voice mail.

"Hi, Abby. This is Elaine Cook," Elaine said. "Jan and I were just driving by your house and it looks like someone is inside. I think you guys are in Florida and I just wanted to make sure you knew someone was there. Anyway, give me a call back when you get a chance." She ended the call.

"We'll see what she says," Elaine said as she tucked her phone back into her purse.

Jan was sure everything was on the up and up. Abby and Burk no doubt knew exactly who was in their house. And she was sure there was a good reason why that person drove the same kind of truck the thief had been driving.

Still, as they drove through the quiet streets, Jan couldn't help but wonder.

CHAPTER THIRTEEN

Jan had woken up before the sun rose on Thursday morning. That wasn't really saying all that much though, since the sun came up after seven at this time of year. Jan loved summer, when bright sunlight streamed in through the windows and soft breezes stirred as she worked on the day's baking, but there was something special about the calm and peacefulness of the dead of winter too. It was a time for rest and renewal. And—she bent down and peeked into the oven—it was perfect for baking. The maple croissants were done.

Jan slipped on pot holders, pulled the pan out of the oven, and set it on the counter. Sometimes the house got too hot in the summer, but in winter, there was nothing like a warm oven, filling the house with the scent of sweet, yeasty treats. Earl Grey pawed at the screen door, and she went over and patted him on the head and tossed some food into his dish.

She took a deep inhale. Her maple croissants were her specialty, and they were the best straight out of the oven. What could it hurt to try one? She'd been so good. Quality control, she could call it.

But she resisted. She would be glad she had, she knew. Recently, her clothes had begun to fit a bit more snugly. Not so much that anyone would notice, but Jan noticed, and it bothered her. It was just that with Bob gone, she'd allowed herself a few too many treats to help make up for his absence. Not that it helped with the loneliness, actually. But it sure did make her feel better in the moment.

Jan used a spatula to transfer the croissants to a wire cooling rack.

But now, Bob would be back in just a few days. She couldn't wait. But also...She gazed down at the little bulge of her belly. Would he be disappointed? Jan wanted to believe that he wouldn't care one way or the other. He loved her. She knew this. And it wasn't like she was doing this for him. She wanted to simply feel better all around.

Still, he would be back in time for the big fund-raiser next week, and she planned to dress up. It couldn't hurt to look her best. If she was good, maybe she could drop a size by then.

Well, she would just keep trying her best. She was already seeing the difference. It had only been a few days, and already her pants were fitting a bit better. She just had to keep it up.

WHEN ELAINE CAME downstairs, Jan was at the table reading the paper and eating what looked like dried twigs and berries with a splash of skim milk.

"How did you sleep?" Elaine asked, setting out the tea kettle.

"Like a rock."

"That's great." Elaine pulled the carton of eggs out of the fridge and set a pan on the burner. Elaine envied Jan's discipline, especially with pans of scones and croissants cooling on the counter around them, but on a cold winter morning like this one, she needed something that would stick to her ribs. Besides, didn't eggs have protein? Wasn't that healthy?

"You?"

"Oh, I slept really well, but I stayed up too late talking with Nathan so I'm tired."

"How's Nathan doing?"

"He's good." Elaine felt a warmth go through her body just thinking about her handsome boyfriend. "He's really busy with this choir he's in, but he's having a good time. And he says he's looked and looked and finally found the perfect Christmas present for me."

"What is it?"

"I don't know. I won't know until Christmas. But isn't that sweet?"

"It sure is." Was Elaine imagining it, or did Jan look dour? Oh, right, she was probably missing Bob. Goodness. She decided to change the subject. "What's the latest?" she nodded at the newspaper.

"The cover story is about the break-in at A Little Something," Jan said.

"Do they say anything we don't already know?" Elaine asked. She dropped a pat of butter into the pan and watched it foam up.

"Not really. Just more speculation and more comparisons to the Grinch story. They don't mention the snowmobile tracks, which is interesting. I don't know if River White didn't know about them or the police decided they weren't important, but there's nothing about them."

"Huh." She tapped an egg gently on the side of the pan. It cracked and she pulled the piece of shell apart to let the egg fall into the pan.

"But they did print a photo of the guy. A still shot from the security footage," Jan said. She slid the paper over and showed Elaine. It was essentially the same shot they had studied the morning before.

"Good. Hopefully someone will recognize him from this," Elaine said.

She took a minute to think through her day. They had some sleuthing to do this morning, and tonight Nathan was taking her out to dinner and to a performance of Handel's *Messiah* put on by the Chamber Choir of Central Maine. Elaine had always loved the music. When Ben had been stationed outside London, he'd taken her to see the London Philharmonic perform the *Messiah,* and it had been an almost spiritual experience. She wasn't expecting the same level of performance here, but she was looking forward to it nonetheless.

"And on a more positive note, here's another story about someone getting a surprise from an anonymous donor," Jan said, pointing at a story in the bottom corner of the front page. "A single mom walked out of her house yesterday to find a brand-new stroller on her porch, just days after the one she'd been using broke."

"That's wonderful." On one level, Elaine knew feel-good stories like this were not exactly hard-hitting journalism. They were designed to boost newsstand sales and make people feel good. But she liked to feel good, and she was thrilled that things had worked out for this family.

But who had left the stroller? Was this the work of the same person who'd helped Garrett? Was it Garrett himself? Did he know this single mom? Were these two stories connected? Maybe she'd have time today to do some digging on that.

"So what's the plan for the day?" Elaine asked as she slid another egg into the pan.

"Well, Bristol wanted to come over to talk about some details for the fund-raiser this morning. The caterer plans to supply the plates and serving utensils and napkins and everything, and I said that was silly since we already have so much of that here. So we're going to go over that and see what we can supply."

Elaine used the salt shaker to sprinkle the eggs liberally. Might as well go all out.

"Then I was thinking this afternoon we would go to the hardware store and try to talk to Cole," Jan said. She ate the last bit of her cereal and put the spoon down.

"Sounds good." Elaine dropped two pieces of sourdough bread into the toaster. "And how would you feel about going to Tag King's shop to ask him about identifying the snowmobile tracks?"

Jan stood and gave Elaine a sly smile. "And ask him about who's staying in his parents' house?"

"Well, you know, if it came up, I wouldn't *avoid* the conversation," Elaine said.

"Sounds good to me."

Elaine took Jan's seat and read through the newspaper while she ate her eggs and toast. Jan was right about the Grinch story. There was nothing new there, at least nothing they hadn't known before. The story about the stroller for the single mom was heartwarming, and the weatherman was calling for more snow today. Elaine finished her breakfast and headed upstairs to get ready for the day while Jan put another batch of muffins in the oven.

As Elaine was getting out of the shower, she heard the doorbell ring. Bristol must be here, then. She heard Jan walk to the door and greet her, and Elaine dried off and got herself dressed and blew her hair dry. A little while later, she went back downstairs, but instead of finding Jan and Bristol chatting about the fund-raiser, she saw Jan sitting alone, huddled over her laptop.

"Bristol is gone already?" Elaine asked as she walked into the kitchen. She could use another cup of tea.

"Huh?" Jan looked up from the screen, her eyes wide. Elaine froze. Jan looked like she'd seen a ghost.

"Wasn't that Bristol at the door?" Elaine asked.

"No." Jan looked back down at the keyboard. "It was Max."

"Okay..." Elaine let her voice trail off. Why was Jan acting so crazy? "Did something happen with Max?"

"Look at this." Jan tilted her computer so Elaine could see the screen. Jan had a photograph pulled up. "He was wearing these boots."

Elaine squinted at the screen and saw what had Jan so worked up. It was a picture of boots. Behind the boots in the picture was their own wooden kitchen floor.

"You took a picture of Max's feet?" Elaine asked. She checked the kettle and saw that it was still half-full, so she turned on the burner.

"I told him I was looking into boots as gifts and liked his," Jan explained. "Look at them."

Elaine looked closer, and she finally saw what had gotten Jan so excited. The boots Max was wearing were Schnee boots. The exact kind that Jan had discovered had left the prints in the snow.

"No way. Max?"

Elaine tried to picture jovial, hardworking Max Arrington dressing up like Santa to break into their home. It was hard to imagine. But then, it was hard to imagine anyone doing it at all.

"How did the thief know where the money would be?" Jan asked.

Elaine took down another Earl Grey tea bag and plopped it into a mug. She thought for a moment. Max had been in their home many times. He had even been to the office to deliver and sign invoices. He had no doubt seen the safe, as it sat right out there in the corner. In some ways, Max being the thief made more sense than many other people. But then, surely knowing where the money was kept didn't limit the thief to people who had been inside the tearoom.

"But wouldn't anyone guess that the money would be in the office?" Elaine asked. "And even if he didn't know we had a safe, it would be a, well, a safe bet." Elaine chuckled at her own joke.

Jan shook her head. "But think about it. Max makes deliveries to all of the businesses in town. He's probably one of the few people who actually has seen the office of every business. He would know where everyone kept their money, as well as the layout of the shops."

Elaine could see her point, and it was starting to make more sense. It did answer something that Elaine had been wondering about. "And because he had been in all the businesses, he knew which ones don't have security cameras."

Jan hesitated. "But A Little Something does have one."

"Yes, but it was brand-new, right? Unless he'd been inside that day, he wouldn't have known about it," Elaine said.

Jan had moved the picture of Max's boots to one side of the screen and had pulled up the picture of the boot print in the snow. "And he drives a pickup," Jan added.

Elaine realized she was right. On his rounds, Max drove the company van, but on his off-hours, Max drove an old, beat-up pickup that had seen better days. Goodness. It really could have been Max.

"Do you know if Max has a snowmobile?" Elaine asked.

Jan looked up at her over the top of the laptop and narrowed her eyes. "Half the people in town have snowmobiles. There's a good chance."

Elaine didn't know if Max knew how to pick a lock or whether he owned a Santa suit. But she supposed they could look into that. The kettle whistled, and Elaine turned off the flame and poured the hot water over the tea bag.

"I guess we should look into Max," Elaine said.

Jan nodded. "I should say so."

"Let's add that to our list," Elaine said.

Just then there was a knock at the front door, and Jan headed down the hallway to answer it. Elaine added a splash of milk and a spoonful of sugar, and Jan returned a moment later with Bristol Payson.

"Hi there." Elaine gave her a wave.

"Hi, Elaine. It's good to see you. How's everything going?"

Jan had been hanging Bristol's coat in the hallway, and she appeared in the kitchen.

"Oh, you know." Elaine shrugged. "Aside from someone terrorizing the town dressed like Santa Claus, just fine."

Bristol laughed. "I'm glad to hear that things are okay aside from that."

"How's everything going with the fund-raiser?" Jan asked.

"You know, I've been really surprised," Bristol said. "We had another large donation yesterday at the box at the church."

"That's fantastic," Elaine said. "Anonymous again?"

"Yes. Someone just left it in the box. Thankfully I've asked people at the host sites to check them every night—you don't want cash just sitting around. Pastor Mike found the large amount of cash and called me right away. He was so excited."

"That's wonderful," Jan said.

"It almost balances out the other stuff going on in town. Sure, what the thief is doing is horrible," Bristol said. "But people are good. It's heartening."

"That's great to hear," Elaine said.

"Now, I don't want to waste too much of your time. You guys are already being more than generous," Bristol said. "I just wanted to go over the caterer's proposal and see what you all have here and what she would need to bring in separately."

"Of course."

It only took about fifteen minutes to go over the list, and Bristol thanked them profusely and gratefully headed back to open up the Bookworm for the day. Once she had gone, Elaine turned to Jan.

"Are you ready to go see a man about a snowmobile?" Elaine asked.

Jan laughed. "I can't wait. Hopefully Tag will have some answers for us."

CHAPTER FOURTEEN

Jan drove up in front of Tag King's shop and pulled into a parking spot. The sky felt low, heavy, and the scent of snow hung in the air. Jan climbed out of the car and navigated around the parts from various vehicles that were scattered throughout the parking lot, half-buried in snow. Tag owned his own mechanic shop and he could fix just about any engine, but he specialized in snowmobiles and motorcycles. Jan followed Elaine across the lot and into the shop. The small office was warm and clean but needed a woman's touch, Jan thought. There was a small waiting area with some magazines for snowmobile enthusiasts and a plant that was on its last legs, and a counter, which was empty. Through the glass wall, they could see Tag working on a maroon pickup truck in the shop.

Elaine went over and tapped on the glass, and Tag turned and nodded that he saw them. He held up one finger, asking them to wait, and started wiping his hands off with a rag. A few minutes later, he stepped through the door and behind the counter.

"I'm sorry about that. I didn't hear you come in."

Tag King was in his twenties and had brown hair and big blue eyes. Jan could see that his nails were rimmed in black, but his demeanor was warm and kind.

"That's quite all right. We're sorry to pull you from your work," Elaine said. "We have a couple questions we were wondering if you could help us with."

"Sure thing." He smiled at them. Tag was always friendly and helpful, and Jan had always appreciated that about him. "You know a lot about snowmobiles, I believe," Elaine said. "You fix them here, and you're a member of the Blizzard Riders Club too, right?"

Tag nodded. "I'm sort of obsessed, if I'm being honest."

"That's what we thought. It's wonderful that you get to run a business doing what you love." Elaine gave him an encouraging smile. Jan always felt kind of useless watching Elaine work in situations like this. Elaine was so much quicker on her feet and better at getting people to trust her.

"It just makes sense. I'd be working on the engines anyway. Might as well get paid for it." He shrugged.

"That's wonderful. You're just the person we're looking for then."

He tilted his head.

"We have a question about some snowmobile tracks left in the snow." As Elaine spoke, Jan pulled out her phone and scrolled to the pictures.

"We were hoping you might be able to tell us if there's any way to figure out anything about the particular snowmobile these come from," Elaine said as Jan handed over the phone.

Tag looked down at the photo. "You're hoping to find the snowmobile that made these marks?" he asked.

"We don't know if it's possible," Jan said. "But we were hoping."

Tag didn't say anything for a moment, just stared down at the tracks. Someone had hung paper snowflakes in the windows, and they rattled in the breeze from the heater. Then Tag turned to his computer. He shook the mouse to wake it up and typed something in. He pulled up a website that seemed to sell snowmobile parts, including the tracks—the circular chain that dug into the snow and moved the sled forward. The piece that would have left the marks in the snow. He clicked on a few options and held the phone close to a few of them.

"Well, here's what I can tell you. I am pretty certain these marks were made by a sled outfitted with Ice Attack treads," Tag said. He handed the phone back to Jan.

"Ice Attack?" Elaine echoed.

"Sounds painful," Jan added.

"Yeah. They all have these tough-sounding names, like Cobra and Ripsaw." He shrugged. "Basically, they all do the same thing, which is grip the snow to pull the sled forward. But the lugs"—here he pointed to the part that stuck out of the track; the bit that made the indentation in the snow—"are different on each model. Some models are for back-country riding, and those have taller lugs that grip further into the snow, since out on the back country you're typically more worried about traction than speed. For racing, there are models with almost no traction." He clicked over to another kind of tread and pointed. This one had tiny lugs that would hardly break the surface of the snow. "Those allow you to get up to great speed, but you give up control."

"What are Ice Attack tracks for?" Jan asked.

"Those are trail tracks. That's most common around here, so that makes sense."

It did make sense. Most people around these parts who rode snowmobiles rode on the trails that snaked through the woods.

"What makes you think these are Ice Attack tracks?" Elaine asked.

"The pattern of the imprints in the snow match are pretty close to what you see here," Tag said. He pulled up a close-up of the treads on the Ice Attack tracks. Jan leaned in and looked at his screen and saw that he was right. He had basically done exactly what she'd done to hunt down the model of boot that left the prints in the snow, but he'd done it with snowmobiles.

"Great," Jan said. "That is very helpful."

"Now, is there any way to figure out whose snowmobile these came from?" Elaine asked.

"That's trickier," Tag said. "The short answer is, not really. If you had a bunch of snowmobiles lined up, you could look at each one and figure out which ones have which treads. But without seeing a machine, you can't really tell who owns what."

Jan had been expecting this answer, but it was still a blow. They would have to go around and talk to every snowmobile owner in town to try and figure out who had which tracks. They had no way to even know who had one, so this seemed pretty pointless.

"Well, thank you for your help," she said. They knew more than they had before, even if they wouldn't be able to track down the thief yet.

"Yes, thank you. We can't say how much we appreciate it." Elaine hitched her purse up on her shoulder and then paused. "You know, we were driving by your parents' house last night," she said, as if she'd just thought of it, "and we saw the lights on. Are they back from Florida?"

"Oh no." He closed out of the website that sold the snow-mobile treads. "Nah, they can't stand the winter." He laughed. "They let my cousin Joe stay there for a while. He moved in late last week. He needed a place to stay."

"That's nice that they're doing that," Jan said.

"You said his name is Joe?" Elaine asked.

He nodded. "Joe Stone." He jerked his thumb at the garage. "That's actually his truck in there. He skidded on some ice a couple days ago and wrecked his tie rod. We just had it towed over this morning. That's pretty much the kind of luck he typically has."

"We will add him to the prayer list at church. And is there anything specific we can help him with?"

Tag looked from Elaine to Jan and back again. "You guys are serious?"

"Yes." Now Elaine seemed surprised. "Why wouldn't we be?"

"I don't know. I'm just always pleasantly shocked by people. You don't know anything about him, and yet you're already talking about bringing him casseroles."

"So a casserole would help?" Jan asked. Of course they did want to help if this man needed a little assistance getting on his feet. And if they learned something about that pickup truck in the process, so be it.

Tag laughed. "Maybe. I guess it can't hurt. But I don't know how much a casserole would really fix. It's kind of a long-term thing."

Jan and Elaine waited. And just as Jan knew he would, Tag went on to fill the silence.

"He had a tough childhood. He grew up outside of Portland but his dad ended up in jail when he was a kid and his mom didn't cope very well. She drank a lot and he was mostly on his own. My mom tried to help them as much as she could—she's his mom's younger sister—but Aunt Tina wasn't particularly receptive, from what I understand. Anyway, Joe always wanted to join the Air Force. That was the only thing he ever talked about wanting to do."

Jan's heartbeat sped up as she heard this. They were looking for someone in the military!

"But I guess he couldn't get in for some reason, and he's been trying to figure out what he wants to do instead but hasn't really landed on anything. He's had a few brushes with the law, but it looks like things might be finally turning around for him."

"Oh?" Elaine asked. She met Jan's eye and then left it at that, and sure enough, Tag started in to fill the silence again.

"He's got a girlfriend who seems to be really good for him. She works at SuperMart over in Waterville, and she got him a job there too. He's kept it for a while now, and both the job and the girlfriend seem to have settled him a bit. Anyway"—he shrugged—"his lease ran out and he needed a place to stay for a while, and since my parents aren't home anyway, they offered their house."

"I'm so glad," Elaine said. "It sounds like he's on his way."

"We all hope so."

"When we drove by last night, there was a pickup truck in the driveway," Jan said. "Is that his?"

"Yep. Or was, until this morning." He looked over at the garage again. Tag scooted his chair a bit closer to the counter. He looked directly at Jan, and then turned and looked directly at Elaine. "And, if you're asking because of this whole Grinch thing, I'll have you know it couldn't be him."

"What makes you think that's what we're doing?" Elaine asked. Her voice showed mock indignation.

"I know you two. You can't resist a good mystery. And if you're asking nosy questions, trying to act all innocent about it, there's probably one very clear specific reason." Tag's voice didn't convey anger, just honesty.

Jan didn't have a response to that, and neither did Elaine, apparently.

"But Joe works nights at SuperMart stocking shelves." He crossed his arms over his chest. "There's no way he could have been behind the thefts because he was at work."

"I'm thrilled to hear that," Elaine said. "You're right, of course. We would love to know who is behind these thefts. But we don't want it to be your cousin, and if he's innocent, that's great news."

"Good then."

Jan could see Tag was finished with the conversation, and she turned to go. "Thank you so much for your help," she said.

"We really appreciate it," Elaine added, and turned to follow Jan.

"Of course. Any time." Tag waved, and the cousins walked out of the shop to the car.

As soon as they were buckled in, Jan turned to Elaine. "So we're going to investigate Joe, right?"

"Of course." Elaine's seat belt clicked into place. "It does seem a bit unlikely, if what Tag says is true and he works nights. Plus there's the fact that our guy is a military man and Joe wasn't in the military. But yes, of course we should look into it anyway."

"Do you want to head to Waterville now and see what we can learn from the store?"

Elaine's eyes flicked to the clock on the dashboard. "As much as I would like to, we should probably get back and get the tearoom going."

Jan reluctantly agreed. Their first customers would be arriving shortly.

"But maybe we can put together a casserole and bring that by soon," Elaine said.

"Definitely." A casserole was a perfect excuse to stop in and see him face-to-face.

"We're getting closer." Elaine said. "I can feel it."

Two HOURS LATER, the tearoom was filled with people talking, laughing, and enjoying Jan's homemade treats. Elaine looked around the west parlor. Rose was taking the order for a table of young moms with babies and making goo-goo faces at the children, and Archie was charming a table of older women by the fireplace. From the snatches Elaine could overhear, he was telling them some story about going to university at Oxford, and they were eating it up. Snow was falling gently again outside, and the soft music made the whole place feel warm and cheerful.

Everything looked like it was in order, so she wandered over to a table at the front of the room where some of her regulars were seated. Macy Atherton, Rue Maxwell, Maureen Oakley, and Kate Pierce all looked up as she approached the table.

"How's everything going here?" Elaine asked.

"The tea is a bit weak," Macy said. Elaine kept a smile pasted to her face.

"Oh, hush," Rue said, shaking her head at her friend. "Everything is delicious, Elaine. Thank you."

"These maple croissants are wonderful, as usual," Maureen added. Maureen was an elegant woman in her seventies and the kindest soul you'd ever hope to meet. A bout of polio when she was young had left her with a limp, but she was always thoughtful and well put together.

"I don't know how you do it, but you always manage to have the most beautiful decorations," Kate Pierce said, gesturing toward a hammered-copper votive holder on the mantel. Jan had punched snowflake-shaped holes in it and light shone through as the candle burned.

"You're very kind. It's all Jan," Elaine said.

"But where's that painting you used to have? The one with the woman drinking tea?" Maureen asked. "I loved that one."

"It's being restored at the moment," Elaine said. *Authenticated* was the correct word, Elaine knew, but she certainly didn't want to tip Macy off that the painting they had probably was done by a world-famous painter. Not until they knew for sure. And maybe the authenticator would make sure the painting was in tip-top condition before returning it to Archie, so it wasn't necessarily untrue.

They had recently come to believe that the painting had been done by Archie's father, who had apparently had a very successful art career under the name Harley Archibald Benningham before Archie was born. It turned out the painting could be quite valuable. Archie had never known his father had been an artist, and though he recognized the symbol in the painting to be his father's, he had no idea who the woman in the painting was. It was a mystery, one that the cousins had been exploring as best they could. But whatever they discovered, both Jan and Elaine loved it for the same reason they'd first been drawn to it—it was a beautiful picture of a woman drinking tea.

"Really?" Macy asked. "Seems like a lot of trouble for a picture you picked up at a garage sale."

"It was a flea market," Elaine said mock defensively. "Now, do you all have everything you need?"

"We're great, thank you," Kate said. Kate ran Kate's Diner down the road, along with her two grown daughters, Patti and Lydia. Kate spent most of her time in the kitchen, but Lydia and Patti were outgoing and welcoming, and they made everyone feel at home, which was a large part of why she always drew a large crowd. The focus on bacon was the other.

"We were just discussing this monster who's terrorizing the town," Macy added.

"Ah." It made sense. It was on everybody's mind these days. "The Grinch."

"Did you see the picture in the newspaper this morning?" Maureen asked. She wore a pink twinset over soft gray pants, and she had pearls in her ears.

"Oh yes," Elaine said. "From the security camera?"

"I was just saying the picture obviously shows Mel Stadler," Macy said. "I don't know why the police haven't arrested him yet."

Elaine almost let out a laugh, but she managed to stifle it. "Mel?" Mel owned the Pine Tree Grill, along with his sister Bianca, and he was the nicest, most welcoming man ever. The very idea of Mel putting on a Santa suit and breaking open a safe with a crowbar was ludicrous. Not to mention Mel was wiry, like a stretched-out noodle, not solidly built like the man in the picture. "What makes you say that?"

"It looks just like him." Macy threw up her hands, and her voice indicated she thought Elaine was a dolt.

"I don't know." Maureen selected another scone from the serving tray perched at the edge of the table. "I think it looks more like Dutch Bigelow, personally."

"Really?" Elaine tried to keep her face neutral as she pondered this. Dutch was several years older than Mel, with a round belly. He was kind and gentle and he spent much of his time carving wooden birds in his workshop.

"Plus, he's a former state trooper, so he knows things like how to pick locks," Maureen added.

Elaine smiled, though she wasn't at all sure that lock-picking was a skill they taught at the police academy these days.

Rue Maxwell shook her head. "Doesn't it seem more likely it's Reggie Anderson?"

"Reggie?" Elaine realized he had not returned her call. He had had a difficult time since he'd gotten home from his second tour of duty, and had come up as a suspect in a mystery Jan and Elaine had investigated last year. He'd been innocent, but there was still something about him that invited suspicion.

"It's not Reggie," Maureen said, softly but definitively. "I am good friends with his mother, Bettina, and he's out of town at the moment. He's on an ice fishing trip in Alberta with some friends from the military. Apparently she'd heard from several people who think it's him, but it's not. If you look online, you can see pictures he's posted, and the mountains make it clear he's not anywhere near here."

Well. That explained why he hadn't returned her call. She'd have to check out the pictures online to make sure what Maureen was saying was true, but that did seem like a logical explanation.

"Well, I for one don't know who the thief could be," Kate said. "But Lydia swears she served the man from the paper in the diner last week."

"How could she tell?" As interested as Elaine was in finding the thief, she was growing a bit weary of idle speculation.

"She said the man she saw looked like the guy in the photo," Kate said. Elaine nodded, but inside she had already dismissed the rest of whatever Kate was about to say. How could anyone possibly identify the man when he had so thoroughly obscured his face with the mustache and beard? "But it was the bracelet that made her sure."

"Wait, what?" Elaine was suddenly paying attention again. "She noticed the bracelet?"

"Sure. That military dog taggy thing? It was right there in the picture," Kate said, shrugging. Well, that was true, but it seemed like most people hadn't picked up on that. "And she saw a guy wearing the same one last week in the diner." Kate gave a little shiver. "To think, he was right there, eating in my restaurant."

"Did Lydia say anything more about this guy?" Elaine asked.

"Not to me. But I'm sure if you wanted to talk to her, she'd be happy to chat." Kate looked pleased to have contributed something that had piqued Elaine's interest.

"Maybe I'll stop by," Elaine said, nodding. It couldn't hurt to hear what Lydia had to say. Maybe she really had waited on the thief at the diner. Anything was possible. And she could probably get some bacon out of the deal.

"I'll tell her to expect you," Kate said.

"I still think it's Mel," Macy said. Elaine wasn't sure how to respond, but just then, the front door opened, and another group came inside, carrying a blast of cold air and a few flakes of snow with them.

"I should go get them settled," Elaine said. She started to move away from the table. "But thanks for the tip."

She would stop by the diner soon and try to find out what Lydia could tell her about the man in the photo. Maybe this would be the clue that finally pointed them in the right direction.

CHAPTER FIFTEEN

That afternoon, Jan and Elaine told Rose and Archie they were going out for a bit, then started for Waterville. They were hoping to talk to Cole Holmberg, the football player in a Santa suit.

As Jan drove, Elaine told her what Kate had said about the guy in the diner and that Maureen was certain Reggie was innocent. She'd also heard back from another of the real-bearded Santa groups, and it wasn't willing to give out the membership lists.

"Oh well. It's probably not one of those Santas anyway," Jan said, and Elaine agreed.

"Maybe we'll get lucky talking to Cole," Elaine said.

"I hope so. And if not, we still need to find out more about Max," Jan said. "And Joe, Tag's cousin. I know Tag doesn't think he did it, but the thefts started right after he arrived in town. That seems like a mighty big coincidence."

"And there's still Garrett Ruth, the disabled veteran whose rent was paid off."

"True." Elaine adjusted the vent so the air was blowing away from her. She was wearing her coat and was suddenly roasting. "Though it seems less glaringly likely to be him now that the single mom with the stroller is in the picture. Maybe someone really is doing anonymous good deeds."

"It's possible," Jan agreed. "But it's also possible that he is stealing the cash, and he had some money left over after paying his back rent. Maybe doing something for someone else seemed like a good way to keep people from pinning it on him."

It was possible, Elaine had to admit. Maybe.

They were quiet for a moment. They were off the highway now, and Elaine could see the shopping center where the hardware store was located a little ways down the road. Then Jan spoke.

"You know what occurred to me this morning?" Jan asked.

Elaine turned her head. Her cousin's profile was silhouetted against the falling snow outside. "I couldn't start to guess."

"A big hardware store would sell crowbars."

Elaine realized with a jolt that she was right. Lock-picking sets too, no doubt.

"Of course anyone could have gone into the store to buy one," Elaine said.

Jan nodded. But they both knew that Jan's point was a good one. Cole could have easily acquired the tools the thief had used while at his job. During slow times, he might have even learned how to use them there.

A few minutes later, Jan and Elaine pulled into the parking lot outside the hardware store in Waterville. The chain store was huge, and the large lot was surprisingly full on this Thursday afternoon. They found a spot and made their way through the gently falling snow toward the door. A man in a Santa suit was standing outside the store, and for a moment, Elaine's heart thudded in her chest. Was it him? But then she realized this Santa was ringing a bell and stood next to a little red bucket. He was collecting money for the Salvation Army. Elaine wondered if she'd ever see a Santa and not be freaked out.

A blast of warm air greeted them as they stepped inside the automatic glass doors. They walked past a display of fake trees and outdoor lights and looked around. It was a big warehouse store, with open shelving and aisles and aisles of stuff Elaine couldn't identify if her life depended on it.

"I guess we ask there?" Jan suggested, gesturing toward the customer service counter.

Elaine nodded and followed her, and they were directed to the appliance section by an older man wearing a reindeer pin with a light-up nose. They found their way to the appliances without too much trouble, and it wasn't too hard to find the teenager. He was tall, and solid—not fat, but muscled—with dark hair cropped close to his head. But the giveaway was the orange apron that had his name printed on the front. They waited while he finished speaking with a woman looking at refrigerators. Her face looked pinched, and her two young children ran up and down the aisles. He said something to her, and she nodded and walked over to the floor models and started opening doors.

Elaine seized the opportunity to step toward him. "Cole?"

He turned and smiled, but his eyes showed that he was confused. He was handsome, in a conventional sort of way. Elaine imagined he was probably quite popular at school. But she remembered what Chris had said, that he had been caught stealing.

"Your name is on your apron," Jan said, pointing at it.

He still stared at them. The words didn't seem to register.

"That's how she knew your name," Jan said.

"Oh, right." His smile spread. "Cool. Can I help you?"

Elaine had already thought about what she would say, and now she came out with, "We were hoping to talk with you. We've been told you're pretty much the toughest guy around, and that you could help us."

"Oh yeah?" The flattery, Elaine could see, was working, as it usually did. His smile got wider, and he nodded a bit. "Who said that?"

Elaine thought quickly, but Jan was quicker. "Everybody," Jan said.

This seemed to satisfy him, and he leaned back so he was resting against a washing machine, and said, "So what do you need?"

It was actually a nice washing machine, Elaine noticed. It was top-loading, with a clear lid, and the finishes were shiny and the face well designed. Elaine looked away and tried not to get distracted.

"I don't know if you've heard about this guy who's been breaking into businesses all over Lancaster," Elaine began.

"Oh yeah. It's, like, crazy funny," he said.

Elaine was so surprised by this response that it took her a moment to figure out what to say.

"Funny?" Jan asked.

"I mean, dressing like Santa Claus as a disguise? That's genius. Whoever would have thought of something like that?" He chuckled a little.

Elaine could see in his face that he was serious. He thought it was funny. Jan looked as perplexed as Elaine felt.

He must have noticed their confused looks, because he added, "I mean, of course it's a horrible thing to do. I don't mean it's cool or anything. It's just that, if you're gonna do something like that, why not do it in a big way, right?"

"I suppose," Elaine said. And then, as if she'd just thought of it, "It does take creativity, I'll admit. It must be hard to find a Santa Claus costume. I don't even know where you'd look for one."

"Oh, they're super-easy to find. I got one at the thrift store here in Waterville for almost nothing. If you find one at the right time of year, they're practically giving them away."

Elaine smiled. He'd just admitted he had one. "Oh, really? Why did you need one?"

"Oh, I got it back in September. I was at Goodwill with my bros looking for T-shirts—sometimes you can find the best shirts with, like, funny sayings on them—and my buddy Jayden found it in the costume area. There were, like, four of them there, and he was like, 'Dude, someone has to get this.' And I was like, 'Totally. This is what I'm being for Halloween.'"

"And were you?"

"Absolutely. I wore it to Eli's party, and it killed. Everyone thought it was so funny."

Elaine pressed her lips together. She didn't consider herself to be fussy, but it baffled her that the expression meant "went over big."

"Have you worn the costume since that night?" Jan asked.

"Nah." He laughed. "There aren't really all that many places you can dress as Santa, you know?" Then he seemed to reconsider. "Though now that you mention it, I bet I could have some fun at the mall if I wore it there." He chuckled again.

No doubt he could confuse more than a few children—and anger an elf or two. Elaine looked at Jan and saw that she was as put off by this guy as she was. But that didn't necessarily mean he'd been behind the thefts.

"One more thing," Elaine said. "We're very interested in finding out more about the guy behind these thefts. You haven't been out and around town at night recently, have you? Maybe you saw something we didn't see?'

Cole shook his head. "Nah. I wish. I've gone home after work every night the past few weeks. My dad's out of the picture, and my mom's health is not great, and I've had to help take care of my kid sister."

Elaine felt a pang of tenderness for him, despite all the ridiculous things he'd said so far. It sounded like he had a hard situation at home. Through the years she'd learned that it was often the case that when someone said harsh things, it was bravado masking some deeper problem, but it was hard to remember that until she was confronted with it.

"I'm sorry to hear that," Jan said. "We'll pray for your mom."

"Thanks," Cole said. "I'm sure she'd appreciate that."

Then Elaine had another thought. Cole had a single mom, and no dad around. He was working an after-school job. Money was no doubt tight in this family. Was it tight enough that he might have gone to extreme lengths to help the situation out?

"So. Back to our initial question," Elaine said. If he had noticed they hadn't actually asked him about anything hardware related so far, he hadn't shown it. In fact, it didn't seem that he'd even realized he was being questioned as a suspect. "We read that the guy breaking in dressed as Santa Claus has been using crowbars to get into safes. We've never seen a crowbar up close. Do you sell those here?"

"Huh." He put his hand to his chin as he thought. "I think they're in aisle 13?"

"Can you show us?" Elaine asked. She did her best to look small and helpless.

He had two customers milling in his own section, but he said, "Sure," and led them over to the aisle where the crowbars were held. Elaine looked at the long pieces of metal laid out in the bins and a shiver went through her. Most were the short kind, eighteen inches or so, that Santa had had tucked into his belt, but there were a few that were several feet long and seemed the stuff of nightmares. She reminded herself that there were many legitimate reasons people needed a crowbar—the contractor had used one when he was demolishing the old cabinets in their kitchen, for instance—but they still frightened her.

"What about lock-picking sets? Do you carry those?"

"Huh." Cole looked up, as if he might find the answer in the heavens. "You mean like a hammer? Or what?"

A hammer? Goodness. A hammer would smash a lock, not pick it. She studied his face. His eyebrows were raised, his forehead scrunched, his lips pursed. If he was pretending not to know what tools you'd use to pick a lock, he was doing a good job of it.

"They sell small kits," Jan explained. "With long, thin tools that go inside the lock."

"Let me check." He held up one hand, and then dashed off toward the end of the aisle and disappeared.

Elaine looked at Jan. "What do you think?"

"I'm wondering if he thinks it's odd that we came specifically to him to ask where to find lock-picking sets when he works in appliances," Jan said.

"I don't think so," Elaine said with a smile. "I get the impression he doesn't think about a whole lot in general."

"Elaine." Jan's voice was scolding, but there was a smile on her face. "Be kind."

"On the plus side, I actually don't think he was behind the thefts. We should try to verify that he was at home the night of the thefts like he says, but he doesn't strike me as a criminal mastermind."

"Elaine." Jan's tone was a little harsher this time, but she grinned, to let Elaine know she was teasing.

"I'm just saying. If he doesn't know how to pick a lock, it doesn't seem likely he's our man."

Jan nodded. "I happen to agree with you." She gave a small smile. "On all counts."

Just then Cole reappeared at the end of the aisle. He walked toward them slowly. Something in his demeanor had changed while he was gone.

"Did you find them?" Elaine asked brightly.

He nodded but didn't say anything.

"Is everything all right?" Elaine asked.

"I've been thinking." Cole stopped in front of them and crossed his arms over his chest. "You guys are asking me all these questions about this stuff. You're not planning to break in and rob people, are you?"

Elaine almost laughed out loud, but then she saw he was serious.

"You mean, are we planning a copycat robbery?" Jan asked.

He nodded, his arms crossed over his chest. "You asked me about the tools you need. You asked me where to buy a Santa suit. I don't know. Seems like you could be."

"No," Elaine said, holding back a smile. "Can you see this one using a crowbar?" She gestured at Jan.

He didn't say anything at first, just looked from one to the other.

"If we were, why would we have come in and asked you all about the tools we need?" Jan asked.

"You want to get the right tools," he said, as if that explained everything.

"I can promise you, we're not planning on robbing anyone." Elaine decided it was time to get out of there. "But we very much appreciate your help."

She turned and headed for the door, and Jan followed a few steps behind her. When they got to the end of the aisle, Elaine glanced back and saw that he was still staring at them, his eyes narrowed.

They hurried out of the store, and when they were safely back in the car, Elaine let out a sigh.

"I suppose if the tearoom fails, we can always fall back on a career as cat burglars," she said, and Jan laughed.

"True. I've always thought I would make a great archcriminal."

"You could bake cookies for all the inmates when we get caught."

Jan laughed and put the car in gear. "On the plus side, we did pick up a clue."

"We did?" Elaine buckled herself in. She couldn't think of anything useful they'd learned, aside from reinforced stereotypes about jocks.

"We sure did." Jan looked in the rearview mirror and then started backing up. "And we're going to check it out right now."

CHAPTER SIXTEEN

It only took a few minutes to pull up in front of Goodwill, the thrift shop where Cole had bought the Santa costume. The lights were off inside, and Jan looked at the dashboard and saw that it was a few minutes after five.

"I see," Elaine said. "You want to ask about who bought the other Santa suits Cole mentioned seeing when he bought his."

"Precisely." Jan tried not to let frustration get the best of her. "But it looks like we'll have to come back another time."

"We'll come in the morning," Elaine promised. "For now, we should probably head back to the tearoom."

Jan nodded. She'd also hoped they could get over to SuperMart and ask about Joe Stone, but it would have to wait for tomorrow. They needed to help Archie and Rose clean up, and she knew that Elaine needed to get ready for her date with Nathan tonight. Jan felt a little sad, thinking about Elaine and Nathan going out while Bob was so far away. It was only four more days until he came back, but it felt like a lifetime.

"We'll come back first thing in the morning," Elaine promised. Jan gave her a sad smile and headed for home.

That evening, after Nathan had arrived to take Elaine to the concert, Jan got to work. She had been serious about bringing Joe a casserole. Or if not a casserole exactly, something to make him feel welcome. When she was growing up her mom had always brought meals to people in the church who were sick or had babies or were new to town. It was a way to look out for each other. A practical way to serve. And, Jan thought, as she covered the lasagna in foil, if it meant she got a little peek at Joe, so be it.

Technically, aside from the fact that he drove a truck, there wasn't any evidence suggesting that Joe could be the thief. But Jan wanted to check him out anyway. The thefts had started shortly after he'd arrived in town, for one thing. That didn't necessarily mean he was behind them, but the timing was pretty coincidental if he wasn't. Added to the fact that he had had brushes with the law, as Tag had so delicately put it, he was worth at least finding out more about.

Jan carried the lasagna, a green salad, and a bag of Rose's cookies carefully to the car, and it only took a couple of minutes to navigate through the gently falling snow to the King house. Abby and Burk's house was ranch style, low and long and painted a modern light gray. The truck wasn't there—it must be still in the shop—but the lights were on inside, and in one of the front windows, she could see the flickering light that meant a TV was on.

Jan parked in the driveway and walked up the path to the front door. She rang the doorbell and held her breath. At first, she didn't hear any movement inside, but then she heard footsteps and a man calling, "Be there in a second."

The door was pulled open, and a big man with dark hair stood on the doorway. He was wearing a long parka and boots and was pulling a hat down over his head. He reared his head back a bit when he saw her.

"Oh." He blinked. "You're not Ainsley."

Was this the man Elaine had seen? Jan studied his face. Was this the guy whose picture had been in the paper, caught in the act?

"No, I'm not Ainsley." Jan held up the lasagna. "I'm the welcome wagon."

He stared at her. She decided to try again.

"I'm Jan Blake. I'm a friend of Abby and Burk, and your cousin Tag told me you were staying here for a while. I wanted to welcome you to town. I brought you a lasagna."

Up close, Jan couldn't tell if this was the thief or not. She'd been hoping there would be some kind of instantaneous recognition, but there was nothing of the sort. He had the right build and the right coloring. But so did so many men around here. Whatever its true intention, the Santa costume had done an excellent job of masking the features of the thief. It could be him, she thought, studying him. But it very well could not. Still, she couldn't rule him out.

"Really?" He didn't move out of the doorway. He wasn't the friendliest guy, Jan noted. But then, most people would be taken off guard if a stranger showed up, especially one who was scrutinizing him the way Jan was.

"Absolutely." Jan pasted a smile on her face. "It's a small town. We do things like this."

For a moment, it seemed like he wasn't sure what to do. But he finally stepped back and gestured for her to come inside.

"Thank you," Jan said. She wiped her feet on the doormat and looked around. She'd been in the Kings' house a few times, and it looked pretty much the same, with the beige carpet, the overstuffed sectional, the white kitchen cabinets. It was warm and comfortable.

"You can bring that in here," Joe said.

She noticed that the television was playing a football game. Then she noticed something else. His boots! They were just like the boots she'd seen online. The ones that matched the prints in the snow outside their house! Jan's heart started pounding. It was him. It had to be him.

Her triumph turned to cold fear. It was him, and now she was inside the house with him. A convicted criminal who now had committed several acts of armed robbery. She had to get out of here. She would just leave quickly, call Dan Benson, and tell him—

And tell him what? Jan thought. That she knew she'd found the thief because he had Schnee boots? She knew enough to know what the police would do with that information. Laugh, most likely. It wasn't enough. She needed proof. Jan forced herself to calm down. She'd need to think this through.

Jan set the lasagna and the other containers on the counter and tried to force a smile on to her face. She had to see if he was wearing that military bracelet. Right now his wrists were covered by the sleeves of his coat.

"How long are you in town?" she asked brightly.

"I'm not sure," Joe said. "Hopefully just staying here a few weeks. We'll see." He opened the fridge and set the food inside. Jan saw that the shelves were nearly empty. That showed that he was having a hard time affording food, or else that he was a bachelor who didn't cook.

"And where are you from?" Jan asked.

"Around here." He shut the fridge and didn't elaborate.

"Well, what do you like to do for fun?" She was hoping he'd make it easy and say something like snowmobiling.

He shrugged. Then he looked around, like he was searching for an escape route. Jan thought quickly.

"What do you do for a living?"

"I stock shelves over at the SuperMart in Waterville. In fact, I need to..."

Jan wasn't about to be shown the door before she had her proof. She needed something. She didn't know what she was searching for, but she knew there had to be some evidence she could find to prove that he was the thief.

"Tag mentioned you had hoped to join the military. Were you ever able to do that?" Jan asked. Maybe he hadn't been able to enlist for some reason, but perhaps he was in the reserves. Something. Anything to explain why he'd be wearing a military dog tag bracelet.

"Nope." He shook his head. "Afraid not. Turns out they don't let you in if you have epilepsy. And ever since..."

Just then, a horn honked outside the house, and he broke off.

"I've never had a family member in the military, but my cousin Elaine was married to a lieutenant colonel in the army. It's quite an adventurous life."

"Look, that's my ride." He nodded toward the front of the house.

"Oh. Well, that's nice. It's nasty out. How wonderful that you don't have to drive."

He laughed. "Yeah. How nice. My truck's in the shop again."

At that moment his phone lit up. The name Ainsley appeared on the screen.

"I gotta go," Joe said. "Thanks for the food. Really. I appreciate it."

Jan knew she had to leave. She turned reluctantly toward the door. She hadn't gotten the proof she needed.

"Please don't hesitate to let me know if there's anything you need. My cousin and I live in that big Victorian on Main Street. The one with the tearoom?"

Jan wasn't sure if she was imagining it, but she thought she saw his eyes widen just a bit when she said that. Was that because he'd been inside the house, trying to rob them blind? Or was Jan so desperate to find proof that she was seeing things that weren't there?

Joe opened the door, and Jan saw a compact car with the engine running at the curb. There was a woman in the driver's seat. Jan couldn't see much about her, but she was watching Jan.

"Nice to meet you, Joe," Jan called as she stepped past him. "Let me know if you need anything."

Jan waved and hurried down the path to her car.

It had to be Joe. She knew it had to be. Now all she needed to do was prove it.

CHAPTER SEVENTEEN

Elaine followed Nathan across the carpeted lobby of the concert hall. The performance had been soul-stirring. Handel's *Messiah* chronicled the life of Christ, and was one of the most beautiful pieces of music she'd ever heard. The soloists had been incredible, and when the whole chorus sang, it was like hearing angels. And when the entire audience rose for the Hallelujah Chorus, Elaine thought her heart might burst. *And He shall reign forever and ever,* the choir sang. *King of Kings, and Lord of Lords. Hallelujah.*

"What did you think?" he asked. Nathan looked especially dapper tonight. He wore a nicely tailored suit with a vest and bow tie. Elaine could never resist a man in a bow tie.

"I loved it," she said, and threaded her fingers through his. He squeezed her hand. "Thank you."

He smiled at her, and then held the door open so she could step out into the night. Elaine pulled her coat more closely around her, and she felt his arm snake around her back. Snow was falling gently, and she walked with him down the steps of the concert hall toward the parking lot. She leaned into him. As they got closer to his car, Elaine noticed something. Someone, really.

"Max!" she called, but he was too far away and the wind carried her voice off so he didn't hear. But it was Max. He was dressed in a nice suit and was holding the hand of his wife, Judith, who Elaine had met once or twice. They must have been at the concert too. How nice. She was glad they were getting out. She knew she shouldn't be surprised that he was at the concert. Just because he delivered packages for a living didn't mean he didn't enjoy music. She simply hadn't known he was into this kind of thing. Then again, he probably didn't know she was either, she reasoned. And the *Messiah* was a great concert whether you were into music or not. She looked down at his feet. He was wearing nice loafers, not boots. But of course that made sense.

Nathan touched his key ring, and his car's headlights turned on. Elaine reached the car a moment later, and watched as Max and Judith climbed into the cab of a shiny new SUV.

Wait a minute.

Max drove a beat-up pickup truck. Possibly the truck that had shown up in the security footage outside their house. When did they get an SUV?

Elaine saw that there was only a temporary license plate on the front of the car. The SUV must be brand-new then. And— was that a Mercedes logo on the front? Unless Elaine was mistaken, this car had cost a pretty penny. She watched as they climbed into the vehicle and pulled out of the parking space.

"Everything all right?" Nathan asked.

Elaine climbed into the car and closed the door. "Yep," she said as brightly as she could. Nathan smiled, leaned over, and gave her a peck on the cheek before he put the car in gear and backed out. Elaine tried to enjoy the afterglow of the concert, the warm car, and the time with the man she cared more about each day. But inside, she was going over and over things in her head. Where had Max gotten the money to buy a brand-new SUV?

CHAPTER EIGHTEEN

Jan was surprised to see Elaine sitting at the table nursing a cup of English breakfast tea when she went downstairs Friday morning. The sky was just starting to brighten on the horizon, and the whole downstairs was cast in a dim silvery glow. Elaine was hunched over her laptop, scrolling through pages of links.

"Oh. Hello." Jan was usually up first, making the day's scones and tarts. What was Elaine doing up? And after the late night she'd had?

"Hi there. I couldn't sleep."

"Ah." Jan moved over to the stove and saw that the kettle was still hot. She put a teabag in a mug and poured the water over it. "Something bothering you?"

She knew it was a ridiculous question. Of course something was bothering Elaine. She'd seen the thief face-to-face when he'd broken into their home. That would be enough to give anyone nightmares.

Jan looked and saw that she was squinting at the website for Mercedes-Benz. Three different models of SUVs were splashed across the page.

"Doing some Christmas shopping?" Jan asked, coming up behind Elaine.

"I wish." Elaine clicked on one and the car enlarged. "I wanted to check something out. I saw Max Arrington last night. He was at the concert with Judith, and he drove away in a brand-new SUV."

"One of these?" Jan pointed at the image on the screen.

"I think this is the same model." It was hard to tell since it had been dark and snowing, but to Elaine this looked like the same car.

Jan pointed at the price listed on the screen and let out a whistle. The base model, with no upgrades, cost almost $70,000. "Looks like the Arringtons are doing all right for themselves," Jan said.

"Yeah. They must be."

"What else have you found out about Max?"

"Not much," Elaine admitted. "He has a Facebook account, but he rarely updates it. He delivers packages. Has a twelve-year-old daughter with his wife. If there's dirt out there on him, I didn't find it." She was scrolling through his Facebook feed, looking for something. "But get this. On Veteran's Day last year, his wife posted a picture of him in an army uniform. Here it is." Elaine pointed to the picture. It was a faded picture of a much younger Max wearing a military outfit. There was an American flag draped in the background and his last name was emblazoned on his left lapel. Underneath the photo his wife had written, *Happy Veteran's Day to my husband, who served his country faithfully.*

"That's an army dress uniform," Elaine said.

"Huh." Jan added milk and stirred in some artificial sweetener. "So he's a veteran."

"It sure looks that way."

"I've never seen him wearing a bracelet though."

"Maybe you haven't been looking."

Jan nodded. That was fair enough. "He's been wearing so many layers every time I've seen him since fall, it's hard to know. He could have been wearing one that was hidden by his jacket." Jan took the tea bag out and set it in the sink. "I guess we try to talk to him then, right?"

"I think so." Elaine turned around in her chair to look at her. "But our first stop of the day should be to SuperMart to find out about Joe, I think."

Jan took a sip of her tea. It was warm and fragrant. She loved the hint of bergamot that gave the tea its characteristic spiciness.

"Sure." After what she'd seen last night, she was anxious to find a way to prove he was behind the thefts. "Let me get some breakfast, and after I make the pastries we can get going."

"Sounds good. Would you like help?"

Elaine looked so earnest, even a bit hopeful. Jan realized she was serious. Jan froze. It wasn't that she didn't want Elaine's help. And she knew that everyone loved to bake, especially around the holidays. It was just that...well, Jan had her routines down.

"Tell you what. How about I knock the day's baking out as quickly as I can so we can get going faster. But Max— little Max—and Riley are coming over tomorrow to decorate Christmas cookies. Maybe you can help with that."

"All right." Elaine nodded and pushed herself up. Jan's six-year-old grandsons were a hoot. "I'll go work on those invoices I've been putting off then."

"That sounds great," Jan said. "We'll head out as soon as I'm done here."

Jan turned on the oven and started gathering the ingredients for the day's scones. Could Elaine be right about the new SUV? Where would Max get money for a purchase like that? Even if he was the thief, could he possibly have stolen enough cash from robbing a few stores to buy a $70,000 SUV?

No, Jan decided. He couldn't have stolen that much. But the sums stolen from the stores were not insubstantial. He could have gotten away with enough to make a hefty down payment on a vehicle.

Max being a thief was so hard to believe. He was so jovial and jolly. But Jan had to admit, the evidence was slowly stacking up against him.

ELAINE SAT DOWN in front of the computer. She checked her e-mail and saw that she had a message from the International League of Real-Bearded Santas, the one Santa trade group she hadn't heard back from yet. She scanned it, but it said basically what she'd expected. They couldn't release a list of their members, citing privacy concerns. However, the writer could attest that no member of his organization would stoop to thievery and taint the name of Santa. Elaine suppressed a smile. You had to love how seriously these guys all took their jobs.

Elaine realized she hadn't talked to her son, Jared, in a while. She checked the time. He would probably be on his way to work, and Corrie would be busy getting the kids out the door for school. But Sasha might be awake. She was a trainer at a gym and kept odd hours. Elaine picked up the phone and dialed. It rang a few times, and then Sasha answered.

"Hi, Mom," Sasha said. She sounded groggy. "What's up? Is something wrong?"

"Oh dear. Did I wake you up?"

"Um...yeah, kinda. It's only 6:30 here."

"Oh." Elaine had forgotten about the time zone thing. Sasha lived in Colorado. "I'm sorry about that. I wasn't thinking."

"So there's no emergency?"

"No, I'm afraid not."

"Uh, Mom? I'm glad there's no emergency."

"Oh. Of course."

Elaine chatted with Sasha for a few minutes, talking about when she was coming home for Christmas and about the snow conditions here as opposed to Colorado, and then Sasha said she had to get ready for work. Elaine hung up feeling bad about waking her, but glad they'd had a chance to talk.

Elaine set the phone down and scrolled through social media. She wasn't procrastinating; she was just catching up on what was going on in the world. Soon she would get right to work on those invoices. But as she scrolled, mentally she was making a list of who their thief could be. She was pretty sure it wasn't Cole after their conversation with him yesterday. She just didn't think he had it in him. But Max was looking more and more likely. She knew Jan didn't want to believe it, and frankly neither did she, but there were so many things working against him. There was also Tag's cousin Joe. He hadn't been in the military, and Tag said he worked nights so he couldn't have been the thief. But surely he didn't work every night. The thefts hadn't happened every night. And he drove a truck, just like the one in the video. She hadn't yet had a chance to ask Jan how dropping off the lasagna had gone.

And there were still so many leads they hadn't had a chance to follow up on. They hadn't found the owner of the boots, or the truck, or the snowmobile. They needed to go to the thrift store where Cole had bought his costume to see if they sold others—and to whom. And they still needed to talk to Garrett Ruth, the veteran whose rent had been paid off. Not to mention the guy Lydia Pierce had seen at the diner, whom she swore looked like the man in the newspaper photo.

Then Elaine realized what she needed to do. The invoices could wait. She could use this time to go talk to Lydia. She would most likely be working right now, Elaine decided.

"I'll be back in a few minutes," she said as she passed Jan in the kitchen.

"Where are you off to?" Jan looked up from the bowl, where she was mixing ingredients with her hands.

"Kate's Diner," Elaine said.

"If you're hungry…"

"Kate mentioned that Lydia saw a man she thinks was the man in the newspaper photo. I'm going to ask Lydia about it."

"Oh. All right then." Jan gave her a mock salute. "Let me know what you find out."

"Will do." Elaine bundled up in her heavy coat and warm snow boots, and she made the trudge down the sidewalk to Kate's. It was only past A Little Something, but in the brutal cold, it felt much farther. Warmth enveloped her as she stepped inside. It smelled like bacon and warm toast and coffee. Even though Elaine had already eaten a bagel and cream cheese back at the house, her stomach groaned.

"Hi there!" Lydia Pierce greeted Elaine. She had a coffee-pot in one hand and a stack of menus in another. "How are you today?" Her smile was wide, and she wore dangly earrings that shook as she spoke. It didn't matter how much caffeine Elaine drank, she wasn't typically that cheerful in the morning.

"I'm all right," Elaine said. She inhaled deeply. "It smells delicious in here."

"The food tastes even better," Lydia said. "Sit anywhere you like."

Elaine hadn't intended to eat anything, but now that she was here, she figured a cup of coffee couldn't hurt. She would need to sit somewhere to talk to Lydia anyway. Elaine looked around. A long counter ran along one side of the small main room, and tables filled up the rest of the space. There was a pass-through window to the kitchen along the back wall, where Elaine could see Kate cooking over the hot griddle. The whole interior was done in maple paneling planks laid horizontally. Elaine had seen something like it in an interior design magazine recently. Apparently this look was all the rage for high-end restaurants in Brooklyn these days, though Kate's had been decorated with function and warmth, not style, in mind.

Kate had thought it was hilarious when Elaine showed her the article.

There were a few people eating at small tables, and Darby Clement, the town road commissioner, sat at one end of the counter. Elaine smiled at him and he nodded, and she took a seat at the other end of the counter. Lydia slid a menu in front of her and went to carry out food to one of the tables.

Soft Christmas music played over the loudspeakers, and the windows fogged up in a way that made this whole space feel warm and cozy.

"So what can I get you?" Elaine hadn't even noticed Lydia appear in front of her, behind the counter.

"Just coffee," Elaine said.

"Are you sure?" Lydia gestured to a glass and wood display case perched on the edge of the counter. "Those maple bacon donuts are amazing."

"Maple bacon donuts?" Elaine couldn't have heard that right.

"That's right. They're freshly baked and seriously delicious."

How could she resist? She had to at least try them. "All right, you convinced me."

"Coming right up."

For a moment Elaine felt bad ordering something so decadent when Jan was being so good at sticking to her diet. But then, Elaine wasn't on a diet, so why was she feeling bad?

As Lydia placed the donut in front of her on a small plate, every thought of guilt vanished.

"This looks amazing."

"Just wait until you taste it." Lydia set a ceramic mug down in front of her and poured coffee into it. "Can I get you anything else?"

"Actually, I did have a quick question," Elaine said. Elaine tore off a bit of the donut. There was a maple glaze covering tiny pieces of crispy bacon on top of the doughy base. "Your mom was in the tearoom the other day, and she mentioned you had seen someone who looked like the man in the photo that was printed in the newspaper."

"Oh yeah. The Grinch guy?" Lydia set the coffeepot down on the burner. "I totally saw him. He was sitting right where you're sitting."

Elaine shifted on her stool.

"When was this?"

"Oh, a week ago, I guess?" She thought for a moment and nodded. "Yes, it was Saturday, because we were really busy, and I didn't have time to chat with him much to see what his story was. And I wanted to, since I'd never seen him before, and we don't get too many visitors around here this time of year."

Elaine nodded and took a sip of the coffee. It was rich and dark and delicious.

"What makes you so sure it was him?" Elaine took the bit she'd broken off and put it in her mouth. Goodness. It was scrumptious.

"He had that look," Lydia said. Elaine was suddenly less certain than she had been that this was going to pan out. "Same build, same dark hair. And, I don't know. His eyes looked, well, haunted, somehow. Like you could tell something wasn't right with him."

Elaine took another bite of the donut. Wow, this was seriously amazing.

"Plus, I noticed his medical bracelet when he was here. It was mostly covered by his sleeve, but I noticed it because my aunt Jean Ann has one for her diabetes. Anyway, you could see the same bracelet in the photo that was published in the newspaper, so I know it was him."

"Wait." Elaine set her donut down. "That's a medical bracelet?"

"Yeah. Sure. A lot of people with serious health concerns wear them. It basically says your name and what your condition is so if you pass out, the paramedics will know how to help you."

Well, that was a pretty dismal thing to think about. But a useful one, in this case.

"You're sure it was a medical bracelet?" Elaine asked. What if the thief wasn't a military man, but a diabetic?

"Yep. It had that symbol with the snakes and wings that medical stuff has. It was definitely a medical bracelet, and I'm certain it was the same one in the picture of the guy in Faith's store."

"Wow." It took Elaine a moment to process this. If Lydia was right, they'd been thinking about this all wrong. "Did you get his name when he was in here?"

"He wasn't very talkative. He told me his name was Paul and he was new to the area but that's all I got out of him."

Paul? They hadn't come across anyone named Paul in this investigation so far. Of course, there was no guarantee that was his real name. And who was to say whether he was really new to the area or not?

"Did he pay with a credit card?" Elaine asked. If he had, and if they could dig the receipt up, it would say his real name on the receipt.

Lydia shook her head. "Cash. A really tiny tip too, which is how I remember."

Well, that was too bad. But there had to be some way to determine who this Paul really was. If there was any chance he was the thief, they had to find out. She took another bite of her donut and realized it was almost gone.

"Did you notice whether he was wearing boots?" Elaine asked.

"Yep." Lydia noticed Darby signal for the check, and she grabbed it and slid it to him without missing a beat. "I did notice, because he didn't wipe them on the doormat when he came in, and it was a slushy day, and he tracked the slush to his seat."

Goodness. Lydia noticed everything that went on in here.

"He had on boots," Lydia said. "I don't know what brand, but they were black and gray. Looked about like the kind of boots everyone in Maine wears this time of year."

It did indeed. But more specifically, they sounded like the kind of boots the Grinch wore. Elaine couldn't think of what else to ask, but she thanked Lydia for her help, finished her donut, and paid her bill.

"Keep me posted on what you find out," Lydia said, and Elaine nodded and promised to do so before heading home. When she got there, Jan was cleaning the baking sheets while scones and muffins cooled on wire racks.

"Did you try the maple bacon donut?" Jan asked, shutting off the water.

Elaine froze. Could she tell the truth? Would that just make Jan upset that she couldn't have one?

"You have some on your cheek," Jan said, a smile on her face, and Elaine laughed and reached for a napkin to wipe it off.

"It was amazingly delicious," Elaine confessed.

"No doubt. How could it not be?" Jan set the pan in the drying rack. "I would kill for one right now."

Elaine smiled. "I'm proud of your resolve! I was hopeless in the face of that donut. Are you about ready to get going?"

"Let me just run upstairs for a minute and then I'll be ready to go." Jan wiped her hands on the dish towel before heading for the stairs.

While Jan was upstairs getting ready, Elaine wandered over to the back door and looked out. Earl Grey was curled up in his little nest, and Elaine opened the door and stepped out. She picked him up. The cat gave a little groan of protest at being woken from his nap, but then settled against her chest and began to purr.

The air out here was cold, but the cat was soft and warm. Elaine stroked his head and gazed out over the lake. It was calm and peaceful right now, with snow falling gently and the whole world a wash of gray and white. It was a beautiful place to live, she thought. Beautiful but brutal. A person could freeze to death out there in a short time. But wasn't that what life was like in general? Beautiful but brutal. No one made it out alive. But boy, it could be wonderful sometimes.

She thought about the faces of her children. Of each of her grandchildren. That powerful love—the kind of love that made you forget yourself and care only for another—that love made it all worth it. She wondered how God felt, sending His own son to be a part of this hard, dangerous, beautiful world on that first Christmas morning. Did He worry about Him, the way Elaine worried about each of her kids as they went out into the world on their own? Did God worry at all? Wasn't that against His nature? But then, how much did we really understand about His nature?

"You ready?" Jan asked from the doorway. "Archie and Rose will be here soon to open for us."

Elaine shook her head and tore herself from her musings. She turned and saw that Jan had her purse slung over her shoulder and had brushed her hair and put on a new sweater and coat of lip gloss. Now Elaine felt underdressed, but she decided it didn't matter for where they were going, so she tucked the cat back into his nest and stepped inside.

A few minutes later, they were driving along the highway. As they drove, Elaine filled Jan in on what she'd learned at the diner.

"So it wasn't a military bracelet. It was a medical bracelet," Jan said. Elaine nodded. "Wow. That changes things."

"Yep. We've been looking for someone with some connection to the military, but we need to be looking for someone with diabetes."

"Or some other serious medical condition," Jan added. "What reasons would make one wear a bracelet like this?"

"I don't know," Elaine said. "And I don't know how we would track this person down. It's not like there's a registry of diabetes sufferers."

"I suppose we could ask around. Maybe Matt McInnis would tell us who he knows of."

"Possibly, but there are laws against sharing that kind of patient information," Elaine said. But there had to be some way to figure it out.

Jan was quiet for a moment. Elaine kept her eyes on the road. Instrumental music layered over the swish of the wipers.

"You know who does have a medical condition? The kind that might lead to a bracelet?" Jan asked.

"Who?" Elaine asked.

"Joe Stone. He told me he has epilepsy."

"That would do it," Elaine said. "In that case, let's go find out if he's our man."

Soon they were parked in the lot of the big shopping center on the outskirts of Waterville and were headed inside the SuperMart. The store was bright and loud and a bit over-whelming, and Elaine's eye was immediately drawn to a display of items under a dollar. She spotted some mini stockings. And they had boxes of candy canes and chocolates shaped like Santa. Maybe she should just—

"You don't need any of that stuff," Jan said, dragging her past the display.

"Of course I don't." Elaine looked back. *Ooh.* There were Pez dispensers with reindeer heads on top. "But I want to buy it."

Jan took her cousin by the arm and pulled her past. "You'll thank me later."

Elaine knew Jan was right, but still. It was hard to pass up the allure of a good deal, even on things she didn't really need.

"So," Jan said when they were safely past the display and the registers. They stood in front of the stationery and greeting cards. Elaine did love to send a good Christmas card, but she'd already bought hers, so she didn't need anything in the section. "Where should we start?"

Elaine had no idea where you were supposed to go to ask if one of your employees was breaking into people's homes.

Jan shrugged and pointed to the customer service counter along the front wall. "Maybe we ask for a manager there?"

"I guess it's a good a place to start," Elaine agreed. There was one woman ahead of them who was trying to return a set of sheets without the receipt. By the time they stepped up at the counter, the woman behind the desk looked ready to take a nap. She was in her midfifties and had black hair that frizzed out around her face. She wore a long tunic that stretched across her hips, and her heavy eye makeup didn't hide the dark circles under her eyes.

"Hello." Elaine kept her voice upbeat and cheerful. "We have a bit of a strange question. We're hoping to talk to someone about one of your employees. A Joe Stone."

"What about him?" The woman's name tag said Delia.

"He stocks shelves. We'd like to know which nights he's worked in the past few weeks."

"Hmm." The woman looked at them for a moment and then turned to the computer on the counter. "You'd need to talk to the manager of his department."

"And where would we find that person?"

Delia grunted and turned to a grubby phone list taped to the wall. She ran her finger along a line and then dialed a number. "I need a manager from inventory," she said into the phone.

The person on the other end of the line mumbled something. The woman nodded and looked up at Jan and Elaine again.

"What do you need this for?" she asked.

"We just want to verify his employment," Elaine said quickly. She hoped that would be enough to get them to talk to someone who knew something.

"Garnishing his wages?"

"What?" Elaine didn't know what to say, but apparently her baffled response was enough information for the woman.

"Mortgage, I guess," Delia said into the phone.

The person at the other end of the line said something, and then she hung up. "All right. Go on through those doors," she said. She gestured to a set of double doors a little ways down the wall. They were marked Employees Only.

A man in a business suit came up behind them in line and sighed.

"Thanks so much!" Elaine said, keeping her voice far more chipper than she felt. They walked over to the doors and pushed them open as if they belonged. They were in a long hallway painted a grayish beige. The linoleum floor was scuffed and the fluorescent overhead lights buzzed and popped.

"Where to now?" Jan asked. Elaine looked around and shrugged. Just as she started down the hallway, a door swung open at the other end, and a petite woman with dark hair came out. Was Elaine imagining it, or did she hesitate for a second when she saw them? Had they met before? Elaine racked her brain, but she couldn't remember ever seeing her before. But then, before Elaine could be sure, the woman smiled and continued toward them.

"Are you the two who wanted to verify employment for one of my inventory guys?" she asked. She was upbeat and cheerful. Pretty much the opposite of the woman at the customer service counter.

"That's us," Elaine said. "I'm Elaine Cook, and this is my cousin Jan Blake, and we're hoping you can help us verify the records for an employee named Joe Stone."

"Sure thing." She used a passkey to unlock a door that branched off to the right, and she ushered them inside what looked like a small office. There was a desk with a computer on it, and two padded chairs across from it. The place was small and had the same beige walls and too-yellow lighting as the hallway, but someone had attempted to warm it up by placing a potted plant, now withered and brown, on the corner of the desk. "You guys are from a bank?"

Elaine didn't know what to say, but the woman didn't seem to mind. "We don't get so many of these verifications these days, now that it's much harder to get a loan, but used to be every other day or so someone was calling to verify someone's work history." While she was talking, she was typing, and Elaine just let her.

Did this woman really believe they were here from a bank, here to verify Joe's income and employment history? They hadn't said anything of the sort, and they certainly didn't look like they worked in finance. Jan was wearing a sweater with dancing snowmen on it, for goodness' sake. Was that even how securing a loan worked? She was doubtful. But if she didn't confirm anything, it was okay, wasn't it?

"What was the last name?"

"Stone," Jan said, and she spelled it out. "Tall, dark hair."

"Good guy. Hard worker." She typed something else in, and then tilted the screen so they could see it. "Here we go."

Elaine craned her neck and saw that the woman was looking at some kind of software that tracked employee schedules.

"Looks like Joe Stone worked Saturday, Sunday, Monday, and Tuesday," she said. "And last night too. Wow. He's been busy."

"What hours were those shifts?" Jan asked.

The woman used a mouse to click on something, then said, "Says here nine to six." She shrugged. "Nine at night to six in the morning, that is. Vampire hours."

Elaine met Jan's eyes. She could tell that Jan was as shocked as she was that the woman had given out this information. But there was something more in Jan's eyes too. Disappointment. Her face mirrored the disappointment Elaine felt. Because if this woman was right—and Elaine was looking directly at the screen; she could see that she was— then Joe had been working when the break-ins happened. He couldn't have been the one to break into their house, and the other businesses in town.

"What about breaks?" Jan asked.

"Yep. A twenty-minute lunch, and two fifteen-minute breaks. You can see where he punched out for those." She ran her finger along a line on the screen. "Funny how they call it a lunch even though it's the middle of the night," she said.

The woman didn't seem bothered by the question, though Elaine couldn't see how any bank representative would care about that. Still, it was good to know. A twenty-minute lunch wouldn't be enough time to drive to Lancaster, rob a business, and get back in time to punch back in. And based on what she saw, his lunches were later in the morning—closer to four—than the break-ins had all been.

Joe wasn't their man. And while on a certain level she was glad that Tag's cousin wasn't the thief, she was starting to wonder if they'd ever figure out who was behind it all.

"Thank you for your help," Elaine said, and turned to go.

"Yep. Let me know if you need anything else." The woman smiled and escorted them back to the hallway, and Elaine followed Jan out the door.

"Well, that was easier than it should have been," Jan said as they walked away. "Did she really think we were there from a bank? Why would a bank even do that?"

"I have no idea. She didn't ask for a business card or anything. I'm a little scared about how simple that was. It's a good thing we only have good intentions."

"True enough. And I'm certainly not complaining," Jan said. "But it does mean that Joe is ruled out."

"I know. And we're running out of suspects."

"We've still got Max," Jan said. Even though they were no longer certain they needed to find someone with a military connection, he still had the boots and the new SUV.

"And Garrett. And if we go over to the thrift store, maybe they'll have some leads for us."

"Let's hope," Elaine said. "Otherwise I'm not sure where to look next."

CHAPTER NINETEEN

The Goodwill was only a few minutes' drive away from the SuperMart, and when they pulled into the parking lot this time, the lights were on inside the store. They went inside and looked around. Jan had been in plenty of thrift stores, and this one looked pretty typical. In front were racks and racks of clothing, and beyond that were household items. Toys were against the far wall, and books next to that. A young woman sat behind the counter looking down at her phone. Shoppers milled around in the distance.

"Excuse me."

The girl looked up as Elaine spoke.

"We're looking for costumes. Santa suits, specifically."

She had dark hair and her sparkly silver-painted nails flew across the face of her phone.

"Sorry, we had a bunch, but that's a popular item this time of year."

"They're all gone?"

"Yep. 'Fraid so."

"Would you be able to tell us anything about the people who bought them?" Elaine asked.

The girl looked at her as if she had two heads.

"Do you keep records of that sort of thing?" Jan asked.

She shook her head. "Nah. We don't keep track of who buys what."

"Would there be any way to find that out?"

Now the woman looked more annoyed than confused. Her eyebrows narrowed, and her forehead wrinkled.

"Nope," she finally said, and turned back to her phone.

Well then. Elaine looked at Jan and shrugged. Jan didn't know what to do, so they turned and walked out.

"That was less than helpful," Jan said as they hurried to the car.

Elaine nodded. "Maybe we can try other thrift stores in the area. Someone has got to remember something."

"I'm doubtful, but I suppose it can't hurt." Jan looked at the time on the dashboard. Archie and Rose would already have opened the tearoom. "But probably not now. We should get back."

Elaine reluctantly agreed, and they climbed into the car and started back toward Lancaster.

"I've been wondering something," Jan said. "Why Santa?"

Elaine shrugged. "Why not Santa? It's as good a disguise as any, I suppose."

"But why wear a disguise? Why not just wear a ski mask or something?"

"I don't know." Elaine sighed. "There's something really twisted about it, isn't there? Saint Nicholas—the real Saint Nick, who evolved into the commercialized version of Santa we know now—became famous for distributing toys to children. This is pretty much the opposite."

Jan nodded, but she didn't say anything.

"And he doesn't wear a coat."

"Huh?"

"It's winter. In Maine. Yet this guy wears only a Santa suit but not, say, a parka. And he stands outside picking locks."

"*Hmm.*" Elaine thought about that. "Maybe he has one on under his costume?"

Jan didn't answer, because she didn't know what to say.

They were most of the way home when Elaine's phone rang. Jan glanced over and saw Elaine digging in her purse. She found it and squinted at the screen. It was a local number, but one she didn't recognize.

"Hello?" she said.

"Elaine? This is Fiona Latimore."

"Oh, hi, Fiona." Elaine didn't know her well, but Fiona was always friendly. She owned Oldies But Goodies, one of several antique stores in Lancaster.

"Bristol said I should call you. She said you're looking into the Grinch thefts going on around town."

"That's right." Elaine got a sinking feeling in her gut. She was afraid she knew what Fiona was going to say.

"Well, in that case, I wanted to let you know that my shop was robbed last night."

CHAPTER TWENTY

When Jan and Elaine finally returned to the tearoom, Elaine felt drained. Shaken. They'd stopped by Oldies But Goodies and talked with Fiona, and it was the same story. Lock picked. Safe opened with a crowbar. Cash missing—a lot of cash. Nearly a thousand dollars, it turned out. Fiona didn't have any sort of security system and no one had seen the intruder and thus could not verify he was dressed as Santa. Yet the known details fit the pattern. It was very likely the same guy, Elaine thought, even if they didn't have any evidence to prove it.

So now he'd hit up three businesses in town, plus the attempted robbery at their place. And they—and the police, it seemed—were no closer to finding him than they were before.

Elaine went through the motions of helping in the tearoom, though her mind was far away. Jan had stepped in to serve in the west parlor for Rose during her lunch break.

"Archie," Rose said, pulling a large covered cake carrier out of a tote bag and setting it on the counter, "check it out. I made this for you."

"For me?" Archie was pulling green linen napkins out of the sideboard, and he stopped and turned.

"Well, maybe more like inspired by you. It's kind of for everyone."

Archie laughed. He didn't seem to mind at all that he didn't get an entire cake to himself.

"We were talking about seasonal menus at culinary school, and I decided to plan out a traditional British Christmas meal."

"Bring on the boiled ham and mushy peas," Archie joked.

Rose shook her head and unlatched the lid. "Actually, I'm going to cook a goose. But that's not what's in here."

"Thank goodness."

"Voila!" Rose lifted the lid and they all turned to look. Returning to the kitchen, Jan joined them in observing a molded brown cake of some sort, topped with a sprig of holly.

"A Christmas pudding!" Archie set down the napkins. A smile spread across his face. "You really made a Christmas pudding?"

"I did." Rose set the lid down on the counter. "I wanted to do a dry run before I make it on the big day. But I had no idea how much work goes into these."

"It really is impressive." Elaine had seen Jan make a Christmas pudding before. After chopping and mixing the flour, sugar, apples, and candied citrus peel, you had to boil it for eight hours.

"Are we going to light it up?" Archie asked.

Ah, right. And then after all that work, you doused the cake with brandy and set it on fire. Such a strange concept for a dessert.

"Maybe not just now," Jan said.

"How about we save that for some other time?" Archie asked. "I've got to get these napkins out there."

Jan laughed and prepared her order. Soon the place was hopping. But in the early afternoon, there was a lull. Elaine thought about using this time to go question Garrett, but Jan was engaged in a conversation with some out-of-town guests. She'd ask Jan about it when she was done. In the meantime, Elaine decided to use the opportunity to slip into the office and call the other thrift shops in the area to ask about Santa suits.

She settled down at the computer, shifted the stack of invoices, and used the phone book to find the phone number for the Goodwill in Augusta. The clerk who answered the phone there was kind, but couldn't tell her anything about Santa suits. He had no idea if they'd sold any in the past few months, and when he asked the other employees, one thought maybe they'd had one at some point but couldn't remember when it had sold and certainly not to whom.

Elaine tried a few smaller stores in neighboring towns, but had no success. She was ready to call it quits. After all, what were the chances the suit had come from a thrift store anyway? If Elaine were going to buy a Santa suit, she'd just go on Amazon and order one. Who would go sorting through racks at thrift stores? Still, there was one more store she knew of, and she decided to give the Goodwill in Portland a call before giving up entirely.

Elaine dialed the store and waited while it rang.

"Goodwill, this is Annette Simons. How can I help you?"

"Oh. Ms. Simons!" She was the one Elaine had spoken with a few weeks back, when she was trying to track down which store the painting done by Archie's father had come from. It turned out that the vendor at Mainely Bargains, where they'd bought it, had purchased the painting at this Goodwill store, but Annette hadn't been able to track down where *they* got it from. But now, the awkward pause on the other end of the line reminded Elaine that Ms. Simons had no idea it was Elaine calling.

"This is Elaine Cook. We spoke a few weeks ago about that painting? The one of the woman drinking tea?" Elaine was glad Ms. Simons had picked up. She had been very helpful before, sending Elaine in the right direction even when there were things she wasn't technically supposed to share.

"Oh. That's right. You know, the funniest thing happened. Just a few days ago, a woman came in here asking about a painting. From everything she said, it sounded just like the painting you were asking about."

"Wait, really? Someone was asking about the same painting?"

"Yeah. It was the weirdest thing. No one ever comes in asking about specific things they bought here, but in the space of a few weeks, two people were asking about that tea picture."

Was it really possible? Was there any chance this woman was confused, and there were two different paintings?

"Who was she?" Who in the world would be looking into the same painting they were?

"I didn't catch her name. She was older, maybe in her seventies or eighties. She had white hair. Well dressed. I told her the same thing I told you—that our records say it came from that antique store that had a fire, but that they have no record of it."

"Did she say why she wanted it?"

"No. She didn't say that. But she was interested in finding out what had happened to it."

"What did you tell her?"

"Well, obviously I can't give away information about our customers, as you know. Their privacy is of utmost importance."

Elaine stifled a laugh. This was Goodwill, not Bergdorf Goodman. But she guessed she appreciated it.

Ms. Simons cleared her throat. "But she did seem quite keen to find the picture. So I admit I did drop a couple of hints that might have tipped her off about where to look."

"What did you tell her?" Elaine wouldn't have minded if Ms. Simons had given out her information. If someone was tracing the painting, she was curious to know why.

"I mentioned that it ended up in the hands of people who had hung it in a tearoom."

"Huh." Elaine wasn't sure if that would be enough for the woman to go on to find them or not. There weren't a ton of tearooms in Maine, but there were enough that it wouldn't be immediately obvious which one she meant.

"Well, if a woman shows up at our door asking about the painting, at least I'll know how she got there," Elaine said. "Thank you for letting me know."

"No problem. I hope you're not upset. I figured the woman might actually be of help to you."

"Not at all."

"Good. Now. What can I do for you today?"

"I have sort of a strange question. I hope that's all right."

"Sure. I'll try to help if I can."

"Great. Thanks so much." Elaine shifted the phone to her other ear. "This time, I'm trying to track down a Santa suit. Have you sold any Santa costumes recently?" Elaine asked.

"Huh." Ms. Simons made a noise at the back of her throat. "That's a good question. I think we did have one here that got bought maybe a week or two ago. I'd have to check, but I'm pretty sure we did have one."

"Would you be willing to look into it?" Elaine didn't want to push her luck, but she wouldn't get anywhere if she didn't ask. "I'm especially interested in learning the name of the person who bought it, if that's possible."

"Huh," Ms. Simons said again. "Well, if they paid cash, we wouldn't know, and like I said, I can't tell you that anyway."

Elaine knew she couldn't. But Elaine also knew that she had been able to drop a few hints last time that had pointed Elaine in the right direction.

"Is there any way to see if there are records?" Elaine asked.

"I can go back and look and see if we have any records."

"That would be wonderful," Elaine said. "I really appreciate it."

"Is this the best number to reach you?" Ms. Simons asked.

"It sure is."

"All right. I'll give a call if I find anything," Ms. Simons said. Elaine thanked her, and then she hung up.

She should probably check on the tearoom. She peeked into the kitchen and saw that Rose was loading up a serving tray with pastries, and the low hum coming from the parlors indicated that their guests seemed to all be having a fine time. Elaine decided she could spend a few more minutes in here working on this mystery. They still hadn't heard from Garrett. Elaine checked the local listings but didn't find a phone number. The couple must be like so many young people these days who didn't have a land line.

She did a search on him to see if there was anything about him she'd missed, but she didn't find much.

What was Garrett hiding? Why wasn't he calling her back? And how could she find out more?

Elaine didn't know, and she felt frustration rising up. Would they ever find any answers?

CHAPTER TWENTY-ONE

Elaine read the paper as she ate her oatmeal on Saturday morning. It was sure to be a busy day in the tearoom, and after she'd done her devotions, she'd come downstairs determined to focus on running the tearoom today instead of being distracted by this mystery.

She'd spent a good chunk of the night tossing and turning, getting more and more frustrated about the fact that they weren't getting any closer to finding answers. The previous night, she and Jan had spent a good hour thinking through all the clues they'd gathered so far. Lydia seemed so certain that the man named Paul she'd met at the diner was the same person in the grainy security photo she'd seen in the newspaper. Even if it was, was there any way to find out who this Paul was?

But this morning, after a bowl of hot oatmeal and a nice cup of English breakfast tea, Elaine was feeling better, and more resolved. The mystery would be on the back burner today.

"Anything good in the paper?" Jan asked from the kitchen. She was taking oversize cranberry spice muffins out of the muffin tin.

"There's an article about the break-in at Oldies But Goodies," Elaine said. "But I am not reading that one. I'm reading one about another kind gesture from an anonymous donor."

"Oh?"

"This one is about three huge boxes of food left outside a home. The father died this summer, and the mom has been struggling with three kids, and there was enough food left on the doorstep for weeks."

"Well, that's wonderful," Jan said. She hesitated. "Do you think...?"

She let her voice trail off, but Elaine knew what she was thinking.

"I don't know. It seems less and less likely Garrett stole all that money and then started giving it away."

Jan nodded. But something was tickling at the back of her mind.

"Anyway, it's a nice story, and that's what I'm going to focus on today. Just good news."

"I support that," Jan said. "Let's focus on only positive things today."

"Sounds good to me." Elaine pushed back from the table and carried her bowl toward the sink.

"Don't forget, Max and Riley are coming over in the afternoon to make Christmas cookies," Jan reminded her.

"Well, I would say that falls squarely into the category of good news," Elaine said. "That will be fun." She pushed herself up. All the more reason she needed to be present today. With Jan distracted by a couple of six-year-olds in the kitchen, Elaine would need to pick up some of the slack in the tearoom. She rinsed her bowl and set it in the dishwasher.

"I'll head upstairs to get ready, and then I'll start making the sandwiches," Elaine said, using her hip to close the dishwasher. She started toward the stairs and had just put her hand on the banister when the phone rang. She started up, but paused when she heard Jan say, "Oh dear."

The tone in her voice said it all. Something had happened. Had there been another break-in last night? She paused and listened to Jan's end of the conversation. "When?...Did anyone else see anything?...Have you called the police?"

Elaine started back down the stairs, and she was waiting in the kitchen when Jan hung up the phone.

"That was Andrea McInnis. She scared away a man dressed as Santa Claus just as he was about to break in to her neighbor's house last night."

Elaine shook her head. It was what she had feared, and exactly what she didn't want to hear. So much for ignoring this whole thing today.

"I'll go get ready to head out. Meet you down here in a few minutes?"

"We don't have to go, Elaine." But Elaine knew her cousin well enough that Jan wouldn't be able to stay away, no matter what Elaine said.

And—well, who was she kidding? She wasn't about to let this new incident go without investigating.

"This can't go on. This guy can't keep terrorizing our town." Elaine felt indignation rising. "I'll meet you back down here in ten minutes," Elaine said. "Let's catch this guy."

When they pulled up in front of the McInnis house—just down Pine Ridge Road, across from Lancaster Community

Church—Dan Benson was just driving away. He gave them a friendly wave as he headed out of the driveway and they pulled in. The McInnis house was a quaint Queen Anne-style home with gingerbread trim, and the kids had built a series of snowmen in the front yard.

Matt and Andrea McInnis ran the Lakeview Medical Clinic. It had been started by Matt's father, Tyson, and was located next door. As they came up the walkway, Andrea opened the door and ushered them inside.

"Thank you for coming," she said. She was a tall African American woman, and she still had the lanky, sinewy look of the sprinter she had been in college. In warmer weather, you could often see Andrea running along the trails that threaded through the woods around Lancaster. Her husband, Matt, was known to be more at home at a concert hall than on a basketball court or football field, but he too was fit and healthy. He was standing in the kitchen in jeans and a striped sweater, and he waved and then gestured that he was heading upstairs.

"Of course." Jan wiped her feet on the doormat and stepped in. The house was not only warm and inviting, but looked like it had come out of a design magazine. A modern, open kitchen with high-end fixtures took up the main part of the first floor, with a long wooden table surrounded by chairs beyond, and a sitting area open to the kitchen on one end. The colors were tasteful and neutral, with a few pops of color that made the space feel bright and inviting, even on this dreary day.

"Matt is helping Anthony practice for his holiday concert," Andrea explained as her husband vanished up the stairs.

"This is lovely," Elaine said, looking around. "I just love that couch." She was pointing at a sectional in a warm gray. Upstairs, Jan could hear the sound of feet and the creak of a violin played by someone who was clearly just learning.

"Thank you." Andrea showed them in and gestured for them to take a seat on the couch. Jan did, and leaned back against a tasteful turquoise throw pillow. "I'm sorry to ruin your morning like this. I almost didn't call, but..."

"We're glad you did," Elaine said. She was adjusting a similar pillow behind her. "We'd love to know what you saw."

"Well, it was very strange," Andrea said. "We had just got Tim and Anthony down for bed, and as I was coming down the stairs, I happened to glance out the window on the landing."

Andrea gestured to the window in the bit of the stairs where they turned.

"And I noticed someone dressed like Santa Claus approaching the doorstep of the Beaty house, right next door."

"Did you get a good look at him?" Jan asked.

"I'm afraid not." Andrea had lowered herself into a side chair in a light blue-and-white striped pattern. "It was dark, and I was so stunned I didn't really stop to think about what I was doing."

"What did you do?" Elaine asked.

"I ran down the stairs and started screaming for him to go away." Andrea looked a little chagrined. "I wish I could say I did something a bit more logical, but I will admit that I just sort of reacted. With everything I've been reading about in the newspaper about this guy breaking into buildings and robbing people, I got a little worried."

"And what did he do?" Jan asked.

"He ran. Just slung his bag over his shoulder and took off."

"He had a bag?" Jan asked. The Santa they'd seen in the footage at A Little Something was also carrying a bag over his shoulder. "What was it like?"

"Just a standard Santa Claus bag, I guess," Andrea said. "Some kind of dark fabric, I think. Again, I didn't really get a good look at him. But when I ran out the front door yelling at him to get away, he shrieked, so I know it was a man."

He shrieked? That didn't mean anything necessarily, Jan thought. But it didn't sound like the seasoned thief they had come to expect either.

"It just about scared Matt to death," Andrea said. "He was washing up the dishes in the kitchen and when I came down the stairs screaming, he almost had a heart attack."

"I would imagine." Jan shook her head. "What did he do?"

"Grabbed the phone and called 911." Andrea nodded. "Not that I knew that at the time, of course. I was out the door."

"How long did it take the police to get here?" Jan asked.

"Fifteen minutes, or something ridiculous like that, before they got here from Augusta. By that time the guy was long gone."

That explained why Dan Benson was just coming by this morning then. They'd sent someone from the main state trooper office last night, and Dan had come by today to follow up.

"You said the guy got away. Did he escape on foot?" Elaine asked.

"No." Andrea was clutching a throw pillow in her hands, pulling at the fringe along the edge. "He got into a car that was parked at the curb. I couldn't tell much about it, unfortunately, because I was running after him..."

"Wait. You didn't just chase him away from the house, you ran after him?" Elaine's eyes were wide.

"Yeah." She looked from Elaine to Jan and back like they were nuts. "What was I going to do, just let him get away?"

"That's fantastic." Jan laughed, picturing this athletic woman chasing down a man dressed as Santa on the icy sidewalk.

"I'm impressed," Elaine said. "When I saw him, all I did was scream and try to hide."

"He's been frightening this town. I wasn't about to let him get away with that," Andrea said. "It was more adrenaline than bravery. But unfortunately, the car was parked in front of the Beaty house, so he had a fair head start. He hopped in his car and got it started before I got close enough to see much of anything about it."

From upstairs, a violin squeaked out notes. "Silent Night," maybe? It was hard to tell.

"It was a car, you said?" Jan asked.

"Not a truck?" Elaine added.

"Definitely a car."

Elaine looked at Jan, who met her eye and nodded. So it wasn't the same vehicle that they'd seen in the footage of the robbery at their place. But that didn't mean the same person wasn't involved.

"A sedan of some kind. I couldn't make out anything about the license plate," Andrea said. "There was one thing I did see though. The car had one of those volunteer firefighter bumper stickers on it."

"What?" Jan thought Andrea had to be mistaken. The town was too small to have a full-time crew at the fire station, so when there was an emergency, members of the volunteer force were notified by phone—often by Des Murphy, who lived close to the fire station. Because they often ended up racing toward the firehouse and parking haphazardly as they rushed to get to the trucks, the members of the volunteer force were given bumper stickers that identified them, and they were given leniency during emergencies. The familiar bumper stickers showed the Maltese cross with a fire hat, ladder, and fire hydrant.

"Are you sure?" Elaine asked.

"I'm certain of it because I thought it was very odd," Andrea said.

"Huh." Jan didn't know what to make of this. The volunteer fire department in Lancaster wasn't very large. They knew pretty much all of the people on it. There was Des Murphy, Elsa Leon, Russell Edmonds, and a handful of other good, upstanding citizens. If the thief was one of the members, it shouldn't be that hard to figure out who, but Jan couldn't believe that any of those people were behind the string of thefts.

"Who lives in the house he was trying to break into?" Elaine asked. Jan nodded. Andrea had said the Beaty house, but Jan didn't know anyone by that name.

"That's the strangest thing," Andrea said. "Joanne Beaty. She's a widow in her eighties. She lives alone. Doesn't get out much. We keep an eye on her and try to check on her as often as we can. But it seems strange, right? Maybe she's secretly got a ton of cash stashed around the house. But judging by the condition of the house and the car she drives, I always assumed she didn't have a lot."

Jan knew you could never really be sure. But she also knew that Joanne seemed an unlikely target for a crime like this one.

"Is there anything else you can tell us?" Elaine asked.

"That's all I can remember, unfortunately," Andrea said. "But if I think of anything else that might help identify this guy, I'll definitely let you know."

"Thank you for calling us," Elaine said. Her plan to not think about the thefts had lasted last less than half an hour, but at least they now had something to go on. She and Jan headed toward the door and waved to Andrea again.

As soon as they sat down in the car, Jan cranked up the heat, put the car into gear, and pulled away from the curb. "Did that seem odd to you?"

"Totally." Elaine held her hands up to the hot-air vents. "I believe Andrea is telling the truth, but the way Santa acted this time is totally different from how he's acted in the past."

"I was thinking the same thing," Jan said. "For starters, she said she'd just put the kids to bed when she saw him. Which means this was, what, maybe eight o'clock?"

"Not much later, I wouldn't think," Elaine said. "And the other thefts have all happened in the dead of the night."

"This was also the first time a home has been targeted. So far it's only been businesses that have been robbed," Jan said.

"Our home was targeted."

"But it's a business as well. And we're guessing the thief was probably aiming for the office, right?"

"Probably." Elaine agreed. "And it's possible that the thief didn't realize we live there, maybe. But still."

"Fair enough," Jan said. Technically this wasn't the first residence that had been targeted. "But I still think it's fair to say this was different. There's also the fact that it was an elderly widow who was hit up. If you were going to rob someone in this town, would that be the first house you'd try?"

"No." Elaine shook her head. "And not only that. Andrea said he shrieked when she ran after him."

"I noticed that too. It doesn't sound like the experienced criminal who appears to have been behind the other thefts." Jan slowed for the stop sign, then slowly turned on to Main Street. There were plenty of people out on this Saturday morning, and the shops along Main were starting to open.

"So what does that mean?" Elaine asked. "Do you think our thief has branched out?"

"Maybe." But that didn't seem likely to Jan. This seemed so different, it didn't seem likely that this was the same person. But it was certainly related. "I suspect this might be a copycat."

"Oh dear." Elaine shook her head. "I suppose that is the most likely scenario."

Jan hated to think it, but it did seem likely to her as well. Someone was borrowing the idea of dressing up like Santa Claus for nefarious purposes.

"But who?" Elaine asked.

Jan wished she had an answer. "I guess we need to figure out who all the volunteer firemen are, and what they drive."

Elaine nodded. "That's probably the best place to start."

CHAPTER TWENTY-TWO

J an and Elaine headed back to the tearoom, and a few hours later the Saturday afternoon rush was in full force, with both of the parlors busy with customers. But the real excitement was happening in the kitchen. Jan looked around and sighed. To be more specific, the kitchen was an absolute disaster. There were bowls of colored frosting spread across the table and colored sugar scattered everywhere. Flour covered every surface, and dirty metal cookie cutters filled the sink. On the counter were four dozen sugar cookies, decorated with drippy frosting and piles of colored sugar. Jan had sampled a few scraps of the dough—she had to make sure it tasted right, after all—but she had been very good overall. In other words, it had been a very successful afternoon baking with her grandsons.

"Grandma, can I have another cookie?" Riley asked.

"I'd say you've had quite enough," Jan said, laughing. The little monkey had green frosting swiped across his cheek, and he was still chewing the last of his second star-shaped cookie.

"But Max got another one," Riley said, gesturing to his twin brother, who was stuffing a cookie shaped like an angel into his mouth at that moment.

"Max." Jan put her hands on her hips and tried to make her face look stern. But the way he was smiling up at her, his eyes wide, not at all guilty, seemingly pleased at his own courage, made her want to laugh out loud.

She knew she should punish him for disobeying, but she couldn't do it. He was too cute. Jan couldn't help it. She'd been pretty strict with her own children, but with her grandchildren, she couldn't bring herself to scold. Those little munchkins had wormed their way into her heart, and no matter what they did, she couldn't bring herself to be upset at them. Let their parents worry about discipline.

"Riley, why don't you take one more cookie," Jan said. "And then that's it, for both of you."

Riley nodded, shoved an angel cookie into his mouth whole, and hopped down off his chair.

"And just where do you think you're going?" Once again, Jan tried to make her voice sound stern, but judging by the fact that he didn't stop, she decided she probably hadn't been successful.

"To find Archie," he said through a mouthful of crumbs.

"Now hang on," Jan said. Both boys loved Archie, who was gentle and kind to them and loved to show them magic tricks. But the last thing the guests of the tearoom needed was a sticky-fingered child on a sugar high traipsing through. Jan lunged after him, but he was already halfway down the hall.

"Archie! Archie!" Max chanted, still clutching half of his own cookie in his hand, and ran after his brother.

"Wait a minute," Jan said, and stepped into the hallway to follow them. Riley was halfway down the hall when the front door opened, and Jan watched in horror as he bumped right into—

"Whoa there. Where are you headed, kiddo?"

Jan breathed a sigh of relief. It was only Amy, thank goodness. Jan's daughter was tall and thin and had shoulder-length blonde hair. She had always been popular and outgoing, and no one had been surprised when she'd caught the eye of Van Kincaid when she went into a bank to apply for a loan to go to business school. Van gave her the loan and asked her out to dinner, and now they were happily married, with two rambunctious boys. Van was the vice-president of the bank now, and Amy had finished business school before they'd had the twins. Though they just lived in Augusta, they had very hectic schedules and Jan didn't see enough of any of them.

"They escaped," Jan said, as her daughter, very used to chasing after her twins, caught one child in each arm.

"I'm not surprised to hear that," she said. She kissed each boy on the head. "How did it go?"

"Great," Jan said, just as Riley shouted, "Awesome!" and Max yelled, "Come see our cookies!"

Jan cringed. She saw Macy Atherton turn, seated in the west parlor, and glare at the noise.

"Let's go back to the kitchen," Jan said, and Amy nodded and directed the boys back down the hall.

"Wow." Amy looked around the kitchen and nodded. "Yep, this looks like my kids were here."

"It's not so bad," Rose said from the sink, where she was elbow-deep in soapy water. "I've definitely seen it worse. And they had fun."

"And they're going to have fun helping clean up too," Amy said. She walked to the pantry and pulled out a dustpan and handheld broom, which she handed to Max. He groaned, but she gestured for him to get to work. She handed a wet paper towel to Riley.

"Thank you," Jan said. She was so proud to see her daughter in the role of a mom. She was good at it too. She handled these two hyperactive boys with a patience and a grace Jan wasn't sure she would be able to manage. Jan pulled a plastic tray out of a drawer and started placing cookies onto it.

"How many do you want to take home with you?" Jan asked.

"Um, none?" Amy had moved to the table and was screwing the lids back on the bottles of colored sugar.

"No can do." Jan continued to move the cookies to the tray. "I don't want them lying around here."

"But I don't want them around our house," Amy said, laughing. "Ugh. It's so hard this time of year, isn't it? There are delicious treats everywhere."

"You don't need to worry about that," Jan said, gesturing at Amy's thin frame. "You exercise all the time, and you look great."

"Well, thank you," Amy said. "I'll take it, even though I've gained eight pounds since Halloween."

"No you haven't." Jan scrutinized her daughter. "You look just the same."

"Well, again, thanks. It's just impossible to avoid gaining weight this time of year."

Jan didn't quite know what to say. Eight pounds was about what Jan had gained. It didn't look like Amy had gained an ounce. Surely it showed up differently on Amy?

"I just try not to worry about it. That's what January is for, right?" Amy laughed. "You just have to enjoy Christmas and worry about it later. Or not at all." She tilted her head. "You look great, Mom."

Did Amy really struggle with this too? Amy always seemed like the kind of person who didn't have to worry about things like weight. Was that why she was so cavalier? Jan wasn't in her twenties anymore. She couldn't just skip a meal and watch the weight fall off.

"Max, don't dump that there," Amy said. "Riley, pick that up!"

Well, there could be another way she managed to stay so slim, Jan realized. Chasing after these two was a workout, and she did it all day.

"Thank you so much for bringing them over," Jan said.

"Are you kidding? Thank you for taking them off my hands. That was the best two hours I've had in weeks."

Jan helped the kids get their hats and scarves and mittens on, and then hugged each of her grandsons before they left. It was always hard to say goodbye to them.

After they marched out the door, the tearoom got a lot quieter and significantly less filled with life. Jan went back to the kitchen and worked on cleaning up the rest of the cookies. She would be good, though they were tempting. Still, somehow, she felt a little bit less alone in this struggle than she had an hour ago.

CHAPTER TWENTY-THREE

The rest of the afternoon was busy, but by about five the tea-room was closed and cleaned, and Elaine and Jan headed back out into the blustery afternoon. Elaine had been thinking about the volunteer firefighter sticker Andrea had seen, and throughout the afternoon she'd tried to figure out the full list of volunteer firefighters and what they drove. Toward the end of the afternoon, after the twins had left and things quieted down a bit, she'd had an idea.

After the warmth and bustle of the tearoom, the afternoon seemed especially cold and gray, but Elaine was heartened by the lights strung up above Main Street as they drove the short distance to Murphy's General Store. They brought along a couple plates of cookies, which sometimes came in handy in setting people at ease. But Elaine felt silly bringing them into a grocery store, and they left them in the car now, and walked into the store. One of the teenage Murphy twins was checking out a line of customers, and the other—Elaine couldn't tell which was which unless she got up close—was stacking cereal boxes on shelves. Elaine looked around and found Des unloading a shipment of vegetables in the produce section.

"Well, hey there," Des said as she and Jan approached. "In the market for eggplants, by any chance? We got a double shipment by mistake." He held out a deep purple eggplant, its skin smooth and taut.

"Unfortunately not today," Elaine said. Jan didn't much like the vegetable, and Elaine saw it mostly as a vehicle for delivering oil and cheese in dishes.

"The price is right," he said, but shrugged and stacked it on top of a pile of other eggplants. "We've got plenty if you change your mind."

"Thanks," Jan said. "We'll let you know."

"So if you aren't here for our extensive selection of purple produce, is there something else I can help you find?" Des added another eggplant to the stack.

"Actually, we wanted to talk to you," Jan said. Though there was no official head of the volunteer firefighter squad, Des was the de facto leader, mainly because he lived next door to the firehouse. He was usually the first to arrive and often sent out the call to summon the other firefighters.

"Is that right?" Des picked up one more eggplant, set it in the display, and turned to face them. "Is this about the robbery again?"

"Sort of," Jan said, hesitating. Des looked at her, confused, and then over at Elaine.

"We're actually acting on a tip," Elaine said quickly. "Involving the volunteer firefighters."

"The volunteer firefighters?" Des kicked at the now-empty box at his feet. "Is one of them involved in this thing?"

"That's what we're trying to figure out," Elaine said. Then she quickly added, "And we thought you might be able to help us. You know, tell us about some of them." It wouldn't do for Des to think they suspected him and get defensive. Though of course that's exactly what was going on.

"I'll help if I can," Des said. "And if it makes you feel any better, I promise I haven't dressed up in any Santa costumes." He winked at them.

"We didn't think you did," Jan said, while Elaine crossed Des off her mental list.

"I'm glad to hear it. But you two do have a reputation, you know," Des said.

Elaine decided to plow on ahead and not dwell on that. "What can you tell us about the men on the volunteer force?" she asked.

"Just the men?"

"For now, yes," Elaine said.

"I can tell you that they're all fine upstanding men," Des said. "You don't really think one of them is behind the thefts, do you?"

"We're just gathering facts," Elaine said. Better to keep things vague. There was no sense starting a rumor that there was a copycat thief in town, at least not until they knew for certain.

"Well, there's Greg Payson. But he's away at college right now."

Elaine nodded. That was Bristol and Mark Payson's son. He'd always been fascinated by fire trucks and joined the squad as soon as he was old enough. But he was away at school, so it couldn't have been him.

"There's also Burk King, but he's away too. So that really just leaves me, Tag King, Jack Weston, and Russell Edmonds. Oh, and Will Trexler."

"Will Trexler?" Elaine asked. He had to be in his eighties. How was he on the squad? She tried to imagine him suiting up and rushing out to fight fires. It was almost comical.

"It's more of a figurehead role," Des said. He cleared his throat. "Will is a very, well, *valuable* member of the team. But he doesn't exactly go out in the ladder truck very often. I'm not even sure he's taken the necessary training, truth be told."

"Ah." Elaine understood what Des was getting at. "In other words, he helps fund the squad."

"That's about the gist of it," Des said. "The boosters try to raise as much as they can, and Will is generally happy to make up any shortfall. In return, he likes to be considered a member of the squad."

"That makes sense," Jan said, nodding. Elaine thought it was endearing, thinking of Will like an overgrown boy who just wanted to play fireman. But Will drove an older SUV, and had for years. It was memorable, because Will could afford to drive whatever car he wanted, and instead he'd been carting around the same beat-up Ford for more than a decade. The sedan that had driven away from the Beaty house was not Will's car. Which only made sense, because it was hard to imagine the millionaire octogenarian breaking in and robbing his neighbors' cash boxes.

Then again, it was hard to imagine Jack Weston, the game warden who was dating Jan's daughter Tara, or Russell Edmonds, the marine postman, or Tag King doing it either. Elaine decided to focus their questions a bit more.

"Do you know if any of them drive sedans?" Jan asked.

"Sedans?"

"Or just any midsized car?" Elaine added.

"Hmm." He set another eggplant on the pile. "Well, the only one I can think of is Russell. But of the whole lot, he's the least likely. He's a stand-up guy."

Elaine had to agree. In the summer, he delivered the mail by boat, and in the winter he worked at the sorting facility in Augusta. He was husband to Kit and father to seven-year-old Marcella, and just an all-around solid guy. She looked at Jan. She looked as skeptical as Elaine did.

"In any case, I don't believe it was any of them. I just can't imagine any of the guys being behind this. None of them would rob, and none of them would rob me specifically. We're a tight-knit group. When you risk your lives together, you have to trust the guys you're with, and I trust each of them."

Elaine could see that he was being truthful. Rightly or wrongly, he believed the volunteer firefighters were above reproach. They weren't going to get anything more from Des Murphy.

"Thank you so much for your help," Elaine said, and Jan nodded and thanked him too. "I certainly hope you're right."

"Thank you," Des said. "I'm anxious to hear what you come up with."

"What do you think?" Jan asked when they were back in Elaine's car.

"I can't help but think he's probably right," Elaine said. This whole mission was starting to feel hopeless. "It's hard to see any of them being our thief, or even our copycat thief."

"I agree." Jan sounded as down as Elaine felt. "So do we even bother talking to Russell?"

Elaine let out a sigh. It felt pointless. A waste of time. A very good way to offend a very good person. But if they wanted to say they'd followed every possible clue, they really should talk to him. "I guess so," Elaine finally said.

"All right. We'll stop by, check it off our list, and say we tried."

"Right." Elaine put the car into gear. "And then we'll keep digging into Max." She tried to figure out what else they could do, and her heart sank when she realized they were just about out of leads.

"And we'll keep trying to get ahold of Garrett, and see if we can track down whoever this Paul person is," Jan added. "The one who ate at the diner. And hopefully we'll hear something from the thrift store soon. Maybe that will give us a new lead."

"Right." Things weren't hopeless. Just...well, a bit bleak.

They were quiet as the car threaded through quiet residential neighborhoods. A few people were out, digging out cars or using snow blowers to clear walkways, but mostly the streets were quiet. They pulled up in front of the Edmonds house.

Elaine looked at Jan. There was a maroon Camry in the driveway, and it had a volunteer firefighter's sticker on it.

"Is that it?" Jan asked, pointing at the car.

Elaine didn't believe it. She didn't want to believe it. "I guess there's only one way to find out," she said, opening the door.

Jan grasped the plate of cookies, and they walked to the door and knocked, and a moment later little footsteps echoed inside the house.

"Who is it?" a little girl called. Elaine was glad to see that she hadn't just flung the door open but was careful. Safety first. It showed that her parents had taught her well.

"It's Elaine Cook and Jan Blake," Elaine said.

"Yay!" Marcella threw open the door. Her long blonde hair curled at the ends, and she wore a T-shirt with some Disney princesses on the front. "Come in. You brought cookies!" The little girl shrieked this last part, and she clapped her hands and hopped up and down.

"Thank you," Elaine said as she stepped inside. It was a small house, but well kept. Kit had a good eye, with simple, clean pieces and neutral colors, but the toys spilled across the living room floor reflected the fact that two working parents and a child lived there. "Are your mom and dad home?"

"Daddy is at work. But Mommy is here. Mommy!"

"I'm coming." Kit Edmonds appeared at the end of the hallway. Her chin-length blonde hair was cut in a stylish bob, and she had a light sprinkling of freckles across her nose. "Oh, hi there, Jan, Elaine. Come on in."

"Thank you." Elaine held out the plate. "We brought cookies. As you might have gathered."

Kit laughed. "Yes, I heard something about that." She took the treats before giving each of them a hug. "Thank you so much. It's so lovely of you to stop by."

"Thank you," Elaine said. Usually when she was investigating, she didn't really have to think too much about what to say, but she was struggling right now. How did you come out and ask someone if their husband had been robbing people?

"Have a seat." Kit gestured for them to head into the living room. She moved aside a few piles of folded laundry and made space for them to sit down. "I'm sorry for the mess. This month has been just crazy with so many holiday events. It seems like I spend most of the weekend just catching up on the housework I didn't get done during the week."

"It's not a problem at all," Jan said, and sat down on the couch. "We totally understand. And we're sorry to drop by unannounced."

"I'm thrilled you're here," Kit said. She set the plate of cookies down on the coffee table.

"And I'm thrilled you brought cookies," Marcella said.

Elaine and Jan both laughed.

"You may take one cookie into the kitchen," Kit said. "And then go into your room and play while I visit."

Marcella took a frosted angel and vanished down the hallway.

"So." Kit selected a wreath for herself. "How are you both?"

"We're good." Elaine said. "Busy. But I can only imagine it must be busier for you."

Kit was a teacher at the local elementary school, and Elaine remembered all too well the crush of concerts and pageants and parties that made the last few weeks of the year busy at schools.

"Yes, and of course it's busy time for Russell as well," Kit said. "What with all the cards and packages people send this time of year. So he's been working a lot, and it feels like we've hardly had any time to enjoy the holidays."

"I know the feeling," Jan said, laughing. "And I'm sorry that we're here taking up more of your time."

"Oh no. A visit from you two is wonderful. And also the perfect excuse to take a break from cleaning the bathroom." Kit took a bite of her cookie and sat back. For all her words, she did look at each of them in turn, as if waiting for them to explain why they'd stopped by.

"We're here for the silliest reason, actually. It's the strangest thing, and we know it's probably nothing. But last night, Andrea McInnis chased a man dressed as Santa away from the house next door to her home, and she swore that the car the man drove away in had a volunteer firefighter bumper sticker on it. And so we've been talking to the people who are on the volunteer force, trying to figure out who it could have been."

"Yeah, isn't it hilarious? I wish I could see a video of her chasing him away." Kit laughed and popped the rest of the cookie into her mouth.

"Wait. What?" Elaine looked at Jan, who looked as confused as she felt.

"Last night. When she chased Russell away. It sounds like it would have been hilarious to see." She brushed her hands together.

"You're saying that it *was* Russell that Andrea chased away?" Elaine asked.

Now Kit looked confused. "Of course. Isn't that what you came here to talk about?"

Elaine tried to absorb this. Had Kit just admitted that her husband was the thief?

CHAPTER TWENTY-FOUR

Jan tried to process what she'd just heard. Kit Edmonds had just admitted that her husband Russell was the Grinch.

"He and Marcella cooked it all up," Kit continued. There was a smile on her face. Wait. Their seven-year-old was involved too? "We meant for it to be a secret, of course, but after it sort of snowballed, I guess it was bound to come out at some point."

Something wasn't adding up. Kit could not possibly be smiling about this. Not if she was really talking about what Jan and Elaine thought she was.

"Why don't you explain how it all came about?" Jan asked. Elaine nodded.

"Well, it was really Marcella's idea," Kit said. "They were talking about helping others in her Sunday school class. Thinking about ways to help those who aren't as fortunate, especially at this time of year," Kit said.

Jan nodded encouragingly.

"And Marcella came home with an idea. She wanted to help people around town who needed help, and she wanted to do it without anyone knowing."

Jan was beginning to understand, and she feared this whole thing was turning out to be a rabbit trail.

"She decided to sell some of her toys to raise the money. So she set up an online shop..."

"By herself?" Elaine asked.

"We helped her, of course." Kit laughed. "She's smart, but she's not that smart. We figured it would be a good learning experience for her, learning about money and all that. Well, it worked really well. She sold most of them."

"And then you used the money to pay off the back rent for the Ruths," Jan said.

"Yes." Kit nodded. "Their landlord, Gabrielle, is an old friend of mine, and I knew they were facing tough times. It seemed like a nice thing to do."

It did indeed. And a pricey one. "That must have been a lot of toys."

"Well, she's the only grandchild. What can I say?" She shrugged. "Plus she had a whole collection of American Girl dolls she didn't play with, and those go for a lot."

"But what about the stroller? And the boxes of food?"

Kit reached for another cookie, a gingerbread man this time. "Marcella had so much fun the first time we decided to do it again. They were people Russell knew. We ended up selling some of our own stuff and used that money for those donations."

"And last night you were bringing something to Joanne Beaty."

"That's right." Kit looked a bit guilty. "A huge bag of books. She's a big reader and we gathered donations from lots of people and were going to drop them off. But Russell was scared away before that happened." She laughed.

"How did the Santa suit come into it?" Jan asked.

"That was Marcella's idea too. She thought it would be a fun way to bring some holiday spirit into it. And Russell thought it would be a good way to disguise himself in case anyone saw him. We really wanted this to be anonymous."

The thief wasn't the only one who'd had that idea, apparently.

"Where did you get the suit?" Elaine asked.

"Oh, they're really cheap online. We ordered it for next to nothing, and two days later it showed up at our doorstep. That's how I do all of my shopping these days. I don't know what we did before Amazon Prime."

Jan tried to figure out how to say this next part. "But...did you ever worry about..."

Kit took a bite and waited for Jan to go on.

"Haven't you read...?" Jan tried again.

This wasn't coming out right.

"Didn't you think people might confuse you with the thief that's breaking into businesses all over town dressed as Santa?" Elaine asked.

"What?" Kit set down her cookie and scrunched up her forehead. "You don't...I mean...Well, honestly, no, it hadn't really occurred to us."

Jan could tell by the look on her face that she really hadn't considered this.

"But we were helping people, not stealing. Leaving things on doorsteps, not breaking in and taking money..." She let her voice trail off. "It really never occurred to me or to Russell."

Jan looked at Elaine. Could they really be that naïve? But then, Elaine was nodding, and her face showed understanding. Was it possible that in their minds they were doing something so different that they hadn't even thought about it?

"Is that why Andrea ran out of the house yelling?" Kit seemed to just be putting the pieces together now.

"Yes. She thought Russell was trying to break into Joanne Beaty's house," Jan said. "She chased him away. Matt called 911."

"But— " Kit shook her head. "But he had a bag he was planning on leaving there."

"The man I saw dressed as Santa had a bag over his shoulder too," Elaine said.

"Oh my."

Jan felt bad. She could see that Kit really hadn't seen or understood the implications of what she and Russell had done. It was an innocent mistake. A silly, thoughtless one, but an innocent one nonetheless.

"Why did you think she was running after him?" Elaine asked.

"We thought she was trying to unmask the guy who'd been going around doing good in town. I don't know. To thank him or something." She laughed a bit, a sad, disheartened laugh. "I guess we should have realized people were going to mistake him for the thief," Kit said. "I just...didn't." She shrugged.

Jan felt bad. Here this family had been trying to do something lovely, and they were being chased down and mistaken for a serial thief.

"It's a wonderful thing you're doing," Jan said. "I've really loved reading about the people you've been cheering up. It's something our town needs more than ever right now," she said.

"But maybe save the Santa costume until after we track down the thief," Elaine said with a smile.

Kit laughed again. "No kidding. I guess we're lucky getting chased was all that happened to Russell. If anyone else had seen him dressed like that, who knows what might have happened."

Jan agreed. People around here kept guns. Bad things could have happened to him if the wrong person had mistaken him for the thief.

"You're doing good things. Please keep it up," Jan said.

Kit looked dubious.

"We won't tell anyone who it is," Elaine added.

Kit smiled and shook her head. "But in any case, thank you for the heads-up."

They said their goodbyes and Jan and Elaine stepped back outside.

"Well, that's one mystery solved," Elaine said.

"Yeah." Jan pulled her coat tighter around her and hurried down the path. "Too bad it was a dead end for the main mystery. Unfortunately, we're no closer to finding the Grinch than we were before."

CHAPTER TWENTY-FIVE

The kitchen was cleaned up after dinner and Jan was curled up on the sofa by the Christmas tree in the sitting room. Snow was gently falling outside. It was peaceful and quiet. Too quiet. She set down her book and her mug of White Christmas tea. Elaine was out at Nathan's choir concert, and Jan was here alone. Maybe, if she was being honest, she was a tiny bit lonely.

Bob was supposed to call twenty minutes ago, but she'd gotten a text ten minutes before the appointed time. He was running late, he said. He'd ring her when he finished something he had to get done.

She decided to call her daughter Tara. She dialed the number and waited as it rang.

"Hi, Mom." Tara sounded breathless. "What's up?"

"Hi, honey. I'm just checking in. How's everything going?"

"It's okay. Look, Mom, I'm with Jack and we're about to go into a movie. Did you need something? Or can I call you back?"

"It's okay. There's nothing urgent." Jan tried to keep the disappointment out of her voice. "I just wanted to say hi."

"Okay. Sorry, Mom, but I have to go. I'll call you tomorrow."

"All right. Have a nice night." Jan hung up the phone, then she sighed and stood up. She was hungry. That piece of fish she'd had for dinner hadn't kept her full for long. And those cookies they'd baked earlier had looked really good. She tried to resist. But she couldn't concentrate. Her mind kept going to Bob, and to the thief—would he strike again tonight? Would they ever find out who he was?

Determined to be good, Jan grabbed her laptop, settled down again, and set it on her lap. Her fingers hovered over the keys as she tried to think about what to search for.

She wanted to find out who Paul was. But how could she find him with only that name to go on? There were way too many people named Paul in the world for that to turn up anything useful. Instead, she typed in the name Max Arrington, but all she turned up was the same links she'd already found before.

She wasn't getting anywhere on this. Well, she did have another problem to solve. She still needed to find Christmas gifts for Van and Paula. Jan went to the online shop for a clothing brand she knew Paula liked. Maybe she'd just pick out something here. There were some sweaters in soft pinks and cherries and deep purples that would look so nice with Paula's coloring. But Paula always seemed to wear the same shades of brown and gray. Did that mean she needed some new colors? Would she be glad for a bright coral or a deep turquoise? Or did she wear dull colors because that's what she preferred?

Jan shook her head. She didn't know what to get. Maybe Brian would come through with some ideas. But she wasn't honestly sure Brian would know any better than she did.

Well, she'd worry about Paula later. What about Van? Jan thought for a minute. Van was smart. Funny. Kind of geeky. He spoke Elvish and was into Dr. Who and all sorts of strange things Jan didn't understand but loved him for anyway. *Hmm*...Then she thought about something. That shirt Chris Cosgrove had been wearing at the library was the kind of thing Van might think was funny. It was his kind of dry, nerdy humor. Where had Chris said he'd found that?

Jan thought back and remembered that Chris had said he'd gotten it from an online shop. Something like Etsy, but just for Maine. What was it? She closed her eyes and thought for a moment. Mainely Made. That was it.

She quickly found the website and discovered it was just as Chris had described it. It was like Etsy, a site where artists could sell their handmade items. Each person selling things had their own shop, where you could see their wares and a picture and story of the artist. There were shops selling everything from pot holders to personalized onesies to hand-knitted scarves and mittens.

She filtered by category and found a number of shops selling T-shirts, and she scrolled around a bit more and found what she thought was the right one. The featured T-shirt showed a pie chart, with half the space taken up by a shaded area with the word *Knowing*. The other half was divided into two pieces that said *red lasers* and *blue lasers*. Brian had watched enough cartoons as a child that Jan understood it was a reference to *G.I. Joe*, an animated kids' show from the '80s. The slogan they repeated again and again on that show was "Knowing is half the battle." The rest, she supposed, was pretty much just lasers.

Jan clicked on the page and found the T-shirt Chris had been wearing without too much trouble. *There are two kinds of people in the world: Those who can extrapolate from incomplete data*

Let's see. Van was probably a medium? He was tall, but slim. Would that...?

Wait a minute. Jan's eye caught on something on the left side of the page. Max. There was a picture of Max Arrington there. Why was there a picture of Max?

Jan clicked on it and saw that it took her to the page of information about the shop owner. This shop was owned by Max Arrington.

Jan couldn't believe it. She read the short bio. *Max Arrington lives in central Maine with his wife and daughter. He has always had a passion for graphic design and for the Tardis, Dig Dug, and all things nerdy, and is grateful for the opportunity to showcase his love of geekdom in these handcrafted designs.*

Max Arrington was interested in all these things? The Max who delivered packages all over town? Jan thought about this for a moment. She'd had no idea. But then, she supposed she'd never really asked him what he was interested in. Usually they'd chatted about whatever she was baking or the weather.

She clicked back to the site and looked through the designs. There were some clever T-shirts, and you could get most of the designs on mugs and bumper stickers as well. She wouldn't be surprised if they were selling well. In fact...

Jan leaned back against the couch cushions. Could he be doing well enough that he would be able to afford a whole new vehicle? And nights out? Jan did some quick math in her head.

The shirts were over twenty dollars apiece. Even after the cost of materials and whatever commission the site took, he was no doubt pocketing a healthy profit on each sale. It was definitely possible if he sold enough, she decided.

Jan added the T-shirt to her cart and checked out. Jan didn't know whether to be relieved or disappointed. There was a decent chance Max wasn't the thief after all. Or, at least, he had a pretty solid excuse for what made him look guilty.

But if he wasn't guilty, who was?

Just then, Jan's phone rang. It was Bob. Jan set her computer aside. She hesitated before she answered—she didn't want to be frustrated at Bob. But she couldn't help that she was. Still, she wanted to talk to him.

"Hi, Bob."

She would find out more about Max tomorrow.

"Hi, Jan. I'm so sorry for the delay."

"That's all right," she said. He was on the line now. That was what mattered. And he would be here in two days. "How are things going?"

"Honestly? They're nuts," Bob said. "This case I'm on, it's coming to trial just after Christmas, so it's crunch time."

"I hope you're not working too hard."

"I don't think I could possibly work hard enough to be ready for this trial. Which, actually, is part of why I'm calling."

"Oh dear." Jan did not like the sound of this. "What do you mean?"

"I'm afraid I'm going to have to stay here a few more days, Jan."

"But you're supposed to come back on Monday."

"I know I am, and I'm even more disappointed than you are. I would give anything to be there with you right now."

She didn't say anything.

"But I'm afraid I just can't. There's just no way. I've already changed my ticket. I'll be home on Thursday."

Jan bit down, pressing her lips together. It kept her from crying. She was being selfish. She knew she was. There was a man sitting in prison for a crime he didn't commit. Bob was trying to prepare for his one chance to get out. What did it matter if he came home Monday or Thursday?

But the thing was, it *did* matter. It mattered to Jan. She had been so looking forward to seeing him, and now...

"Thursday?" Jan hated the quaver in her voice.

"I'm sorry, Jan. I know that's disappointing."

He was going to miss the fund-raiser if he came home Thursday. She'd been so excited about seeing him all dressed up. About him seeing her all dressed up. She'd even gone down a few pounds, and now—

He would still notice when he came home Thursday, she told herself. A party didn't matter as much as this man's life. But still...

"Jan, are you okay?"

She didn't answer for a moment. This was the man who'd wanted to marry her. She wanted to see him. She hated being apart from him. And...she hated to think it, but the thought came unbidden. Here he was, choosing his work over her once again.

"I really wish there was some way around this," he said.

Then a thought ran through her head. She knew it was crazy, but once it was there, she couldn't dislodge it. Was Bob staying away because he didn't want to see her? Was it because of the couple of pounds she'd put on? Maybe he'd been so repulsed when he'd seen her last month that he wasn't going to come home for Christmas after all.

"I'm looking forward to seeing you," was all she said. And she meant it, mostly.

They talked for a few more minutes before saying good night. Jan hung up, and for a moment she sat still, staring straight ahead. Her stomach rumbled. She really wanted those cookies now more than ever. What was the harm, really? It was Christmas, after all. She pushed herself up. If she couldn't have Bob, at least she could have a few cookies.

CHAPTER TWENTY-SIX

On Sunday morning, the service at Lancaster Community Church ran a bit long, but Jan didn't mind. There had been the lighting of the Advent wreath, and they had sung several of her favorite carols, and the choir had sung a gorgeous rendition of "In the Bleak Midwinter," a carol that felt entirely appropriate up here in Maine. And the children's Christmas pageant had been part of the service, a tradition Jan adored. Her own children had played various roles throughout the years, and seeing the new crop of children always brought back so many memories. This year's Mary had looked terrified sitting up there on the stage holding a doll awkwardly under one arm, but the little girls dressed as angels—wearing tiny white sheets and wearing tinsel halos and wings—had clearly enjoyed dancing around the stage.

"I think there were more angels on that stage than in heaven that first Christmas night," Jan said as she and Elaine made their way down the aisle.

"You can't really blame them," Elaine said. "The angels do have the best costume by far, and they get to dance. All Mary gets to do is sit there."

"I suppose," Jan laughed. "My favorite was the donkey though." A little boy who couldn't have been more than three had apparently gotten tired of standing in the background and decided to lie down right next to Mary. He'd rolled around with his donkey ears and sighed a lot, and generally stolen the show, especially when the wise men had had to step over him to get to Jesus. The whole church had been rolling in the aisles.

"That's the beauty of having children act out the pageant," Elaine said, chuckling. "You never know what they're going to do."

They headed down to the fellowship hall afterward to grab a cup of coffee and say hello to their friends and neighbors. Pale winter light shone in through the high windows, and the room was crowded with people wearing festive suits and dresses. Every year, Sarah Ryder set out quite a spread for the coffee hour the day of the pageant, but Jan managed to avoid snagging the iced breads and Roberta Thompson's famous chocolate babka. She poured a cup of coffee from the metal urn and was just reaching for the cream.

"Jan!"

She turned and saw Bristol Payson standing next to her, filling a plate with cookies.

"I'm so glad I caught you." Bristol straightened up and turned toward Jan. "I wanted to see if Monday afternoon would work for the delivery from the florist. I had asked for Tuesday, but they're closing early that day for a big event, and they wanted to deliver a day early. I know that means you'll have to deal with a bunch of flowers sitting around, so I wanted to check."

"You mean we'll be stuck enjoying flowers for an extra day?" Jan asked. She added a splash of cream and hesitated before adding sugar. She should skip it, she knew. But what good was coffee without sugar? "I think we can handle that."

"Thank you so much," Bristol said. "If you can use them in the tearoom, please go ahead and do so. It's mostly poinsettias, but there are supposed to be some more exotic bunches in there too."

"Sounds lovely," Jan said. She decided to skip the sugar and moved away from the table before she could change her mind. "How is everything else with the fund-raiser overall?"

"It's really, really great," Bristol said. "Like, shockingly good."

"That's wonderful to hear." She took a sip of her coffee. *Blech.* How did people drink this stuff without sugar?

"It's amazing just how generous people have been just with the donation boxes," Bristol continued. "We got another big donation just Friday."

Something pulled at the back of Jan's mind. "Cash again?"

"Yep. I don't know where it keeps coming from, but it's incredible."

It was incredible. The timing was almost too good to be true.

"Can I ask how much?" Jan asked.

"Just over a thousand dollars was what was left Friday," Bristol said. "At the donation box at the town office. When Tasha called me, I almost fell off my chair."

Nearly a thousand dollars in cash. The day after the latest break-in, when more than a thousand dollars had been stolen from Oldies But Goodies.

"Would it be possible to get a list of the major donations you've gotten so far? And when they came in?" Jan asked.

Bristol blinked, and then she nodded. "Of course." She took a bite of one of the cookies. "You don't think…"

"I don't know," Jan said. "I'm just working through an idea."

"All right. Anyone else and I would be confused, but I know better than to question you. I'll send a list over this afternoon."

"Thank you," Jan said. It was just an idea at this point. But it was worth investigating.

SUNDAY AFTERNOON, AS Elaine was washing up the lunch dishes, she turned to see that Jan had returned to the kitchen, her laptop in one hand and a notebook in the other. She barely looked up, but set her things on the table and sat down.

"Everything all right?" Elaine asked. It wasn't like Jan to be so transfixed. It must be important.

"Yes. I'm sorry, I'll help with cleanup in just a minute," Jan said. "But Bristol just sent me something, and I want to check it out."

"It's fine," Elaine said. "We didn't use many dishes." She used a soft sponge to clean a Royal Albert Old Country Roses teapot. The handle was a bit chipped, but the blush-pink color was so pretty. "But I will admit I'm curious." She rinsed and set the teapot gently on the drying rack.

Jan didn't say anything for a moment as she copied something from her screen on to her notebook. Then she looked up and said, "Bristol mentioned that they had another large cash donation Friday."

"That's wonderful."

"Yes." Jan write something else in her notebook. "It's also exceedingly convenient timing."

"What do you mean?"

"I asked her to send me a list of the large donations that have shown up in the donation boxes since she started the fund-raiser," Jan said. She squinted at something on the screen.

"And did you find something interesting?"

"Yes."

Elaine waited for Jan to go on. When she didn't, Elaine cleared her throat. "What did you find?" she asked.

"The large cash donations were all made the day after a burglary," Jan said, sitting back in her chair.

"What?" It only took a split second to understand what Jan was getting at. If Jan was right, this couldn't be a coincidence.

"Yep. The first one came in Monday, in the donation box at the library. The day after Murphy's General Store was robbed," Jan said. "Over twelve hundred dollars. I called Des to ask, and it turns out that twelve hundred dollars was, not surprisingly, the rough amount taken from the store that night."

"Wow." Elaine rinsed a plate and set it down to dry. "Wow."

"The next big donation was Wednesday, in the donation box at the church. Over five hundred dollars."

"Was that the amount taken from Faith's safe Tuesday night?" Elaine asked.

"I don't know. But I'm guessing it is. The big donations match up precisely with the thefts."

Elaine tried to wrap her mind around this.

"Which means that the thief isn't robbing stores just to pocket the money for himself," Elaine said slowly.

"If I'm right, he's not," Jan said.

Elaine thought Jan was indeed right. "He's doing it to come up with money for the fund-raiser."

"Which kind of goes against the spirit of giving to charity, if you ask me," Jan said. "If you have to steal to get it."

Elaine nodded. "Oh, certainly. But it does mean he might not be the Grinch after all. It's actually kind of sweet."

"I don't think so. It's still breaking and entering, grand theft, destruction of property, and probably a whole host of other crimes."

"It is all those things," Elaine agreed. She dried her hands on a dish towel. "But it's also more like Robin Hood than the Grinch. Robbing from the rich to give to the poor."

"Except we're not rich. And it's not his money to give."

"I agree," Elaine said. "I don't condone what he's doing. I'm just saying it casts a whole new light on things."

"I suppose it does," Jan said. She sat back and let out a sigh. "But it doesn't change one major thing."

Elaine nodded. "The fact that we still have no solid leads as to who he is."

"Exactly."

AFTER DINNER, ELAINE and Jan settled into the sitting room on the second floor. They had the tree lights turned on again, and Jan was working on writing notes on her own Christmas cards while Elaine curled up under a blanket with a book.

Elaine had brought up a mug of chamomile tea and some of the cookies the twins had made the day before. They weren't much to look at, but they tasted delicious. Elaine took a bite, then settled in under the blanket and found her place in her book. The room was warm and peaceful, and as the wind picked up outside, she was cozy and relaxed.

They'd been enjoying the peace and quiet for a while when Elaine realized Jan was sighing every so often. Elaine looked up from her book and watched her for a moment. Jan didn't even seem to realize she was doing it. Every time she finished addressing a card, she glanced over at Elaine's plate of cookies and sighed a little.

"Jan?" Elaine said. "Would you like a cookie?"

"Oh no, thank you," Jan said. She gave Elaine a smile and turned back to her cards.

"Are you sure?" Elaine pushed the plate closer. "You keep looking over at them. I don't mind sharing."

"No. Thank you, but I don't want any." Jan's voice was a little harder. "I mean, yes, of course I want some, but no, thank you. I'm trying so hard to be good. And I cheated and had some last night."

Elaine placed a bookmark in her book. She studied Jan. Jan looked upset. Genuinely troubled. About a few cookies.

"It's okay that you had cookies, Jan," Elaine said. "You don't have to be upset about it."

"I'm not upset about it." But the way her voice rose indicated that she was indeed getting distressed. "I just wish there wasn't so much temptation this time of year."

Elaine set her book down. Jan had known there would be temptation this time of year. A normal person would have waited until January and started her diet then, along with half the women in America. Elaine watched her cousin for a moment, trying to understand what was really going on.

"When did you have cookies last night?" Elaine asked gently.

"When you were out with Nathan. Bob was supposed to call, but he was wrapped up in something so he was late." Jan set her pen down. "And then he told me he's not coming home tomorrow after all."

"Oh no." Jan had been so looking forward to seeing him. "When is he coming home now?"

"Thursday." From the forlorn way Jan said it, it might as well have been never.

"I'm sorry, Jan." Elaine understood how disappointed Jan must be feeling. She knew how lucky she was that Nathan lived nearby. If she went a day without talking to him, it felt like a week. She didn't know how Jan managed Bob living so far away.

Jan nodded. "I know it's silly. I'll still get to see him before Christmas."

"It's not silly at all. You were looking forward to seeing him. Of course you're disappointed. Cookies were certainly in order."

Jan gave her a sad smile. And then Elaine saw what she hadn't before.

"You were trying to lose weight before Bob gets home, weren't you?"

"I...," Jan started, but then she stopped.

Elaine understood now. This whole thing was about Jan's complicated relationship with Bob. Of course it was.

"It's not really about Bob," Jan said. "It's about me."

Elaine nodded. "I'm sure it is." And she meant it. "You want to feel good, and to know you look good, when he comes back."

Jan nodded reluctantly. "I've"—she coughed—"put on a few pounds since he left. And I just...I was hoping to get back to where I was before. So I feel better when I see him again." Jan looked down at her lap.

Elaine took a sip of her tea and slid closer to Jan.

"It's okay, Jan. You don't need to be embarrassed. Any woman would feel the same way."

"Not any woman."

"Most women." She hated that it felt true. Most women Elaine knew of paid attention to things like their weight, while she didn't know of too many men who gave their bodies as much thought. It was societal pressure, she knew. Women were judged by how they looked in a way that men weren't, and there was no getting around that. No matter how laid back and comfortable in your own skin you were, most everyone struggled with this, Elaine felt sure.

She racked her brain, trying to come up with the right words to say. Elaine thought about her own weight more than she cared to admit. And not for Nathan. For herself. She wanted to look good and feel good, and it had very little to do with what he thought. But of course she thought about it. It was just that Christmas was a special time, and she gave herself more freedom to enjoy the season than she normally would.

"I understand how you feel," Elaine said gently. She'd spent longer than she cared to admit picking out what she would wear to the fund-raiser, and she'd settled on a silver top because

Nathan had said he liked it last time she wore it. What woman didn't want to look nice?

Jan nodded, but didn't say anything.

"I know this probably won't help, but I'll say it anyway: Bob loves you for who you are. Just the way you are."

"I guess."

"Not *you guess*. It's true. He proposed to you, Jan. He loves you. He doesn't care if you gained a few pounds."

Jan didn't say anything. She appeared to be thinking this through.

"He did love me. But what if he doesn't now?" Jan asked quietly.

Elaine was so flummoxed she didn't even know what to say. Was Jan seriously worried about this?

"If he doesn't love you anymore because of a few pounds of winter weight, he is not worth your time in the first place," Elaine said.

Jan didn't move for a minute, then nodded.

"But I promise you, he won't even notice. He'll be so glad to see you that he won't notice anything else," Elaine said.

Jan was still quiet. Was any of this sinking in? Making her feel any better? Elaine couldn't tell.

"I'll tell you what," Elaine said. "Come January, I'll change my diet and cut out sweets along with you."

Jan looked over at her. "You will?"

"I won't do it before Christmas. That's just madness."

Jan laughed at this.

"But after the holidays, sure. It would be good for me."

"Really?" Jan asked.

Elaine nodded. "As long as you promise to give yourself a break over the next few weeks. It's not the end of the world if you let yourself enjoy the best time of the year."

Jan smiled, then slowly nodded. "All right." She reached out and took her cousin's hand and gave it a squeeze. "Thanks, Elaine."

CHAPTER TWENTY-SEVEN

A snowstorm blew in on Sunday night. Elaine lay in bed, listening to the wind whipping in off the lake and around the house. Snow swirled. She was grateful, more than ever, to have a safe, warm home and a soft bed. Eventually, she drifted off to sleep. When she woke up Monday morning, more than six inches of snow had fallen, and the world was coated in a clean blanket of white.

Elaine spent some time praying, thanking God for this home and this life, and then tied her robe and put on her slippers and trudged downstairs.

"I've been thinking," Jan said as Elaine entered the kitchen. Jan was mixing up a bowl of some kind of cranberry batter. Muffins?

Elaine laughed. Jan spoke as if they'd already been having a conversation.

"About what?" Elaine headed straight for the kettle and filled it.

"We should go out and talk to the people at the donation boxes and see if they can tell us anything about the people who made the donations."

"Weren't the donations anonymous?" Elaine set the kettle on the stove and looked out the window over the sink at the drifts of snow. She'd grown up in Maine and wasn't afraid of a little snow, but trudging out in it didn't seem as inviting as staying here and getting ready for what would no doubt be a busy week.

"Yes. The cash was just left there. But it's possible that someone at one of the donation points saw something."

"I guess anything is possible." Elaine didn't relish the idea of heading out into that snow. But she had to admit she could see Jan's point. If they really believed the donations had anything to do with the thefts, they should investigate. "What are all the places the donations were made?"

"Well, one was at the library. There's also the town office and the church."

"The church office will be closed today." The office was closed Mondays, since the pastor worked Sundays. "But the other places will probably be open."

Jan nodded. "I had the radio on earlier, and the schools are starting late, but they'll be open."

"Poor kids." Elaine wanted to laugh. Most places in the country would probably be shut down entirely after six inches of snow. But out here in rural Maine, it was business as usual. "They don't even get a snow day."

"They'll be glad come June," Jan said. "Why don't we head out after I get the baking done?"

That sounded fine to Elaine. She would use the extra time to address the Christmas cards she'd been meaning to get sent out for a couple of weeks.

"Oh, and by the way, your mother called," Jan said.

"When?"

"A little while ago."

"But it's barely seven."

Jan shrugged. "She said it wasn't an emergency. She just wanted to catch up."

"At this hour?" But even as she said it, she thought about her early-morning phone call to Sasha. Maybe the apple didn't fall far from the tree after all.

She carried a mug of tea and one of Jan's freshly baked scones up to the sitting room and called her mom back. Her mother, Virginia Willard, lived in an assisted living facility in Augusta. She was in good health and enjoyed her life and all the activities at the senior community.

"Hi, Mom," Elaine said, settling down against the couch.

"Well, hello there."

"How's everything going at Millpond?"

"Oh, they make it nice this time of year. They've got a big tree and all sorts of events. Ronald is taking me to the carol sing this evening."

"Who's Ronald?" Virginia always had a group of men buzzing around her, and Elaine could never keep them straight. Virginia seemed to just be having fun, and Elaine didn't see what was wrong with that at her age.

"You've met Ronald. He's got glasses and a beard."

"Mom, that could be anyone."

"Well, maybe you haven't met him, I don't know. Anyway, he's nice, and he is a good dancer. You'd be surprised how valuable a talent that is around here."

"I can only imagine." Elaine chatted with her mom for a few minutes and made plans to pick her up Christmas morning to celebrate with the family. After hanging up, she spent a pleasant hour writing notes and addresses on the cards she'd picked out this year, which had a beautiful painting of the manger scene with a white-steepled New England church in the background. Then she got dressed in her warmest wool sweater and pants lined with fleece and headed downstairs.

"I peeked out the front, and it looks like the library is open," Jan announced. "And I saw Linda Somes drive past, so I assume the town office is open."

"I'm ready whenever you are," Elaine said. She had her stack of envelopes stamped and ready to mail. "As long as we're heading that way, let's stop by the post office."

"That sounds great." Jan looked around the kitchen, nodded, and took her apron off. "Where to first?"

Elaine followed her cousin down the hallway and cast one last glance back at the warm, cheerful kitchen.

"I guess the library." She slipped her feet into boots and pulled her warm parka on. It took her a few minutes to bundle up with her hat, scarf, and gloves, but then she followed Jan outside. They headed across the street to the library. But Priscilla told them that she hadn't seen who had made the large donation, and that no one else on staff had either. She did have the information about charities that worked with veterans, and they didn't have the heart to tell her they didn't need it anymore.

Next they trudged down the snowy sidewalks toward the town office, which was just beyond the post office and next to the fire station. Inside the town office, Linda Somes told them the same thing. No one had seen who made the large donation.

"If no one at the church office saw who made the donation, we've hit another brick wall," Elaine said as they trudged back.

When they made it back to the tearoom, she was pleased to find Archie had cleared the sidewalks and was working on the driveway, while Rose was setting the tables in the east parlor, where a fire already crackled in the fireplace.

"What would we do without you two?" Elaine asked, sliding off her coat.

"Oh, you'd do just fine," Rose said. "But I'm glad to be here nonetheless. By the way, you got a phone call. Abby King said she's sorry it took her so long to get back to you but she'll be available the rest of the day if you want to give her a call."

"That's nice," Elaine said. It didn't really matter so much anymore, since they'd eliminated her nephew Joe as a suspect, but it would be polite to call her back and see how things were going in Florida.

Elaine took the phone into the office while Jan helped Rose and Archie get the tables set up. She dialed the number Abby had left, and while it rang, she scrolled through her e-mail. Nothing interesting.

"Hello? Elaine?"

"Abby!" Elaine was happy to hear her voice. "How are you guys? How's Florida?"

"It's great. It's eighty-five here today, and Burk and I just got back from the pool. How's everything back there?"

"Oh, you know. About the same."

Abby laughed. "I bet. I saw on the news there was a storm last night."

"Not a big one by Maine standards," Elaine insisted. "A light dusting."

"Have I mentioned I was just swimming at the outdoor pool?" Abby asked, chuckling. "You're welcome to come visit any time, you know."

"I appreciate it." She had to admit that it did sound appealing. Instead of shivering up here, she could be relaxing under a palm tree. But as much as she dreaded the cold, she couldn't see giving up this beautiful part of the world, even under this much snow. Especially under this much snow. There was just something about a good old-fashioned white Christmas that made palm trees seem sad.

"But anyway, you were calling about the lights on at our place. I appreciate your looking out for us. But that's just my nephew Joe. He's staying there for a little while."

"We ended up talking to Tag, and that's what he told us," Elaine said. "I'm so glad to know it's someone who is supposed to be there."

"Me too." Abby said. "Joe's a good kid. He's just had some trouble, so we try to help him out if we can."

"Tag mentioned he'd had a tough time of it growing up."

"That's an understatement," Abby said. "And then he was kind of floundering after he couldn't get into the Air Force. He got into some trouble but has mostly gotten back on his feet. We've tried to help as much as we can, but there's only so much you can do. This new girlfriend, Ainsley, is a smart cookie, and she seems to have been good for him. Anyway, when he needed a place to stay, we were happy to let him stay at our place. Otherwise it was just going to sit empty anyway."

"Jan met him, and she thought he seemed nice," Elaine said. Jan was shaking her head from the other seat, but Elaine just smiled. No sense alerting Abby to what Jan really thought. "I hope he's able to use this time to get his feet under him. It's great that he has someone like you to help him out."

"That sister of mine didn't really set him up very well, so we're glad to do it." There was some noise on the other end of the line. "Oh, Elaine, I'm sorry but I have to go. It's time to leave for our salsa competition."

Elaine laughed. It sounded like the community where the Kings spent the summer was a hoot.

"I hope you win," Elaine said.

"I just hope I beat Burk," Abby said. "Tell everyone I said hi. We'll see them in a few months."

"Talk to you soon," Elaine said, and ended the call. She sat there for another minute, turning the phone over in her hand, thinking the conversation through. Something had stood out. Something she should have picked up on. What was it?

She nearly jumped when the phone rang again. She saw that it was a Portland number.

"Hello?"

"Hi, Elaine. This is Annette Simons. From the Goodwill store?"

"Oh. Hello. Thank you for calling back."

"Of course. I was intrigued by your question, because I was pretty sure I remembered that I'd sold a Santa costume recently. Anyway, we did, and it was a week and a half ago today."

"Wow." Elaine felt her pulse race. The timing was just about perfect. This could be their Santa suit.

"Would you be able to tell me who it was sold to?" Elaine asked.

"I can't really do that, I'm afraid," Ms. Simons said. "I'm sorry. Privacy and all that." Elaine bit her tongue. "But I can tell you that it was paid for with a credit card."

"All right," Elaine said. "Thanks." She couldn't do anything with that unless she had more information.

"I'm sure when he puts on the suit, he'll be like a whole new person," Ms. Simons said.

"Okay." Elaine wasn't sure what to make of that. Was that supposed to be a clue of some kind? Or was she just thinking out loud?

"It might be almost like a road-to-Damascus moment, you might say."

There was an awkward pause.

"All right." Once again, Elaine was confused. Was she trying to tell Elaine something?

"Well, I have to go. But let me know if you need any more help."

Elaine thanked her and hung up, rolling around what Annette Simons had said in her mind. Road to Damascus. She recognized it from the book of Acts, when Saul met Jesus on the road...

Oh. It hit her all at once. Of course.

When Saul met Jesus, he'd been transformed. Not quite like putting on a Santa suit, but it didn't matter. She got it now. Ms. Simons had been trying to tell her the man's name.

After Saul's conversion on the road to Damascus, he was a new person. And he had changed his name to Paul.

The man who bought the Santa suit was named *Paul*.

"Everything all right?" Jan popped her head into the office.

"Yeah." Elaine put the cordless phone down on the desk. "Sorry. I'll be right there to help out."

"That's all right. We're okay out here. I was just asking because you looked pensive."

"I am pensive."

"Any particular reason?"

"The man who bought the Santa suit at the Goodwill store in Portland was named Paul."

"Oh." Jan's eyes widened. "Like the guy at the diner?"

Elaine nodded.

"So it's the same guy."

"Looks like it."

Jan hesitated. "Something else is bothering you, isn't it?"

Elaine wasn't sure what to say. Something was tickling at the back of her mind.

"What is it?" Jan asked.

Elaine hesitated. Did this sound nuts?

"Abby King mentioned the name Ainsley. Apparently that's Joe's girlfriend."

"Yeah. I think that's who was picking him up that time I visited him." Jan stepped into the doorway. "I didn't ask who she was, but it seemed likely that was his girlfriend."

Elaine nodded. She couldn't prove anything. But something still wasn't adding up.

"Ainsley was the name of the manager we spoke to at SuperMart the other day."

"Huh?" Jan cocked her head.

"She was wearing a name tag." She indicated the area on her chest where the store's name tags went. "It said Ainsley."

"Okay." Jan wasn't seeing what she was getting at. Elaine wasn't exactly sure what she was getting at herself.

"It's not the most common name."

"No, it's not. But it's probably his girlfriend. We know she got him his job at the store. I never actually saw her clearly at his house, so I can't say if it was her or not."

"Right." Elaine couldn't put her finger on why exactly this was bothering her so much. But something didn't seem right.

"Isn't it strange that his girlfriend would be his manager?" Elaine asked.

"I guess." The classical music they often played kicked on in the parlors. "It's bad personnel management. But it's not a sign that either of them had anything to do with the break-ins."

"Maybe not." But Elaine wasn't so sure. "But if she's his girlfriend, not just his manager, why should we trust her? Wouldn't she have motivation to lie about when he was working?"

"Ainsley showed us the program that recorded Joe was working the nights of the robbery. The proof was right there in the system."

Yes, there was that. Joe *had* to be innocent. The proof really was right there in the system. But knowing that didn't erase her fears. Somehow, they seemed to increase them.

"You never saw Ainsley clearly at Joe's house, but did she see you?"

Jan thought for a moment. "Yes, I think she probably did."

Elaine didn't know what to say. But something didn't feel right.

CHAPTER TWENTY-EIGHT

J an hadn't slept well. Despite herself, she was nervous about the details of the fund-raiser tonight coming together. It didn't matter that the caterer was supposed to be taking care of everything, or that the flowers had been delivered yesterday and looked beautiful. Jan and Elaine were still the hosts, and Jan still felt responsible. She'd also had a hard time sleeping because she was disappointed that Bob wasn't back yet. She couldn't wait to see him.

And of course she was anxious about this whole Grinch thing as well. Every creak and groan of the old house sounded like someone coming up the stairs to Jan. Would a security system make her feel any safer? Or would it only make her feel more vulnerable, more exposed?

When she finally got up, she saw that she had a text from Elsa Leon. There had been a break-in at the Whisper Art Gallery last night. Elsa had discovered it first thing this morning. It followed the same pattern as the other thefts. Jan sighed. He'd struck again.

Fortunately, as she'd tossed and turned through the long night, she'd had an idea. And last night's robbery fit in with her thoughts perfectly.

"I've been thinking," Jan said as she and Elaine drove through town in Elaine's car that Tuesday morning. The sun had come out, casting brilliant sparkles on the glittery white snow.

"Look out, world," Elaine said, laughing.

"It isn't all that rare, actually," Jan said. "But this time, I think I have a pretty decent idea."

"Let's hear it then."

They were on their way to the church, hoping to ask whether Pastor Mike Ryder had seen the person who dropped off the cash donation. Jan knew the chances were slim, but they at least had to try. They'd already stopped by the gallery and talked with Elsa and Rachel, and hadn't uncovered any new clues. But they had become more certain that the same thief was behind this break-in, considering the locks had been picked and the safe opened with a crowbar.

"If we're right, and the person doing the robberies is going all Robin Hood on us, will he show up at the fund-raiser tonight?"

"Huh." Elaine slowed for a stop sign and seemed to consider this. "Why would he?"

"Because he seems to care a lot about the organization. Because there was a big piece in the paper reminding everyone that every dollar donated at the event would be matched. And because he struck again last night, which means he has a large amount of cash to donate."

"Huh."

Jan waited for her to go on, but she didn't. "You already said that."

"I'm thinking," Elaine said.

"Look out, world."

"Hey!" Elaine laughed. "The real question is, do we want him to show up?"

"I don't know," Jan admitted. On the one hand, she did want him to so they could have the police arrest him. But they would need to figure out who he was before then, of course.

"Let's think about it," Elaine said as she pulled into the church parking lot. "There may be a way to lure him there."

Jan glanced at Elaine. Did she really want to lure the man back to their home? The man who'd already broken in and tried to rob them?

She followed Elaine across the frozen parking lot and through the front door of the church. They stepped inside and headed down the hallway that branched off. The wooden floor creaked as they walked in the open doorway that led to the small church office. While they chatted with Pastor Mike Ryder in his study, he admitted that the church was left unlocked most of the day and he often didn't see who came and went. He said he hadn't seen who had left the large donation, and the only other people that day who might have seen anything were members of the moms group that met in the basement.

"You could ask Melissa Webster. She leads that group, and she might be able to tell you," the pastor added.

Jan and Elaine knew Melissa. She was in her early forties, and she and her husband owned The What-Not, an antique store here in town. They had two kids, a rambunctious seven-year-old boy and a sweet four-year-old girl.

"Thanks so much," Jan said. "We'll give her a call." It wasn't a lot to go on, but it was something.

Back at the house, Jan whipped up a triple batch of scones for the tearoom while Elaine went into the office to call Melissa Webster. She had just closed the door behind her when the doorbell rang. Jan wiped her hands on her apron, walked down the hallway, and opened the door.

"Got another one for you."

It was Max. He held up a box and grinned at Jan. For a second, Jan froze. Max! All the thoughts she'd had about him in the past week came rushing into her head. But then she remembered that she had crossed him off her suspect list.

"Max. How are you?" Jan gestured for him to step inside. He stomped the snow off his boots—the same Pac boots she'd noticed before—and came inside the hall. She took the box. It was heavy, and addressed to Elaine.

"Keeping busy, that's for sure." He pulled his scanner out of his pocket and scanned the barcode on the box.

Jan wanted to ask about the website she'd found, but didn't know how to bring it up casually. But he was already turning to go. He probably had a whole truck full of packages to deliver. Before she could think of what to say, she blurted out, "How long have you been selling T-shirts?"

Max stopped and turned back to Jan, a wide smile on his face. "How did you find out about that?"

"I was shopping for a present for my son-in-law and found your page on Mainely Made. It's really great stuff," Jan said.

"Well, thank you." Max pretended to tip his cap at her, though he was only wearing a beanie. "It's something I've wanted to do for a long time. I've always had a passion for graphic design, and I'm kind of a nerd, and last year about this time I decided to just do it. It was my New Year's resolution—to finally do something about the ideas I've had banging around in my head for so long. So I did it."

"That's wonderful." Jan had finally realized her own dream when she and Elaine had opened this tearoom, and she loved to hear of others who had embraced their dreams. "I didn't know you were into all that stuff."

"Nerd stuff?" He laughed.

"Hey, I'm a nerd too. I mean, not all the sci-fi stuff. You lost me with all the Tardis and Klingon jargon. But I love science, and I thought some of the shirts you make are really funny."

"Now, see, I didn't know you were into science." He looked at her appraisingly. Jan knew she didn't look like a science geek. But she'd wanted to study engineering in college, except that she couldn't afford it.

"I guess we should talk more," Jan said. "But can I ask…" How did she phrase this politely? "How did you end up delivering packages?"

"You mean, instead of being a scientist or graphic designer?" She nodded.

"The usual way, I suppose. When Judith found out she was pregnant, all of the plans I'd had went down the tubes. Don't get me wrong, I love that little girl to the moon and back and I wouldn't change a thing. But we were just college kids. I dropped out and joined the army. Yardley was born, and supporting her and Judith was all that mattered. I did two tours in Iraq, and when I left the army, I got the best job I could get. Driving a truck wasn't what I had envisioned for my life, but it pays decent and it has good benefits. That's what matters at this stage."

"But then you decided to finally try your hand at your dream."

"Yeah. Well, at least one version of it. I had this idea for a shirt that I thought was funny. The G.I. Joe one?"

Jan nodded. She'd seen that one when she was shopping for Van.

"And I figured other people might too. So I created the graphic and had some shirts printed, and lo and behold, it worked. People bought them."

"I'm not surprised. They're clever."

"Thank you." He gestured toward the truck at the curb. "Well, I should get going. I have a truckload of packages to deliver."

"It was nice chatting with you." Jan closed the door behind him and looked down at the package in her hands.

She carried the package back to the kitchen and set it down on the counter just as Elaine came out of the office.

"Max isn't the Grinch, for sure," Jan said.

"That's all right." Elaine's eyes were wide and shining with excitement. "I just got off the phone with Melissa Webster. She saw the guy who made the big donation at the church."

"Oh yeah?" Jan didn't want to get too excited.

"Yep. And even better, I know who it is."

CHAPTER TWENTY-NINE

Jan listened as Elaine explained what Melissa Webster had told her while they drove to Waterville. Archie and Rose had assured the cousins that the two of them could handle opening the tearoom, as they had many times before.

"Melissa said she was there the day the donation was made. She said she and the other moms were downstairs, with the kids running around the fellowship hall, and it was chaos like always. But she came upstairs to take her daughter Bean to the bathroom. Apparently Bean is particular and only likes the upstairs restrooms."

"Bean?"

"Don't ask me. I don't pretend to understand what people name their kids these days."

"Anyway, what did she see?"

"She said as she came up the stairs she saw a big guy with dark hair walking toward the collection box. He had an envelope in his hand, and she saw a medical bracelet on his wrist."

"Sounds like our guy." Jan couldn't believe it. It really was him. It had to be.

"It sure does." Elaine flipped on her blinker and made a turn. "And there's only been one suspect we've encountered so far who matches that description."

"But Joe has an alibi," Jan said. "He was working. We saw the store's records."

But even as she said it, doubt was creeping in. Elaine had already pointed out that his girlfriend was his manager, so there was reason to believe not everything was on the up and up. Was there any way the store's software could have been manipulated?

"So Melissa says that when she saw the guy, Bean ran up to him and asked his name."

"So much for not talking to strangers."

Elaine shrugged. "It's a church. And frankly, I'm glad she did. The guy said his name was Paul."

"Paul." Jan mulled this over. Who was this Paul guy they kept running into? Did Joe have a twin? Wouldn't Abby or Tag have mentioned this?

"It just seemed too crazy to not be connected. Right after Joe shows up in town, the thefts start happening, and people start seeing a guy named Paul around. It has to be the same person, right?"

Jan nodded. "Plus, he has epilepsy, so it's likely Joe wears a medical bracelet like the guy in the picture in the newspaper."

"And there's Joe's background."

"He's had brushes with the law."

"Yes, but more importantly, he had a dad in prison," Elaine said. "This whole charity is about helping kids whose parents are in prison."

This last point clicked in place for Jan. It wasn't too difficult to imagine this was a charity he would feel strongly about. If his sense of right and wrong had been warped, you could see how he might see stealing as a valid way to get what he needed to help those kids so they didn't suffer the way he had. It was possible.

"I'm with you," Jan said. "But why the Santa suit? That's never made sense to me."

"It's a pretty good disguise, you have to admit," Elaine said. "It's shocking, for one. If anyone sees you they have a hard time describing anything about *you* because all they see is the Santa. And it covers your whole body and most of your face."

Jan thought for a moment. "But so would a parka and ski mask."

"But those don't have the same shock factor, which, you have to admit, is part of the reason we haven't figured this thing out yet."

"What if it's not so much that as the fact that he's weirdly into Christmas giving?" Even as Jan said it, she knew how ridiculous it sounded.

But Elaine was nodding. "Maybe. Or maybe he just saw the suit at that Goodwill store and went with it. It was a matter of convenience. The right camouflage presented itself."

"Camouflage. Maybe that's the right way to think about it. At this time of year, no one is surprised to see Santa Claus."

"Unless he's breaking into your safe with a crowbar. That's surprising."

"True," Jan said. "Okay, say it is Joe, and maybe he stumbled across that Santa suit at the thrift store and decided it would be good cover for what he wanted to do. I can buy that. But we still don't have proof."

"We have plenty of circumstantial evidence that says Joe and Paul are the same person, and Joe is the thief."

"But no proof. And very good evidence that says he's not."

Jan shifted in her seat. Maybe they'd have that proof soon. They were on their way to SuperMart in Waterville to try to see if someone—Ainsley or Joe, or maybe even someone else— had manipulated their records system to prove that Joe was at work when he wasn't. She wanted to be very sure before she started making accusations. She pulled her phone out of her purse.

"What are you doing?" Elaine asked.

"Trying to get proof." Jan dialed the number for Abby King and waited while it rang. She held her breath, and let it out when Abby picked up. "Hi, Abby. It's Jan Blake."

"Hi, Jan. We're out for our walk, so forgive me if I sound a bit winded."

"It's totally fine," Jan said. Abby didn't sound winded at all, and the idea of walking outdoors for exercise sounded lovely right about now. But she tried to not let herself get distracted.

"I wanted to ask you one more question about your nephew Joe, if that's all right."

"Of course," Abby said. "Is he in trouble?"

"Not that I know of." Jan decided evading the question was the best strategy. He wasn't in trouble. Yet. "But I was wondering—does he ever go by the name Paul?"

"Oh yeah. Paul's his first name," Abby said. "He's always gone by Joe, short for Joseph, but that's his middle name."

Jan couldn't believe it. Her heart started racing. "Does anyone call him Paul?"

"Probably. He's always been Joey to me, but I would imagine he would use Paul on anything legal or official. That's what's on his birth certificate and probably his official ID, so I'm sure he must use it sometimes."

"Thank you so much."

He would use the name Paul on anything legal or official, or if he was trying to hide his real identity. Most people who used a fake name, Jan knew, didn't simply pick one from thin air. They used one that they had some connection to. If he was trying to keep people from finding out who he was—say, a nosy waitress at a diner—it wasn't a stretch to imagine he might give her a name that was close to right but not really what he was known by. "I have just one more question."

"Of course."

"Tag mentioned that Joe had kind of a rough childhood, and you helped him out."

"We did as much as we could," Abby said. "Though he had a rough start. My sister—well, she always was a bit rebellious. But still, when she ended up pregnant, we were all surprised when she went and married the guy, Marty. On the other hand, no one was really surprised when he ended up in jail, sadly. And poor Joe—he was such a scared kid, always afraid of everything. My sister—well, she had her own demons, I guess. She was usually on drugs, living with one boyfriend or another. She wasn't always very receptive to our offers of help, so we just tried the best we could. And Joey was such a sweet kid. He was always trying to keep positive, and he was so funny about things."

"About what things?"

"Oh, things like believing in the tooth fairy and the Easter bunny long past the time most kids stopped. Like, he was holding on to those things because they made him happy, maybe because everything else in his life was so bad."

Well, that was interesting. "What about Santa Claus?"

"Oh yes. He loved Santa Claus. Always did."

Was that enough, Jan wondered, to explain why he would choose to dress like Santa while robbing businesses? It seemed like quite a stretch.

Jan thought about how to phrase this. "Would you say the fact that his father was in prison affected Joe much?"

"Oh yeah. No question. He has such a good heart. Even as a little boy, he always wanted to do the right thing. But he had no one to really show him what the right thing was. He needed a stable man in his life, and he didn't have one. But it affected him other ways too. Financially, emotionally, mentally. Not having his dad around absolutely was a huge deal for him growing up, and he knew it."

So he had a reason to want to support the charity, then. He wanted to help kids who were in the same position he had been in. And, apparently, since he didn't have money to give, he did what he knew best and got some. It was totally twisted reasoning—robbing people to get money in order to give it to other people—but she could see that there was a sort of logic there anyway. If stealing and lying was what he knew, maybe it wasn't such a big surprise that he resorted to that now.

"People keep saying that he got into trouble with the law. Can you tell me what kind?"

"Oh, you name it." Abby sighed. "It started with small stuff when he was thirteen. Stealing little things from stores, that sort of thing. Then it escalated. He started hanging out with a rough crowd, and he got into drugs. Breaking and entering. Assault."

"It must have been so hard for you to watch that happen to someone you love."

"It has been hard. But we just do the best we can. We pray for him a lot." Abby sighed again. "But judging by the fact that you're asking so much about him, I'm guessing he's gotten himself into some kind of trouble up there."

Jan didn't know what to say. She certainly didn't want to add to Abby's burden. "We're not sure," Jan said. She saw Elaine giving her a look from the driver's seat.

"Has he done something illegal?" Abby asked.

Jan hesitated, then said, again, "We're not sure."

"All right." Abby sounded resigned. "I'll see if Tag can fill me in on what's happening in town. In the meantime, please don't hesitate to let me know how I can help."

"Thanks so much."

Jan hung up and looked at Elaine, who had obviously over-heard the entire conversation, judging by the look on her face.

"Is that enough proof for you?" Elaine asked.

They still wouldn't be able to prove it to the police yet. But Jan felt confident they could soon. "Let's go."

CHAPTER THIRTY

When they stepped inside the SuperMart, Elaine went directly to the Employees Only door and walked inside. "You can't just go in . . . ," Jan started, but Elaine didn't listen.

"Excuse me," Elaine said to a young man in a blue-and-yellow SuperMart polo shirt. He was just coming out of a door at the far end of the hallway. He jerked up, startled to see them there. "Where would I find the general manager?"

"Huh?"

"The boss. Who's in charge here? I want to speak to that person please. Would you be able to help me find him or her?"

The guy froze. He had acne sprinkled on his cheeks and peach fuzz along his chin. "Hang on." He turned and vanished back through the doorway. Elaine knew Jan was not thrilled about her strategy, but she didn't want to risk being directed toward Ainsley again. The seconds crept by, the sickly overhead lights buzzing and popping. Then the door opened again and the boy came out, followed by a tall African American woman in a business suit and high heels.

"Hi, I'm Hallie," the woman said. She had smooth dark skin and deep plum lipstick, and she had a smile on her face. "Thank you, Jonah."

The kid scurried down the hallway and out into the main part of the store.

"I'm Elaine Cook, and this is my cousin Jan Blake," Elaine said, sticking out her hand.

"What can I help you with today?"

Hallie seemed pleasant enough, but Elaine knew she had to phrase this carefully.

"We have a question about one of your employees. We asked about him recently and spoke with a manager of his department, but we've uncovered some discrepancies we wanted to ask about."

"Discrepancies?" Her brow wrinkled. "Why don't you follow me."

She led them through the door at the end of the hallway and into another hallway that branched off to the right. They passed a few people in blue-and-yellow shirts, but for the most part it was quiet back here. They followed her into an office, much larger than the one they'd been in before, and with a real wood desk and lamps. Hallie gestured for them to sit down in modern plastic-and-steel chairs.

"What's the name of this employee?" she asked.

"When we were here before, we thought his name was Joe Stone. But we've discovered now that his real name is Paul Stone."

"Let me take a look." She had deep-purple nail polish on her fingernails, and they flew over the keys. She was quiet for a moment—long enough that Elaine began to worry something was wrong. Still, she forced herself not to interrupt.

"Hmm," Hallie finally said. But she kept typing, and using her mouse to toggle back and forth between screens. Elaine held her breath. What was she seeing? What did *"hmm"* mean? She clasped her hands together, forcing herself to wait.

Finally Hallie went on. "Well, I found something interesting," she said. "You said his real name is Paul Stone?"

"That's right. It's Paul Joseph Stone."

Hallie continued staring at the screen and nodded.

"What did you find?" Jan asked.

"It turns out there are two employee IDs for him," Hallie said. "One under the name Joe, and one under the name Paul. Different names, different ID numbers, but the same address and same department."

"Inventory," Elaine said.

Hallie nodded.

"How is that possible?" Jan asked.

"That's what I need to figure out," Hallie said. "I mean, on one level, it's pretty simple. A manager creates your ID on your first day. Obviously a manager created two different IDs for him at different points. But this one ID, the one for Joe, has never been submitted for payroll."

"What does that mean?" Jan asked quietly.

"It means this Joe has never been paid for his work, though his hours have been entered."

"Why would that be?" Elaine asked.

"My guess is because it's not a real ID. His real record is the one set up under the name Paul." She stared at something on the screen. "Payroll would probably have noticed the same person getting paid twice. But it's unlikely anyone would have noticed an extra employee ID in the system if it never came up for payment."

"So you think the Joe entry is the fake one." This made sense to Elaine. Abby had said that he might use the name Paul on anything official, so that things matched his legal paperwork. And the Joe entry was the one Ainsley had showed them, to throw them off the trail.

Then Elaine got a sickening feeling. Was the whole Joe ID created just so he would have an alibi, in case anyone ever checked into him? Some way to show that he'd been at work when he was actually out robbing people? If it was true, that meant Ainsley was in on it. But as his girlfriend, she had a reason to want to protect Joe.

"Can you tell me something?" Elaine asked. "Does it show that Paul and Joe worked different hours?"

"Yep. Sure does." Hallie blew out a breath. "They appear to have worked different nights altogether."

"Meaning the nights Joe was supposed to have worked, Paul actually didn't?" Jan asked.

"There is some overlap, but yes, for the most part," Hallie said.

Jan met Elaine's eye. There it was. Ainsley must have set up the separate employee ID number in order to give Joe—Paul—an alibi for the nights the thefts happened.

And it had worked. When they'd come to ask about his hours, she'd simply pulled up the fake schedule. No wonder she had been so willing to hand that information out. She didn't care if they weren't from a bank. In fact, had she known who they were? Ainsley had seen Jan the night she'd brought the lasagna to Joe. Would she have remembered? Elaine wasn't sure, but if she had, it would have been even easier to imagine how she knew to pull up the fake employee record.

"Did Paul actually work on Sunday, Monday, Tuesday, Thursday, or last night?" Elaine asked.

Hallie hesitated, then shrugged her shoulders and shook her head.

Jan looked triumphant. Elaine was pleased too, but she'd already moved on to their next problem.

They now knew that the thief was Tag's cousin Joe, who sometimes went by his real name, Paul.

But what were they supposed to do about it?

CHAPTER THIRTY-ONE

J an and Elaine stopped by Trooper Benson's house on their way home and explained what they'd learned. He promised to have some officers head down to the store in Waterville and talk with Hallie.

"Are you going to send someone over to the King house to arrest him?" Jan asked.

"Not yet," Dan said. "We need to investigate."

"But we need to stop him before he robs someone else," Elaine insisted.

Dan sighed. "I am sure you two did a very thorough job of researching. But you're not police officers. I can't just go around arresting people without investigating properly."

Elaine knew he was right, but it still upset her. "When do you think you will be able to arrest him?"

"I don't know."

Elaine bit her tongue. There were so many things she wanted to say, but none of them were helpful.

"I can only tell you that we will be investigating, and that we will act with appropriate measures as quickly as possible."

Elaine followed Jan out, more frustrated than ever.

WHEN THEY GOT back to the tearoom, Jan threw herself into getting everything ready for the fund-raiser that night. The tearoom was a bit slow, and she was grateful for that, because Archie and Rose handled everything while she spent much of the day sorting through the plates and utensils the catering company had delivered. She couldn't get started setting up for the fund-raiser until they closed for the day, and trying to do both was making Jan crazy. But honestly, she was grateful for the distraction, as it kept her mind off whatever was happening on the Joe front. Elaine had called Dan Benson to check in around two, but Dan had simply said that they were still investigating.

Finally, it was time to close up for the day. By the time Elaine ushered the last customers out and sent Rose and Archie home, the catering team had already arrived and was placing the tables in the dining room, where they would be out of the way. Then the doorbell rang. Jan assumed it was another person from the catering company, here to help set up for the party, but when she opened the door she found an elderly woman in a neat camel wool coat and a lavender brimmed hat.

"Oh. Hello." The woman seemed uncertain. "Is this Tea for Two?" Her face was lined and her hair a soft gray. She seemed frail, but solid somehow.

"It is. But I'm afraid that we're closed now and having a special event tonight…"

"Oh, I'm not here for tea," she said.

Jan stopped. Why was she here then?

"I'm here to ask about a painting."

Jan didn't know what she'd been expecting, but it wasn't that. Then she remembered Elaine had mentioned that someone had asked at the Goodwill about their painting. Was this that woman?

Jan hesitated, and then, unsure of what else to do, she stepped back. "Come in."

"Thank you. I'm Geraldine." The woman wiped her feet on the welcome mat and stepped cautiously over the threshold. Inside, she looked around and nodded. "This is beautiful."

"Thanks." Right now, people in black pants and white button-downs were scurrying around setting up chafing dishes and setting out platters of appetizers. "It's not usually this chaotic."

"I would imagine not." She stood taking in the lit fireplace, the decorated trees, and the greenery threaded through the candles on the mantel.

"You're here about the Harley Archibald Benningham painting?" Jan asked. That was the name Archie's father had painted under. "The tea painting?"

Geraldine tilted her head, but she nodded. "I don't know who painted it, but yes, there is tea in the painting. There's a woman in it, and she's looking out a window over a park."

The woman had seemed vaguely familiar somehow. Had Jan seen her on television maybe?

"That sounds like our painting," Jan said. "It usually hangs right there." She pointed to the spot on the wall in the west parlor where it usually hung. "But it's away being restored right now."

"Oh." Geraldine pressed her lips together.

"I'm sorry," Jan said. She didn't know why she was apologizing exactly. It was just that this woman seemed crestfallen that the painting wasn't here.

"It's all right." She seemed to recover herself a bit. "It's just that, you see, I recently moved to an assisted living facility over in Augusta. My son...he meant well. He was trying to help, I know. But in the process of 'clearing things out'"—she used her fingers to make air quotes—"he managed to get rid of several things that were very special to me."

"Including the painting," Jan said.

She nodded. "Yes. The painting I'm looking for hung over my crib when I was a baby. It has a lot of sentimental value."

"Oh dear." Jan loved the painting. And since they'd recently discovered that it had almost certainly been painted by Archie's father, a famous artist, and could be quite valuable, Jan and Elaine had discussed giving it to him. But this woman had obviously worked very hard to track this painting down. If it had rightfully belonged to this woman...

But there was no sense getting ahead of herself. Plus, perhaps Geraldine was a link to more information about the painting, and more importantly, about Archie's father. Could she know something? Jan didn't think it was right to ask these questions without Archie here.

"We expect to get the painting back perhaps in a few months," Jan said. "And actually, the painting also happens to have sentimental value to one of our employees, Archie Bentham. Do you know him?"

She shook her head. "Not that I know of."

"Well," Jan said, "I know he'd love to meet you and learn more about your connection with the painting. Is there a number where I can reach you when he returns?"

"That would be lovely." The woman reached into her black leather purse and pulled out a calling card engraved with the name Geraldine Lawrence and an Augusta number. Goodness. Jan hadn't seen one of these things in years.

"We'll give you a call soon," Jan promised, and the woman thanked her again, then headed out the door.

Jan shut the door, but she stood there in the entryway for a few moments, thinking over the encounter. Who was Geraldine Lawrence? What did she want with the painting? And how had Archie's father's painting been hanging over Geraldine's crib when she was a baby? Was she sure it was the same painting? Jan realized in that moment that she had forgotten about the 11x14 picture of the painting that they had printed, which would have been more than enough for Geraldine to confirm whether it was or wasn't hers. Oh well. That would give them another reason to call her for a second visit.

Just then, the door opened once more and Archie stepped inside. His jacket was unbuttoned, and his hat was askew.

"Oh. Hello." It took Jan a moment to focus. "Did you forget something?"

"I think I left my phone on the counter," he said. But even after he closed the door, he too stood in the hallway for a moment, like he wasn't sure what to do. Normally, Archie would make some self-deprecating joke. But now, he just stood there, lost in thought.

"Is everything all right?" Jan asked.

"Oh. Yes." He seemed to come back to the present. "My apologies. I just..." He looked back at the door and shook his head. "I just saw a woman coming down the walk."

"Geraldine Lawrence," Jan said. "She was here to ask about your father's painting."

"She was?"

"Yes." Jan studied him. "Is everything all right?" she asked again.

"Yes, I'm sure it is. It's just that..." Archie paused, shaking his head again. "It's just that seeing her was like seeing a ghost."

"What do you mean?" Jan asked.

"The woman. The one who just left? It's the funniest thing." He took a deep breath. "She looked exactly like my father."

CHAPTER THIRTY-TWO

J an had been distracted for the first bit of the party, and Elaine worked hard to pick up the slack. Jan had tried to tell her something about an older woman asking about the Benningham painting, but Elaine was too focused on the fund-raiser to concentrate on anything else right now.

She knew Jan was dubious, but Elaine really thought there was a decent chance Joe might show up tonight, if the police hadn't arrested him yet. And if Dan Benson's exasperated tone when she'd called and asked for an update was any indication, Joe was still at large, for the time being anyway. Elaine tried to figure out what she would say when she saw him. Would she confront him herself? Maybe she could call him Paul, just to see how he reacted?

Bristol Payson showed up about an hour before the party was set to begin, and she *oohed* and *aahed* over the food and the decorations. They had cleared away a spot under the Christmas tree in the east parlor where people could leave wrapped presents to be donated to the charity, and there was also a wicker basket on a nearby table where cash could be placed. It would be monitored throughout the night and counted at the end of the party, and the anonymous donor—Elaine was almost certain it was Will Trexler—would match the total.

"It's beautiful," Bristol said.

"And you should try the food. Those mushroom bites are out of this world." Elaine gestured to where a waiter was placing a tray of stuffed mushroom caps down on a table.

Bristol reached over and grabbed one and popped it in her mouth. "Thank you for doing this."

"We didn't do anything except open our doors. And we're glad to help out such a worthy cause."

It wasn't long before both parlors were filled with guests, each of whom made a donation to the cash basket, and most had brought along a present to put under the tree as well. It looked like half the town was here. Elaine waved at Gavin and Annie Richardson, and she'd already had conversations with Anita Picard and Maureen Oakley. Nathan was here, chatting with Heather Wells. Jan's daughter Tara was here, looking mighty cozy with Jack Weston. Candace Huang was here from the *Penzance Courier* to report on the event, and Tag King and several of his friends from the Blizzard Riders Club had driven across the lake on snowmobiles to get here. Elaine had shown them where to park, at the back of the house on the yard that sloped down to the lake. They'd laughed about needing dedicated snowmobile parking spots. Macy Atherton had brought Shane and Zale, and all three had loaded their plates high with appetizers, but Elaine couldn't complain about that because they'd also left a thick envelope in the basket.

"Your phone has been ringing," Jan said, coming up next to Elaine beside the fireplace in the east parlor. She had Elaine's cell phone in one hand and a cup of eggnog in the other. Jan had changed into a red sweater and black pants and put in some candy cane earrings. Elaine was wearing a long black skirt and a shimmery silver blouse, along with the pearls Ben had given her for her fiftieth birthday. Jan handed Elaine the phone.

"Ah. It's nice not to be the ones serving, isn't it?" Jan took a canapé off a passing tray and smiled.

"It sure is. And thanks." Elaine had turned the ringer off and left the phone on the counter in the kitchen so she wouldn't be distracted during the party. Now she took the phone and looked down at the screen. She had two missed calls from Trooper Benson.

"It's Dan."

"Oh." Jan took a sip. "You should call him back."

"I think I will, if you don't mind." Elaine set down the cup of eggnog she'd been drinking and started toward the kitchen.

"Wait," Jan said. She was looking at something on the far side of the room. Elaine turned to see what she was looking at. Mike and Sarah Ryder smiled at her, and she smiled back and craned her neck. What was she looking at?

"Who's that?" Jan asked.

Elaine took a step so she could see Jan's line of sight. From here, the wall wasn't blocking her view, and she could see that Jan was looking at a tall man in a blue jacket and a knit cap. He was moving through the crowd quickly, not stopping to talk to anyone. And he was headed toward the tree.

"Is that...?" Jan was squinting at the man. He was the right size, and his hair was the right color.

"It's hard to say for sure from this angle," Elaine said, but she felt her heartbeat speed up. It was Joe. It had to be! She knew he'd show up.

"He's still wearing his jacket," Jan said.

"He's not planning to stay very long." Elaine watched him move through the crowded room toward the Christmas tree. Her phone chirped again.

"It's Dan Benson again."

"Well, answer it, for goodness' sake," Jan said. Elaine nodded, stepped into the kitchen, and held the phone to her ear. "Hello?"

Young men in catering attire rushed around the kitchen, setting food on trays and pouring juice into champagne flutes.

"Elaine? It's Dan. I wanted to warn you that we're on our way."

"On your way here?" Elaine's heart was pounding now. This was it. They were finally going to get him.

"That's where Joe Stone is, right?" There was some garbled speech from a scanner on his end of the line. "We had an officer stationed outside his house and when he left, the officer followed him there."

"He's here," Elaine confirmed. "But I don't think he's planning on staying for too long. Hurry."

"We're just a few minutes away. I had to wait for backup to arrive from Augusta."

"Should I take this to mean you've got your proof that he's behind the thefts?"

"We can discuss all that later. Suffice it to say that after the general manager at SuperMart talked with him, he appears to have made some hasty plans to leave town."

"He's running?"

"He knows he's been caught," Dan said. "That's why we have to get him before he gets away. So I'm sorry to crash the party, but..."

"Just get him before he gets away."

"We'll do our best."

"I appreciate it...," Elaine started to say, but he had already hung up.

Elaine set the phone down and walked back into the west parlor.

"The police are on their way," Elaine said.

"Here?" Jan's eyes widened. She set her eggnog cup on a tray from a passing waiter. "Why are they coming here?"

"They couldn't wait until after the party," Elaine said. "Joe's about to skip town." She could see that the man they'd seen earlier was now walking away from the tree, back toward the door.

"He's running from the law, and he stopped at a party to make a donation to a children's charity on his way?" Jan was watching him carefully. "In a house he tried to break into, in a room full of people he's robbed?"

"I didn't say it was especially smart of him," Elaine said. "But we do know that he's made some incredibly poor decisions out of apparent loyalty to the charity. I guess he just really wanted his last donation to be doubled?"

"He's almost at the door," Jan said, already moving in that direction. Elaine followed one step behind. They were not letting him get away.

"Excuse me," Elaine said, pushing through a small crowd that had been gathered around the punch bowl. She saw Rue Maxwell reach out to grab Jan's arm, but Jan just shrugged it off and kept going. By the time they'd threaded their way through the crowd, he was just about to put his hand on the door.

"Hello! Joe Stone! It's so good to see you," Jan said, her voice bright and enthusiastic.

Caught, he was forced to stop and turn back to Jan.

"Jan Blake. I brought the lasagna over? How are you doing?" Jan didn't give him a chance to answer. "I'm so glad you made it. Have you met my cousin Elaine?" Jan moved so Elaine could step forward, in the process putting herself between him and the door. His eyes darted between them. He recognized them both. He was scared. Well, good.

"Elaine Cook." Elaine held out her hand. "I'm so glad to finally meet you. I've heard so much about you. Abby and Burk speak so highly of you." It was funny, seeing him up close like this. The image of him creeping into the house had kept her awake at night. In her memory, he was huge, hulking, terrifyingly strong. But up close like this, he was just a normal guy. He had a few days' growth of stubble, acne scars, and a mole on his right ear. He wasn't actually so scary when he wasn't breaking into your home in the middle of the night with a crowbar.

"Thanks," he said. His voice was quiet but deep. "I appreciate it. And thanks for the lasagna." He looked at Jan. "It was delicious. But if you'll excuse me, I have to go…"

"Don't be silly! You just got here. Come, come." Elaine threaded her arm through his, and Jan moved directly in front of the door. If he wanted to go through the door he'd have to get past her. "I'll introduce you around. The people in this town are so wonderful." She tried to move him away from the door, but he didn't budge. He was solid, that was for sure.

"I'm sorry, but I really do need to get going," he said.

"But there are so many yummy things to eat." Elaine tried again. "When was the last time you had home-cooked food? A bachelor like you? Though I guess we actually didn't cook this food. Ha!" Elaine tried to keep her voice light, though she could feel him resisting her efforts to steer him away from the door.

"Look, the police are here."

Elaine heard someone in the west parlor say it. She looked out the front window and sure enough, red and blue lights were lighting up the snow in front of the house. Elaine counted three cars, and saw officers climbing out. She sure hoped they'd hurry.

Joe started to pull away, and Elaine held on as tightly as she could. But then he yanked his arm free and turned toward the back of the house.

"Wait!" Elaine called, but he didn't stop. He pushed his way through the crowd. She saw him bump his shoulder against Alan Oakley, sloshing eggnog over the side of his cup. "Stop him! Stop Joe!"

She saw a lot of confused faces turn toward her. This was a party. No one was expecting a bad guy trying to get away. She had to make them see. "Joe Stone! He's the Grinch!"

Finally, Jack Weston sprang into action and dashed out the back of the west parlor.

"Joe?" Tag King called, confusion evident on his face.

"Grab him!" Elaine heard Jack yell, and Elaine could see a few of the catering guys in the kitchen lunge toward him. Elaine forced her way through the crowd and made it into the kitchen just in time to see Joe run out onto the back porch.

Just then, the front door blew open, and what seemed like a half dozen state troopers, led by Dan Benson, streamed inside.

"He just ran out back!" Jan called from the hallway. She flattened herself against a wall, and they all ran past her into the kitchen, and then out onto the back porch.

Everything in Elaine wanted to run after them and try to catch him herself—no one wanted him behind bars more than she did. But Elaine knew that a fiftysomething woman was not going to outrun the state troopers and Jack Weston, and she would likely just get in the way.

Still, she moved out onto the porch to watch what would happen. It was hard to see in the dark night, but the full moon was reflecting off the snow, and Elaine watched as Joe disappeared around the side of the house, followed a moment later by the state troopers. Jan appeared beside her a moment later, just as the sound of a motor rang out in the still night.

"Is that…?" Jan started, but before Elaine could answer, they saw what it was. A snowmobile came flying around the corner and out toward the lake, its headlights creating a small patch of light directly in front.

"Tag is not going to be happy about that," Jan said.

Elaine had to laugh. That was the understatement of the year. Joe had stolen a snowmobile—either Tag's or one of his friends'—and was now racing off toward the frozen lake.

Elaine heard shouting from the side of the house. The officers realized what had happened. A moment later, she heard the screech of another snowmobile motor turning on, and then another state trooper appeared on a snowmobile, also borrowed from the snowmobile lot. All six officers were on the four remaining sleds that had been parked at the side of the house.

They watched as Joe stormed onto the surface of the ice, and then, seconds behind, a swarm of police officers followed him right onto the ice. They knew Joe was familiar with snowmobiles—it was how he'd gotten to and from robbing A Little Something, after all, after his truck had broken down. But this wasn't his, and he wasn't used to this ride, and Elaine prayed that difference would be enough to slow him down. She watched, horrified and transfixed, as Joe led six officers across the frozen lake on a high-speed snowmobile chase.

"I hope that ice holds," Elaine said.

"It will." But it sounded like Jan was trying to convince herself as much as Elaine. "They made it over here on it."

"That's my sled!" one of the snowmobilers yelled. But none of his friends seemed concerned.

"The police will bring him back," Tag King said. "They needed them to catch..." He shook his head. "Man. Joe? It was Joe?"

No one answered him. Soon the riders all disappeared from view. A few moments later, the lights also vanished into the murky night.

"Where are they?" Elaine asked.

"They'll be all right. They'll get him."

Elaine looked up and realized it was Jack Weston who had spoken, and that he had his arm around Tara and stood next to Jan. She also realized that Nathan was next to her, his arm around her waist, and Mark Payson was behind him, and that half a dozen other people were also standing with them on the small porch. Everyone held their breath and waited and watched.

"I wish we could see what was going on," Jan said. Tara moved closer to her mom.

Finally, after what seemed like an eternity, the slightest hint of light penetrated the darkness over the ice. Bit by bit, a little at a time, the beam of a headlight emerged. Soon, others appeared around it. The darkness of a bleak winter night had been overcome, and slowly, painfully slowly, the state troopers made it back to shore. There were five sleds.

"Did they get him?" Jan asked, though no one knew the answer.

The snowmobiles roared up to the back of the house. Slowly, people started climbing off. And that was when Elaine saw it.

Joe, handcuffed on the back of one of the snowmobiles. An officer helped him off, as his hands were cuffed behind his back.

"They got him!" Elaine said. The cheer that went up around her was overwhelming. But it was nothing compared to the rejoicing in her own heart. It was over. The Grinch had been caught. The thief that had threatened their small town was in handcuffs.

"You did it," Nathan said, pulling her closer.

"We did it," Elaine said, glancing at Jan. Jan gave her a smile and nodded.

The Grinch had not stolen Christmas after all, Elaine thought. But that was the point, wasn't it?

He never could. Christmas was bigger than decorations or carols or pageants or presents. Christmas was about Christ, entering the world as a baby, coming to save all of mankind. No one—no Grinch—could take that away.

But still. They'd caught him. Elaine couldn't help but smile.

CHAPTER THIRTY-THREE

Jan tried to keep her heartbeat at a normal pace, but she couldn't help it. She was too excited. Bob had texted that he was only a few minutes away, and every minute that creaked by felt like an eternity. She couldn't wait to finally see him.

Elaine was doing her best to keep her from going crazy, even as traffic and a delayed flight had pushed his estimated arrival back more than an hour. As they cleaned up the kitchen, Elaine had been chattering away about plans for the Christmas Eve service at church, and about her daughter Sasha's training for the Olympic trials, and about a funny conversation she'd had with Avery today. They'd talked through every topic Jan could think of. Now Elaine was saying something about the new diet she wanted to try out in January.

"You know, I've been doing some reading, and a lot of the new research says that cutting back on fat isn't the best way to lose weight," Elaine was saying. "These days experts are more into eating whole foods, as close to nature as possible, and eating it all, but in moderation."

Jan had read something about that too, but it seemed too good to be true. How could a healthy diet include whole milk and butter? Elaine kept chattering away about free-range eggs and organic vegetables, and Jan was grateful, but she couldn't focus on that now. She was too excited. Bob would be here any minute.

Then, finally, a knock at the door. Jan pushed herself up, took a deep breath, and looked at Elaine.

"What are you waiting for?" Elaine asked. She gestured toward the door. "Go!"

So Jan went. She made her way down the hallway. She couldn't believe he was home. Jan unlocked the door, put her hand on the door handle, and pulled it open.

And there was Bob. Even more handsome than she remembered. Snow swirled behind him in the dark night, but the porch light cast his face in a warm glow.

"Hi, Bob," Jan said.

"Jan." He held out a bouquet of red and white calla lilies. "You look beautiful."

Jan gestured for him to come inside, and he stepped in. As he pulled her into a warm hug, she felt herself relax against him. All the things she'd dreaded about this moment now seemed so silly. Bob was home, and that was all that mattered. She threw her arms around him. She wished she never had to let go.

Bob was here, and it was almost Christmas. He drew back and looked at her, then pulled her into another hug.

"I missed you so much," he said.

"Me too." Jan wasn't sure what the future held for them. But she did know that he was home, and that because of that, it would be a very merry Christmas indeed.

ABOUT THE AUTHOR

Elizabeth Adams lives in New York City with her husband and two young daughters. When she's not writing, she spends time cleaning up after two devious cats and trying to find time to read mysteries.

ROSE'S EASY GERMAN *LEBKUCHEN*

1⅓ cups honey

⅓ cup packed brown sugar

2 cups all-purpose flour

1 teaspoon baking powder

½ teaspoon baking soda

¼ teaspoon ground ginger

½ teaspoon ground cardamom

2 teaspoons ground cinnamon

¼ teaspoon ground cloves

¼ teaspoon ground allspice (optional)

¼ teaspoon ground nutmeg (optional)

1½ to 2 cups all-purpose flour

1 cup candied mixed fruit

1 tablespoon light sesame oil (be sure it is the light variety, or it will overpower the spices)

Preheat oven to 325 degrees. Grease a ten-by-fifteen-inch glass pan with a non stick spray.

Using a glass measuring cup, heat the honey and brown sugar in a microwave for one minute. Blend well, then transfer this mixture into a medium mixing bowl.

In another bowl, sift together two cups of flour, baking powder, baking soda, and spices. Add to the honey-brown sugar mixture. Blend well. Add and mix in by hand the candied fruit and oil. Add 1½ to 2 cups more flour and knead to make a stiff but moist dough. Spread into pan. Lightly score the dough into squares, then bake for twenty minutes until inserted toothpick comes out clean.

Cut into squares. May be frosted with sugar glaze (a favorite recipe or see below) or eaten plain. Flavor will intensify over a few days. Can be stored for up to two weeks in an airtight container.

Easy Sugar Glaze:

1 cup confectioners' sugar
1 tablespoon light corn syrup
2 tablespoons water

Optional: A few drops, to taste, of almond, orange, or other favorite flavoring

Stir together the confectioners' sugar, corn syrup, and water till smooth and blended. Add flavoring if desired. The glaze must be stirred each time you use it for best appearance.

Read on for an exciting sneak peek
into the next volume of Tearoom Mysteries!

A Monumental Mystery
by Amy Woods

Elaine Cook stole a brief moment to step back and survey the morning's progress in the Lancaster Public Library, and smiled at the result. "It looks wonderful, doesn't it, Archie?" she asked, clasping her hands together, unable to contain her excitement.

"It does indeed," Archie Bentham answered, turning toward her. She and her cousin, Jan Blake, had hired the older British man some time ago as an employee at Tea for Two, the Victorian tea shop they owned and operated out of their shared home. "Everything looks just right—I'm certain Nathan will be pleased, and the board will be thrilled once they discover the big surprise." Archie's hazel eyes shone with satisfaction at a job well done.

Elaine nodded with shared enthusiasm and the two set off in separate directions to finish getting everything ready. She and Archie had left Tea for Two before dawn to decorate and prepare a library meeting room for what she hoped would be a very special day.

Her beau, Nathan Culver, an auctioneer, had been selected to appraise and locate a permanent place to display a recently rediscovered statue of the famous Maine author, Phillip Camden. She'd rarely seen Nathan so excited—being entrusted with a task of such magnitude had brought out the young man in the nearly sixty-year-old—and he seemed to have a little extra pep in his step these days. Antiques were more than just a career to Nathan—they were a passion—and the statue was by far the largest and most valuable piece he'd ever been hired to handle.

Elaine and Jan had been over the moon when he'd asked their growing tea and pastry business to cater the event, and the two women had spent weeks developing the perfect menu and curating decorations that would give the unique occasion the spark it deserved.

Dubbed by critics "the Charles Dickens of rural Maine," author Phillip Camden was considered a hero in the town of Lancaster, having grown up there and written and set most of his books locally and in surrounding areas. His stories had enchanted both children and adults for decades beyond his death in the early twentieth century, and all of his books were still in print and continued to grace best-seller and academic reading lists alike.

Elaine cherished many fond memories of her father reading Camden's stories to her at bedtime, a tradition she'd carried over to her own children when they were young. She still kept treasured copies of several of Camden's books, and even owned a first edition of her all-time favorite, *The Wind Speaks Softly*. The story held Camden's trademark blend of mystery and intrigue, hope and forgiveness, loss and love, faith and friendship. Elaine made a mental note to pull it out and read it again soon—what a wonderful way to spend a January afternoon, tucked under a blanket on the sofa in the upstairs sitting room with a steaming mug of tea.

Until recently, the location of the antique bronze likeness of Camden was unknown. It was only upon the death of its reclusive owner that the statue had been rediscovered, and the owner's will decreed that the sculpture be placed in Lancaster, the town he felt would most appreciate it and benefit from owning it. Since that time, it had rested safely in Nathan's care.

The unveiling party, on the other hand, was in Elaine's, and she couldn't wait for the library board to see what Nathan had in store for them this morning! Just as she'd been thinking of him, Nathan joined her at the long conference table, where she fussed with the garland surrounding the centerpiece she'd commissioned from a Portland artist—an ice sculpture of a single shelf holding gorgeously carved depictions of Phillip Camden's most famous works.

"That is truly a thing of beauty," Nathan complimented, placing a gentle hand on Elaine's shoulder as she nervously arranged and rearranged a single piece of dark-green foliage. "But it can't compete with my view," he said.

His words pulled her out of distraction and she turned to offer a smile at the sight of his tall, slim frame and light-brown hair, sprinkled here and there with little flecks of grey. He really was very handsome, she thought, feeling her cheeks grow warm as they always seemed to do when Nathan was around.

Friends since childhood because their fathers had been good pals, she and Nathan had officially been dating for several months now. Having lost her husband just over two years ago, she had found great comfort in Nathan's companionship in recent months, but it had taken the man no small effort to convince her that the two of them would make a wonderful couple. Of course, he'd been right, and now his presence never failed to brighten her day.

"Well, I'm so glad you like the decorations," she said, glossing over his flirtatious compliment. "I just hope the board feels the same."

Nathan's eyes softened and Elaine caught those dear little crinkles of age and laughter at the corners. "I have no doubt that they'll absolutely love it. Once again, you've outdone yourself, and Tea for Two can add another success to its growing repertoire."

"Now don't you speak too soon, Nathan," she chastised, shaking a finger. "The meeting hasn't even started yet."

He only winked before heading over to the podium to review his notes one last time. But, she had to admit, it was difficult to maintain modesty as she quickly checked her watch and took one final glance around the beautifully decorated room.

Earlier, when Nathan had told Elaine about the statue and his role as its caretaker, he had also informed her of his plan to surprise the board with such a gift. Keeping the secret from locals at the tearoom had taken some work. Phillip Camden's fame would make Lancaster the home of a great treasure, and it could even boost tourism for years to come. She couldn't wait until the whole town knew.

It was an honor to have a chance to take part in the secret statue's unveiling and, with hard work, she and Archie had transformed the ordinary conference room into a loving tribute to Camden's lifetime of writing. Framed prints of the Maine wilderness the author had loved so much adorned the walls, and streamers made from the pages of old recycled books hung from the ceiling. The large center table was lit by candles in antique brass holders, rendering the ordinary room a passage into Camden's Victorian-era America.

Jan had gone all out with the cooking and baking. There were little triangle-shaped cucumber and cream cheese sandwiches, cupcakes adorned with tiny colorful stacks of fondant books, and black tea macarons with honey buttercream, just waiting to be savored. Elaine's cousin had labored for hours over those macarons, shooing anyone who dared interrupt her away from the kitchen until she'd finished meticulously piping rich buttercream between each fragile cookie. The impressive end result was definitely worth the effort.

And their other employee, Rose Young, had chosen a light, fruity herbal tea blend of lemongrass, rose hips, and pink peppercorn that she'd named The Wind Speaks Soft-Tea, after the book of Camden's that Elaine loved so much, to accompany the culinary delights and to provide a break from the frigid winter air outside the library doors. Jan and Rose had stayed back at the tearoom to serve the bustling breakfast crowd that morning, but Elaine knew they would be just as proud of the outcome as she was.

On that note, she pulled her cell phone out of her apron pocket and took a few hurried snaps of the room, eager to show Jan and Rose the fruits of their labor when she returned to Tea for Two later that afternoon.

In moments, the library board—a fancy name, really, for the simple collection of townsfolk who helped Priscilla Gates, the librarian, oversee the care and function of the facility—would arrive, and the statue would be revealed. The board members had no idea what was coming their way, and already the room held an unmistakable sense of anticipation.

"All right then, it's just about time," Nathan said, eyes sparkling with unbridled eagerness. "All set?" he asked, glancing between Elaine and Archie.

The two nodded at each other and Archie said with an exaggerated flourish of his hand and a little bow, "Ready when you are. Go ahead and show them in."

Nathan nodded and sent an anxious look in Elaine's direction, his features presenting an odd mix of excitement and nerves. Her heart went out to him, and she said a silent little prayer that God would bless the statue unveiling and allow things to proceed without a hitch.

Positioning herself near the front so that she could welcome the board members and point them in the direction of refreshments, Elaine pulled in a deep breath. Soon enough, they began to file in, their faces pleasant but bemused—wondering, no doubt, what Nathan had in store for them.

The board consisted of six volunteers, most of whom either had a particular interest in books, were simply invested in the health and well-being of their local library, or, in a few cases, both. Katelyn Grande Conrad, the youngest and newest board member, was the first to walk into the meeting room, her pretty eyes lighting up behind dark-framed glasses as she absorbed the decorations.

"Wow!" she exclaimed, doing a little spin so as not to miss anything. "This is delightful."

Elaine beamed and ushered the young woman toward Archie, who held out a cup filled to its brim with steaming tea.

Bristol Payson, owner of the Bookworm bookstore, and Will Trexler, octogenarian inventor of a very effective—and very lucrative—insect repellant, and the library's most generous donor, followed. When Macy Atherton, owner of Green Glade Cottages and member of the Bookworm Book Club sauntered in, she crossed her arms and squinted at the decorations.

"Well," Macy said, her tone giving away the slightest hint of judgment and suspicion, "I don't know what on earth you've got planned here, but I hope the surprise doesn't give any of us a heart attack, if you know what I mean." Macy glanced briefly in Will's direction and winked.

Elaine caught herself just in time to prevent an audible gasp. "I'm sure that's not likely to happen," Elaine said, patting Macy on the arm as she directed her to the refreshments area, where Archie continued to serve up sizeable helpings of treats. "It should be a good surprise rather than a shocking one."

"I suppose we'll see soon enough," Macy said, heading off to the pastries with a huff.

As Elaine turned back to the door to welcome the last few folks, she indulged in a little pride on Nathan's behalf at the full turnout. Though there were only a handful of board members, she knew from chats with Priscilla that most meetings were missing a person or two, presumably because the older woman in charge of reading the minutes had a slight tendency to go on about them for longer than necessary. She was known for taking copious notes and, consequently, for reading through them meticulously and, well...slowly. As if on cue, that very person, Margaret Childers, entered and made a beeline for Jan's macarons, with a small wave to Elaine serving as her greeting. She was followed shortly by Priscilla.

"Well, hello there, Elaine," Priscilla said in her soft voice, offering a friendly smile. "How are you?"

Elaine took the librarian's hand and shook it gently. Initially, Jan and Priscilla had become good friends, and Elaine had wished for a stronger friendship with the librarian, but for some reason she hadn't taken to Elaine in quite the same way at first. But recently, she and Priscilla had been forging a wonderful friendship. "I'm just fine, and you?"

"Oh, I'm well enough." Priscilla looked around the room with large, curious eyes, tucking a strand of chocolate-brown hair behind one ear. "I just can't wait to find out what Nathan has up his sleeve. He talked to me about this surprise weeks ago and, after some coaxing, I agreed to let him keep it in the storage room. I know it's huge, but I can't for the life of me figure out what he's got hiding in there."

Elaine grinned. "Believe me, you won't be disappointed."

"In that case, I'm even more eager to know. I do enjoy a surprise now and then," Priscilla said, the slight rise in the pitch of her voice hinting at her exhilaration. Then she leaned in closer to Elaine and whispered, "Speaking of surprises, I see this meeting has greater than average attendance already."

The two women chuckled in unison.

"I guess all it takes to bring more folks out to our gatherings is a little mystery," Priscilla said.

"I'd say you're right on the nose." Elaine winked at the librarian and then pointed her in the direction of the table at which Archie was serving tea. Elaine was happy to see that, in addition to their teacups, almost everyone now carried a plate of goodies. After about twenty minutes, the visiting chatter began to quiet down, and the group gradually settled into their chairs at the long mahogany table.

Elaine and Archie quickly cleared snack debris away from the refreshments area and moved to stand at the back of the room, doing their best to be as quiet as church mice. Nathan caught Elaine's eye and she gave him a thumbs-up, hoping her encouragement would quell his nerves.

Priscilla officially called the board meeting to begin, Will seconded the motion, and after they took their seats, Nathan cleared his throat and welcomed the attendees. The board members focused their full attention toward his podium and Elaine was pleased to hear laughter as he made a little joke to set his listeners at ease. After a few introductory comments, he began to speak about Phillip Camden's influence on Lancaster and on the whole of literature—how the author's work was and continued to be a testament to the rugged and pure, but often harsh, beauty of outdoor Maine, and its parallels to the challenging ups and downs of life itself. Elaine felt herself drawn in by the descriptions of some of her favorite novels, their beloved characters, and the scenery each evoked, and when she looked around she could see that the board members were equally enthralled, waiting with bated breath to discover what Nathan's speech would lead up to.

"Finally," Nathan said, his eyes shining as he held on to the last few seconds of his secret, "we've come to the moment you've all been waiting for."

Even though Elaine already knew the secret, Nathan's contagious eagerness made her feel as though she were hearing it for the very first time. She looked over at Archie, whose right hand rested in a fist over his mouth, as though he couldn't wait any longer for Nathan to spill the beans.

"I recently received the great honor of managing the placement and future welfare of a very special gift, bestowed to the town of Lancaster by Jonathan Frost, a collector of antiques and a lover of the author about whom I've been speaking. Unfortunately, Mr. Frost is no longer with us. However, he has endowed this town with something very special from his private archive, something I think Lancaster residents and visitors will enjoy for years to come. This long-lost antique is bound to quickly become a treasure for our great town. Also, I would like to propose, if everyone is in agreement, of course, that the existence of it be kept mum, and that the board officially unveil the gift to the whole town at the upcoming annual library fund-raising event. Nothing has ever been more certain to bring in donations than what I'm about to present to you."

At that, Nathan called toward the back of the room, "Archie, if you would be so kind as to let Chris in."

Archie hurried to the entrance and pulled open the heavy wooden door, fastening it to its built-in stopper. As he stepped aside, Chris Cosgrove, a part-time work-study library assistant and also the quarterback of the Claremore Raiders football team, pushed a low, wheeled metal cart into the room. Atop the cart was a huge object—taller than Chris himself and several feet wide—hidden by a burgundy velvet coverlet. Chris stopped the cart close to Nathan's podium and stood back to wait for further instruction.

All eyes were glued to the form hidden underneath that cover.

"As many of you are aware, a well-known but not often seen commemorative work of art regarding Phillip Camden has been missing for decades. Sculpted by an obscure but talented artist and last spotted in the latter part of the twentieth century, that piece was assumed missing—or, worse, destroyed—until very recently. I am pleased to tell you today that this piece of art, thanks to Mr. Frost's estate, now belongs to the town of Lancaster, and I am certain it will be an absolutely wonderful decoration at the Lancaster Public Library's entrance, as well as a beloved attraction for locals and tourists alike, for generations."

When Nathan paused, Elaine saw several mouths open wide as the board members slowly began to realize what they were about to behold. The room was suddenly so silent that Elaine could hear the winter wind howling outside the thick library walls.

Nathan stood poised to reveal the gift, months' worth of pent-up energy threatening to burst out of him. Elaine could almost feel him buzzing with it, even from all the way across the room.

"Without further ado…," Nathan said, motioning for Chris to pull off the cover.

Chris complied, the young man's lanky arms reaching for the corners of the dark-red velvet. His motions were slow and Elaine could sense the board members' growing anticipation. Even she, having heard Nathan talk about the piece but not actually laid eyes on it yet, could hardly stand to wait any longer.

Nathan reached out both arms as the coverlet rose up, up, up, and, finally, off the object it covered. "I give you the mysterious statue of the late, great author, Phillip Camden."

And in that moment, the previous silence disappeared, replaced by the collective intake of breath of every board member seated at the table, along with Elaine, Archie, Chris, and Nathan himself, as they all noticed the same unfortunate, terrible truth.

There was no statue to be found underneath that cover.

The stunned gasp quickly built to a loud rumble, questioning what on earth had happened and whether they were all the unfortunate witnesses of some sort of bizarre prank. Elaine gazed at what stood in place of the beautiful bronze statue they had all been expecting: an old clothing mannequin, dressed in a T-shirt, overalls, and a lumberjack hat.

Her body immobilized by shock, Elaine moved her eyes until they met Nathan's, which were full of despair, and she sensed him reach a conclusion at the same time she did—that the very valuable, very special statue of Phillip Camden…had been stolen.

FROM THE
GUIDEPOSTS ARCHIVE

This story by Gerry Steinbock Parmet of Prescott, Arizona,
originally appeared in *Angels on Earth*.

Baking Christmas cookies!" "Our big tree!" "My favorite part of Christmas is the presents!" My first-graders and I were discussing what we liked most about the holidays. "How about you, Bradley?" I asked. He hadn't said a word. Bradley just shrugged his shoulders. "I don't believe in Santa Claus and I don't believe in Christmas."

The room went quiet. I didn't know what to say. I'd never heard anything so sad. And I'd only made it worse by putting him on the spot.

While the children packed up their desks for Christmas break, Bradley's comment hung in my mind.

What would make a little boy give up on Christmas? I knew Bradley lived in a rough part of town. His single mother worked to try to make ends meet. As the "man of the house" Bradley had to take on many adult responsibilities, including caring for his younger brother. He often seemed tired—too tired for a first-grader. Somewhere along the way Bradley stopped believing that Christmas was for boys like him.

I sent the children home to get on with their celebrations and watched Bradley leave the room. *Lord, won't you do something special for his Christmas this year?*

The next day I still couldn't get Bradley off my mind. I phoned my friend Lucille, who was president of the PTA. If there was anyone who'd understand, it was her.

"We can't fix everything," Lucille said. "But we can do something."

Even for a little boy like Bradley? I wondered. He stayed in my prayers the rest of the break.

School resumed the Monday after New Year's. One by one, I asked the kids about their Christmas. I skipped Bradley. Why add insult to injury?

"You skipped me!" he shouted.

"Well, I know you don't believe in Christmas," I said.

"Now I do!" he said. "We came home after grocery shopping and found a huge wreath on our door. I thought we were at the wrong apartment, but it was my door. And when I opened it, I couldn't believe what I saw. Santa had been there! He put up a tree that touched the ceiling. With presents!" Bradley jumped up and spread his arms wide: "He left a card that said Merry Christmas and Happy New Year. And he signed his name." The kids cheered.

At the end of the school day, I ran into Lucille in the hallway. "Bradley had quite an exciting Christmas. I thought you might have had something to do with it."

"What makes you think it wasn't Santa himself?" she asked.

"I have a feeling it was an angel."

Lucille grinned. She and the PTA had turned Bradley's modest apartment into a Christmas wonderland. Bradley saw that the magic of Christmas belongs to every child, thanks to that child who was born in a manger, bringing hope to the whole world.

A NOTE FROM THE EDITORS

We hope you enjoyed Tearoom Mysteries, published by the Books and Inspirational Media Division of Guideposts, a nonprofit organization that touches millions of lives every day through products and services that inspire, encourage, help you grow in your faith, and celebrate God's love.

Thank you for making a difference with your purchase of this book, which helps fund our many outreach programs to military personnel, prisons, hospitals, nursing homes, and educational institutions.

We also create many useful and uplifting online resources. Visit Guideposts.org to read true stories of hope and inspiration, access OurPrayer network, sign up for free newsletters, download free e-books, join our Facebook community, and follow our stimulating blogs.

To learn about other Guideposts publications, including the best-selling devotional *Daily Guideposts*, go to Guideposts.org/Shop, call (800) 932-2145, or write to Guideposts, PO Box 5815, Harlan, Iowa 51593.

Sign up for the
Guideposts Fiction Newsletter
and stay up-to-date on the books you love!

You'll get sneak peeks of new releases, recommendations from other Guideposts readers, and special offers just for you . . .
and it's FREE!

Just go to Guideposts.org/Newsletters today to sign up.

Guideposts.

Visit Guideposts.org/Shop
or call (800) 932-2145

Find more inspiring fiction in these best-loved Guideposts series!

Mysteries of Martha's Vineyard
Come to the shores of this quaint and historic island and dig into a cozy mystery. When a recent widow inherits a lighthouse just off the coast of Massachusetts, she finds exciting adventures, new friends, and renewed hope.

Tearoom Mysteries
Mix one stately Victorian home, a charming lakeside town in Maine, and two adventurous cousins with a passion for tea and hospitality. Add a large scoop of intriguing mystery and sprinkle generously with faith, family, and friends, and you have the recipe for Tearoom Mysteries.

Sugarcreek Amish Mysteries
Be intrigued by the suspense and joyful "aha!" moments in these delightful stories. Each book in the series brings together two women of vastly different backgrounds and traditions, who realize there's much more to the "simple life" than meets the eye.

Mysteries of Silver Peak
Escape to the historic mining town of Silver Peak, Colorado, and discover how one woman's love of antiques helps her solve mysteries buried deep in the town's checkered past.

Patchwork Mysteries
Discover that life's little mysteries often have a common thread in a series where every novel contains an intriguing whodunit centered around a quilt located in a beautiful New England town.

To learn more about these books, visit Guideposts.org/Shop